PRINCE & PATRUAN

PART ONE

OF THE

ZARAPATHINEON SERIES

BY

IAN RUTTER

A Grizzly Dare Publication

In association with RutStuff Publishing

Copyright Ian Rutter 2017

Grizzly Dare Books
London UK

British Library Cataloguing in Publication Data.
A catalogue record for this book is available
from the British Library

Edited by Grizzly Dare
Co-edited by Oxford Editors

Typesetting and Origination by Grizzly Dare

Cover design concept Grizzly Dare and RutStuff

Cover digital artwork, production and imagery by SK Howson

Additional artwork and processing by Grizzle London

Acknowledgements

Thanks to Rachel - my rock, my inspiration - your love, faith, patience and assistance in seeing this book come to fruition has been nothing short of phenomenal.

Thank you, to the Editing and Creative team at Grizzly Dare and to Cherry of Oxford Editors.

To all those who proof read, helped and guided me, with particular thanks to Tom Carpenter and Dave Dale.

A huge thank you to my family and friends whose input and advice was, as always, invaluable.

I'd also like to thank S K Howson for helping transform the artwork into a great front cover and Grizzle.London for additional artwork and assistance.

Finally - thanks to Tommy Rockett for the website.

PROLOGUE

Eleven centuries ago the Umarian Empire was at its zenith, a huge civilisation that dominated the known world - A society of modern thinkers and warriors, but one built upon tyranny and the enslavement of others.

The Peninsoola Sotra was one such occupied territory, the many nations that made up its southern headland forced into slavery to feed the belly of the Umarian Empire above it.

Hearthonzarra, an ancient kingdom within this southern peninsula, was the last to be conquered. It was a noble land with a reputation for courage and virtue; qualities that would see many of its males selected from adolescence, to be trained and utilised within the Umarian slave armies.

After three hundred years of occupation, like countless generations before him, one such Hearthonzarran male was chosen to serve the Umarian banner.
His name was Caprasees.

A gifted soldier and natural leader, Caprasees quickly rose through the slave ranks.
Granted his first command at the age of twenty, he soon amassed a number of significant victories for his masters.
Stories were told of his deeds conquering the barbarians.
The Umarian courts grew to love him, honouring him with promotion and wealth until he reached the highest status a slave could achieve, *Secondary* Citizen to the Umarian Order.

Granted limited freedoms, he could own property, travel freely and even marry into an Umarian family with the permission of the state. He was a hero, hosted and entertained by great families when returning from battle.

However, as his influence and prowess grew, many in the High Senate deemed Caprasees to be a threat, the ruling elite within the capital, Uma, beginning to fear the great warrior slave - Fear that would see the politicians plot his demise.

As the Umarian Order pushed further east, a new enemy had been stirred - a race known as the Herdecian - a society that more than made up in numbers what it lacked in military skill.

They had taken back a far-flung outpost, scattering the small Umarian force that had been left to defend it.

In such a victory, the High Senate found worthy cause to see Caprasees sent to his honourable end.

He was made High General of his own Sixth Army, an honour never before bestowed on any *Secondary* in the history of Umaria. A title that would give him control of not only slave battalions, but Umarian commanders and soldiers of the First Citizen Order.

One such man was the newly promoted First General, Algamon. He was an orphan of noble birth, celebrated for his victories as a commander in the Northern Territories.

Together, they were to take back the fort and hold the outpost until the Third and Fourth great armies could march from the western borders to reinforce them.

It was a suicide mission, and those who understood soldiery knew it.

The slave general was to be a martyr to the Umarian cause, and never again would the Senate allow one of such lowly station to rise through their ranks so prominently.

It was a flawless plan.
Unfortunately, it was a plan doomed to fail.

Not only did Caprasees understand his master's intention, he also won the impossible fight. Using attrition, inspiration and courage, he scored an unprecedented victory against the Herdecian, taking back the outpost and fortifying his position.

He then held it against impossible odds, as the two great armies supposedly sent to his aid were delayed time and again.

His men, slave and free alike, revered him for his leadership and courage, loved him for keeping them alive, for delivering honour and victory from certain defeat and death.

Understanding he'd been sent there to die, Caprasees then took the fight to the Herdecian.

He advanced deep into their land, plundering their treasures and armouries, scattering their number far and wide. He then returned to the fortified outpost ready to make history.

Caprasees decreed the slaves within his army free and declared his intent to rebel against Uma in a bid for self-determination. With gold in their pockets, he permitted all to return home if they so wished, honouring them for their commitment and bravery in battle. Each slave to a man swore allegiance, and while thousands of Umarian soldiers left, two-thirds remained. Betrayed by their Senate, their lives cheapened like sacrificial lambs... they joined Caprasees's freed men to create a formidable, new kind of legion.

Of the Umarian commanders under Caprasees's banner, all but one took the offer of safe passage home - He who remained, being the highest rank of them all, Algamon.

In the beginning he'd been a reluctant second, but had since marvelled at the integrity, cunning and bravery displayed by the slave general. Algamon witnessed how he'd saved them all from certain doom and vowed to amend his Senate's betrayal by giving his life to Caprasees' cause - a cause soon to be put to the test.

As word of treason reached the High Senate in Uma, the delayed Third and Fourth armies were immediately mobilised toward the slave general's position.

They marched quickly to unite, but not quickly enough...

Before the forces could meet, Caprasees smashed the Fourth Army with a swift attack.

The Umarian command had expected Caprasees to prepare for a siege within the fort stronghold he'd already won...

In the confusion, the Fourth was scattered.

Message was sent to the thousands of slave soldiers within the retreating ranks encouraging them to become part of the slave general's cause - Most were quick to join rather than return defeated to their Umarian masters.

A number of these defectors were sent toward the approaching Third Army, to supposedly re-join the Umarian fight.

Once absorbed into the ranks, they spread word of Caprasees' intention, and of the ease in which he'd just destroyed the Fourth.

Rumours quickly infected the rank and file and when the slave soldiers mutinied, Caprasees wasted little time, routing the Third, as he had the Fourth.

Again, he honoured the Umarian command, granting the captured free passage back to Uma to spread word of the reckoning to come.

Panic gripped the capital - as the first cracks to the perceived invincibility of the Umarian Order began to show.

As Caprasees and Algamon marched south, the Second and Fifth armies were sent to intercept.

Stripped of their slave soldiers for fear of further rebellion, the legions were amalgamated as one Umarian force.

Without time to adjust to the new tactics, the force was slaughtered. The momentum and battle readiness of the slave general's ranks proving superior on every level.

Uprisings spread as Caprasees marched on, infecting the Umarian Order like a virus - seeing thousands more flock to his banner.

As the nervous capital awaited its once celebrated hero, vast numbers were conscripted to bolster the ranks of the First Army, the elite garrison charged with defending their city.

When Caprasees encamped outside Uma, his army numbered fifty thousand. The readiness of his troops and thirst for revenge of those loyal to him - both in and outside the walls of Uma - ensured the advantage was with the former slave general.

With the city's slaves in rebellion and mutiny on the streets, Caprasees took the exterior walls in only three days... this time showing no mercy.

His forces marched through the avenues of the outer quarter, as those within the inner sanctum prepared for the worst.

The unthinkable defeat of the Umarian Order was inevitable.

Many who had flocked to Caprasees's cause demanded Uma be burned to the ground. However, what he and Algamon did next surprised everyone.

They sent message to those cowering within the inner citadel… A peace was to be negotiated.

The Senate was suspicious, but after the General of the First Army and defence commanders - many of whom had served under Caprasees - met with the warrior slave, the news was positive. As long as Uma agreed to surrender its arms, a treaty would be put in place - the citizens of the great empire spared catastrophe, but only under certain conditions.

Two days later, Caprasees and Algamon marched their army to the Senate steps and delivered these terms to the city.

The Umarian Order would prevail on the condition the Peninsoola Sotra be freed and placed under Caprasees' rule, with a decree that any slave or citizen would be permitted to live within the liberated peninsula to become part of this new society.

The Umarian Navy was to be sailed south by its freed slave sailors, to a new home within the Peninsoola Sotra - all Umarian trade to remain under the navy's protection.

If any ship, soldier or Senator were to ever raise arms against, or threaten the free peoples of the Peninsoola Sotra, the slave general would return to finish what he'd started and burn Umaria from the pages of history.

With terms agreed, Caprasees turned his conquering force about and marched them south to their new lives - thousands more joining his cause along the way.

Greeted as a hero by the freed nations of the southern peninsula, Caprasees returned home to Hearthonzarra where the confiscated navy awaited his command. With great ceremony Caprasees was proclaimed protector of the Peninsoola Sotra and his beloved Hearthonzarra renamed, Thiazarra - *Free Kingdom.*

The army and navy were expanded. For ten years they trained, ready to defend the narrow corridor into the southern headland, preparing for a fight never to come.

Revered for his mercy by the Umarian people, his massive forces of land and sea so feared by the Uma Senate, the once slave general was to see the terms of his treaty honoured, leaving him free to begin construction on a different kind of empire.

The newly named Thiazarra proclaimed Caprasees as... Zarapathineon - *King of the Free.*

The leader appointed a High Council to govern under his stewardship, answerable to the Zarapathineon, as he would be answerable to them.
The new moral guidelines born from stories of their occupation and liberation became the faith all Thiazarrans would hold dear.
Freedom, truth, honour and justice. Peace and equality for all.

Caprasees rewarded his most trusted second, Algamon, with the office of Patruan - *Of the True.*
Like the Zarapathineon, it was to be an office set in blood.

Thus, the idea was born; the two bloodlines would never be severed - King and faithful Noble House, protectors of the freedom. Together with the council, they would rule fairly and for the people.

Watching these events transpire, many of the countries surrounding the newly created kingdom flocked to be amalgamated into the cause and over the next two decades a new unified nation formed, unlike any seen before.

The Kingdom of the Free - Zarrapathia - was born.

To help protect this new land, the Pathan Order was created... Spiritual elders were instructed to form the Garpathan Brotherhood - A force committed to upholding the moral codes of the new society, and to see it protected from enemies near and far. Warriors from all corners of the land would be trained from early adolescence - given trials to assess their worth - Taught the codes of combat and valour, to honour all they were born to protect.

At the age of seventeen, the best of these would be taken into the temples of the Garpathan Brotherhood where they would spend the next four years honing their skills until ready to undertake the Pathantral, the final assessments which would see them anointed into the Pathan Order.

Graduates who wished to join the Warrior Monks of the Garpathan Brotherhood were bound by oath to the fortress monasteries, the remainder sworn in as Pathan Knights... the elite soldiers of the realm.

All took the sacred vow to protect and hold dear the values of Zarrapathia, to embrace the gods as an example by which to measure one's deeds, so that men may live as gods in peace and perfection - the Zarrapathan Way.

When Caprasees, the first Zarapathineon died, Algamon governed the kingdom until the King's son was ready to take the Pathantral. Only when the trials of the Pathan Order were completed was he anointed Zarapathineon.

Henceforth the great tradition was created - Never would the Patruan and Zarapathineon households rival each other...

Their sons were raised as brothers, their daughters raised as sisters. If no male heir were available to the throne, then a Queen would govern under the protection of the Patruan house until a new Zarapathineon male was ready to rule.

After suffering centuries of slavery, they worked hard to maintain freedom and peace.

Neighbouring realms unified to Zarrapathia's banner, and the nation continued to grow, until eventually its borders reached from ocean to mountains - from the desert to forests and swamp. From here it was decreed Zarrapathia would grow no more, that all countries beyond these natural defences would become part of a united alliance, the free nations of the Peninsoola Sotra.

A great wall was built across the most northerly point of the Kingdom of Danton, Zarrapathia's northern neighbour, the border of which protected the narrow entry that connected the Peninsoola Sotra to the mainland. It was a century in the making, a high fortress, ninety miles across, sealing the narrow peninsula from the vast landmass above.

With the Hundred Year Wall and vast Zarrapathan Navy and military elite, the Peninsoola Sotra flourished - safe for a thousand years - while those above it wrangled and burned.

CHAPTER 1

Our story begins through the eyes of a Pathan eagle, as she swoops down through bright clouds into blue sky below...

Soaring over glistening ocean, where strong white surf crashes against rugged red cliffs.

She turns, soon over the Inpenetra Fostra, its dense woodland and swamp eventually giving way to the yellow sands of the Barrum Maxim desert.

She rides the thermals, descending over the rolling dunes that ripple with the breeze like a great golden pond.

She soars over the endless peaks, their spell interrupted by the sparkling silhouette of a rider brushing across them, heading north toward the distant walls and fertile lands of the first great city, Prima.

She cries out as she glides over the rider below.

He acknowledges her call, the eagle the very symbol of all he holds dear. For this is the Prince of the bird's domain, first in line to the throne of Zarrapathia, eldest son to the Zarapathineon - King of the Free.

*****

As they reached the hilltop, the magnificent sight of a distant Prima came into view.

The mare snorted as Cappa brought them to a halt on the plateau, "Easy now, Kazar." He patted her warm neck and smiled. This was Cappa's favourite view in the world, the approach a dramatic one after the majesty of desert led onto the fertile Thiazarran plains.

Prima's walls graced the horizon, standing proud with high ramparts protecting the township within, cut only by its three open gates and surrounded by a deep moat, which took its irrigation from the passing Artaeous River.

The sun was splendid and Cappa could feel the warmth on his light torso armour, the polished plate making him dazzle like a distant star.

As he petted the fine mare he beamed, for there in the distance, flying high for all to see, were the Royal Standards proclaiming from every turret that his father, the Zarapathineon, was now in residence.

"He's early," Cappa whispered into Kazar's ear, "Shall we go and greet him?"

The head of his dark horse lifted as if offering an optimistic response. He patted her again then dug in his heels.

*

"The Prince returns," a guard cried out.

"The Prince returns," another echoed from the interior battlements.

Capatheous cantered onto the bridge beneath the shadow of the south gate, Kazar's hooves playing a drumbeat on the wooden floor below.

The heads of his soldiers bowed, as did those of his male subjects, partnered by tilts from the women, and eager waves from the children.

Cappa smiled brightly as he passed, returning their gestures with greetings of his own.

The bridge was left behind, Kazar's hooves echoing into a melody of hard stone as they passed under the arch, entering the great walls of the city's perimeter.

He rode on through the main avenue beyond - his subjects happy to see his return as he headed for the inner fortification, protecting the central castle.

There was an energy charging the air - The First City's inhabitants clearly excited the King now sat in residence within Thiazarra's capital, the Zarapathineon's spiritual home.

The Prince approached the castle; its imposing walls made of the same grey Coba stone as the exterior fort now some three hundred strides behind him.

The hooves prattled across the cobbles as the tunnel gate was raised seeing him journey through toward the inner courtyard of the grand palace.

A stable boy quickly followed the Captain of the Guards, both respectful as they approached.

Cappa dismounted, "Cool her with vinegar before you brush her down." The stable boy took the reins and nodded.

"Oh and, Aethon." The stable boy turned. "Give her those salt licks I know you've been saving for her." The stable boy flushed into a smile before leading the magnificent mare away.

"Your father arrived early this morning on the Royal Barge," the Captain began.

His report was quickly interrupted, "Thank you, Udraeous, that will be all." The interruption came from the shadows with imposing authority.

The Captain turned to see the High Patruan, second to the King, announce his presence.

"My lord," the Captain bowed.

"Thank you, Udraeous." Cappa echoed as the Captain took his leave. Cappa turned toward the mighty old warrior now headed his way. "How are you, Haandos, it's been a while?"

Haandos ignored the bright enquiry. "I'm told nobody said anything about camping in the desert overnight."

The Prince smiled as the Patruan approached. He wore leather sandals complete with shin guards of polished metal, the footwear died blue to match the fine silk of his skirt. The armour plate covering his torso was emblazoned with the plumage of the Pathan eagle and the midnight blue of his cape swooped weightily to the floor. His hand rested on the hilt of the fine old sword, passed down the generations of his family's Patruan tradition.

"I know, I know," the Prince began, "But Kazar was tired from the sands, and you know how much I love the moon over the dunes this time of year."

"With respect, your highness, I don't care if the moon loved you so much in return it leaned down and kissed you goodnight, you should not be out in the desert alone!" Haandos was clearly not amused, "Where was your Patruan escort?"

"Your son was with Helaena, the girl of his..."

"My son should have been with you!" Haandos interrupted.

"It was I who dismissed him. He did not..."

"Your highness, you know the code," Haandos declared, "You know how we operate."

"Of course, but it was only one night. I hardly think it qualifies as a risk. Who would harm me within my own lands?"

"In light of recent events, the answer to such an enquiry is something you should not need from me. Besides, there are snakes, creatures of the night..."

Cappa grabbed Haandos by his shoulder, "You worry too much old friend."

Haandos raised an eyebrow at the remark. "That's precisely what a Patruan is supposed to do." He shook his head, "Come, your father awaits." The High Patruan turned to lead the way.

The Prince followed, his bright smile never abating.

*

Capatheous Lutho Antragon IV had proved predictably pleased when greeting his son - the Zarapathineon had been equally predictable, however, in showing his dissatisfaction of Cappa's carefree trip into the desert.

"Your Patruan should never leave your side in such circumstance," he'd insisted, "You never disobey the code."

Cappa was humble in the presence of the King. "I'm sorry, father, it will not happen again."

This seemed to sway the ruler somewhat after his initial chastising. "I just hope you and Laonardo take on board all that will be said to you today."

Laonardo was Cappa's greatest friend, his Patruan, eldest son of Haandos. Laonardo had also received a stern reprimand some hours before Cappa's return.

"Potentially dangerous times lay ahead, my son. A lapse in focus should not be something you wish to begin nurturing at this stage of your learning."

Again, Cappa begged his father's pardon.

It was a little over the top, but his father was right.

The world into which Cappa had been born was indeed under possible threat, albeit a distant one, brewing in faraway lands for the first time in centuries.

The Zarapathineon had just returned having spent four months in the Umarian Midlands. Their allies had grown concerned over developments in the lands north of the Peninsoola Sotra, where petty attacks on Umarian farmlands had become more frequent.

Those responsible were the Hoerdici.
Descendants of the Herdecian Empire - the Hoerdici - had ruled east of the northern hemisphere for half a millennia.

Until recently, they'd shown little interest in the lands south of their borders. However, as raids became more common, the

Zarapathineon deemed it necessary to reassure the Alliance. With such assurances fulfilled, the King had returned to neighbouring Danton's capital, Dantuun, located a short ride from the One Hundred Year Wall.

With a garrison of Pathan Knights stationed within its shadow, both the King and High Patruan had been keen to return home, to spend time with their heirs.

The coming days would be their last chance to do so before both boys would enter the Hidden Temple, wherein their full Pathan apprenticeship would begin.

The Zarapathineon smiled on his eldest, content no further berating was needed. He turned to Haandos, "Call Laonardo back in. I think it's time our boys were brought up to speed with all we have learned beyond the wall."

CHAPTER 2

The first year spent within the Hidden Temple had been an arduous one. No leniency was shown for those of noble blood.

If anything, both Capatheous and Laonardo were treated more harshly than their peers.

It had been the same during their earlier years within the Garpathan temples.

From the age of eleven Zarrapathan boys would spend their winters and summers undergoing the *jumal* – junior trials that would assess their worth and determine the fate of those wishing to later enter the order as full apprentices.

For those selected, senior training began in the seventeenth year. However, for Patruan and future King - things were not always so simple. Since tradition dictated both served their apprenticeship together, adjustments would often prove necessary as nature played its course. Cappa and Laonardo were born fourteen months apart, which meant Laonardo had entered the Hidden Temple in his nineteenth year.

If on occasion, no male heirs of the dual dynasties were born within five years of one another, the two royal houses would see uncles, cousins, even fathers make up the partnership, in order to maintain the Pathan Way - a rare scenario not called upon in nine generations.

As was the case in their younger years, both Prince and Patruan had excelled in this first year of their apprenticeship, the youths well ahead of their classmates.

Of course, Cappa and Laonardo had been trained hard since birth, and as such were expected to be as well qualified as their position demanded. However, with Laonardo and Cappa, even the Garpathan Monks were quietly pleased.

Their aptitude, spiritual awareness and, above all, skill in combat were beyond most in recent memory, particularly in the case of Cappa who was by far their most gifted student.

Over the past decades it had been the Patruan line that excelled, particularly in combat, however in this instance the son of the Zarapathineon had stood head and shoulders above all.

Cappa was as gifted a warrior, tactician and scholar as any of the elders had seen, but what really impressed was his deep spiritual understanding, his ability to focus and utilise his intuition. Gifts very much encouraged within the Pathan Code.

As the first year's graduation dawned, Poentrikas, the Garpathan High Elder, was more than pleased to report such findings to the Zarapathineon and High Patruan, who had arrived to witness the ceremony.

"Rest assured, my lord," Poentrikas explained to Haandos, "Laonardo's development is well beyond the norm… but Capatheous," Poentrikas shook his head, "Why, the only one close to him at such a young age was you yourself, High Patruan."

The Zarapathineon smiled, "Poentrikas, you know I'm no longer a student but ruler of this land. When will you learn it may fair you better to at least pretend it was I who was superior back in the day?"

"My King," Haandos grinned, "I told you then as I tell you now, I'd wager my weaker left against your stronger right any day of the week."

The Zarapathineon grinned, "It's true you are indeed gifted in combat, but as always it's your humility that is lacking."

The three men laughed.

"As such I must lay a wager," Haandos declared, "That out of the blue, my boy will trample Cappa in the trials. For you'll soon realise he has held himself back solely due to my instruction, so I may take gold from your purse once more."

Haandos knew the futility of his jovial statement. As High Patruan he'd trained both boys since infancy and had always been astounded at Cappa's natural ability in all he undertook.

"Good-Poentrikas," the Zarapathineon turned to his old teacher, "Can you remind me where it is written in our great constitution that my supposed trusted second, would decree it good morals to continually fleece the King's purse?"

The warrior monk smiled, "In this case, it appears your Patruan is taking sympathy for any past gambles lost. For as good as his boy has proved, such a wager is like donating money to the pouch on your belt."

The deep vibration of the temple's gong brought the humour to an end. The trio looked on from their perch and observed as eight Garpathans entered the arena below; behind them followed Cappa and Laonardo.

It was the first time either youth had been seen by their respective fathers since entering the temple, its high walls hidden within the Inpenetra Fostra, close to the western coastline.

They took a deep breath as their sons entered.

Both appeared more defined, stronger and honed.

The Zarapathineon and High Patruan looked to one another, made proud by their old master's comments, words which would never be uttered unless true to the core.

They remembered their own first-year trials, and wondered where the time could have possibly gone.

CHAPTER 3

Another year had passed since the Zarapathineon and
Haandos had last seen the inner sanctum of the Hidden
Temple. On that occasion, their heirs had done them proud,
passing the first phase of the Pathantral with ease.

The past year had been a fruitful one.

Haandos and his wife, Yoalensa, had received a healthy
baby girl, while the sister of Unaasi, Queen to the
Zarapathineon, had welcomed a baby boy.

Trade profits had been high and perhaps most important of
all, the raids on the Umarian Midlands by Hoerdici bandits had
ceased.

To reaffirm the good omens, both the King and High Patruan
were now seated in the Temple Hall, listening to Poentrikas as
he confirmed Cappa and Laonardo's rapid advancement
through the Pathan-Code training.

"Both have been separated from their peers these past nine
months, trained only by the monks of the temple." Poentrikas
smiled, "Your boys have excelled beyond even my high
expectations."

The two fathers were clearly delighted.

"Laonardo's improvement has been astonishing, while
Capatheous," once again the old teacher smiled, "Well…you'll
see." Poentrikas turned as eight Garpathan warriors led
Laonardo into the chamber.

He was dressed in the midnight blue of the Pathan. His arms, chest and shoulders were padded, and he carried the helmet of a Pathan apprentice. It bore no plumage, it's highly polished metal surface covered in bruises, any dents meticulously beaten out each night to be presented for inspection.

The Garpathans were armed with a variety of weapons, their faces like stone.

The warrior monks spread out into a large circle surrounding the determined youth in the centre. A chant rang out across the ranks and immediately Laonardo dropped to one knee. He closed his eyes, steadied his breathing… focussed his soul.

Laonardo had no weapon of his own. His initial task would be to take one from the first attack.

He stood slowly, opened his eyes and let out a long, steady breath as he put on his helmet.

Poentrikas nodded toward a Garpathan in the far corner, who stood immediately, striking the large gong to his right.

Laonardo's trial had begun.

*

Laonardo's assessment had lasted the entire morning, Cappa's much of the afternoon, yet to the proud fathers observing, the day had flown by at a spectacular rate.

Both Laonardo and Capatheous had indeed advanced beyond their years, but the manner in which Cappa had repelled the Garpathan attacks had been spellbinding.

His clarity and movement were as good as anything either ruler had seen in one so young. His strength was something to behold, and all present knew he would match any Pathan or Garpathan when he reached full manhood.

"A most worthy display by both apprentices wouldn't you agree?" Poentrikas smiled, "Laonardo will be in the Presentation Hall in a few moments. Shall we head down?"

*

On completion of the bathing ritual, Cappa felt exhausted. The trial had been far tougher than expected.

They'd trained hard these past months, both spiritually and physically and as he pulled on his tunic, he felt the twinge of an injury sustained a week earlier. He sighed.

Cappa had reached the half way stage of his Pathan apprenticeship, but upon completion of this most arduous second year, he questioned what more he could possibly learn. He and Laonardo had improved vastly this past term, but over the last two months neither felt they were really advancing.

Both he and his Patruan believed they'd peaked, and as a result, both worried about their capabilities.

His father and Haandos had trained the boys since their youth, and although the monks had taken this training to another level, Cappa was at a loss to see how they could possibly grow much further within a training environment.

One thing was for certain; the next two-year phase was to be a most demanding, drawn-out affair.

He dressed quickly into the required simple garbs of the ceremonial Pathan underclothes.

Another heavy sigh followed.

His father and Haandos awaited in the presentation hall, where he was to be honoured - and not for the first time, he secretly wished he would be leaving with them.

As in the winters and summers spent in such institutions as a child, he missed the outside world, and yearned to begin living his life again. He chastised himself, '*Control your weakness, focus. Don't give thought to such self-indulgence.*'

There was a gentle knock at the door, "Capatheous, your father awaits."

"Thank you, I'm on my way." He straightened himself and headed to the exit.

*

The Presentation Hall was dimly lit, the evening sun lost to the forest outside, with only candles warming the room.

As Cappa entered he was surprised at the number of Garpathan Monks present. All stood on the outskirts of the large rectangular chamber, in full ceremonial battle dress. Standing at the far reaches was his father, Haandos and Poentrikas. There was a distinct grandeur to proceedings and Cappa appreciated immediately that passing year two of the trials was clearly to be a more profound affair than the completion of the first.

He approached the three great warriors wearing his simple apprentice's tunic, carrying his highly polished, well-maintained helmet, his Pathantral sword worn high on his hip.

Flanking his rear, to the immediate left and right, two Garpathans followed, dressed in the robes of the Brotherhood.

Cappa's heart beat a little heavier.

There was something not quite right about all of this.

He approached his father and knelt on one knee.

A low rhythmic chant passed around the monks, ended by a gong being struck.

Cappa's eyes followed the sounds then returned to Poentrikas as the old monk spoke. "Capatheous Lutheno Antragon, first in line to Zarrapathia, protector to Thiazarra, brother to the Pathan Order, lay down your arms before this gathering."

Cappa's confusion grew. He knew of this ritual, and it was not what he'd expected.

He placed his helmet as far in front of him as he could stretch, the eye-slits facing the three before him.

He unfastened his sword and repeated the process.

"Submit honour to the Garpathan Brotherhood," Poentrikas continued.

Cappa adjusted onto both knees, pressing his elbows to them before lowering himself forward. His forehead touched the back of his hands as he pressed his palms and forearms flat to the floor. He controlled his breathing, determined his bewilderment would not take hold. In the following silence, he could hear his breath return at him from the polished floor.

"Capatheous son to the Zarapathineon, future of our great tradition, do you swear oath upon the Pathan Code, do you vow to protect, honour and endorse its teachings, to give your life to the fulfilling of its order, so that your house and the people it protects may prosper?"

More chants sang around the room. The striking of the gong was this time Cappa's cue to slowly rise into an upright posture, his palms now gripping the tops of his knees.

His mouth dried as he remembered the words he was bred to speak. "I give my oath to the Pathan Code, honour the Pathantral from which I've been delivered, and swear to protect all our Pathan tradition holds dear." Cappa noticed a slight smile appear on his father's lips.

Poentrikas gave the faintest of nods and immediately the stirring sound of an unseen Garpathan choir rang out, hidden from view on the balcony to Cappa's rear.

The hairs on the neck of the young apprentice pricked and he swallowed hard as realisation dawned.

This was no subtle test or mind game, and certainly no halfway stage in his Pathantral.

This was his inauguration into the Pathan Order.

He swallowed hard as two Garpathan Monks came into view, what they carried between them confirming his suspicion. It was the chest armour of the Zarapathineon's heir, its reflective steel emblazoned with the Pathan eagle, its left talon gripping an effigy of the sun, symbolising him as the dawn, next in line to the throne. One day, its right talon would have the moon etched beneath it, but only when he succeeded his father to inherit the kingdom.

Surrounded by the emotion of the event, wrapped within the voices of the stirring choir, he stood to have the armour fitted to his body.

Two monks then presented a large wooden chest at the feet of Poentrikas and the rulers.

The old Master reached inside and took out the midnight blue cape of a Pathan Knight. He carried the weighty garment toward Cappa, who had to fight back tears as it was fastened around his neck, allowing the rustle of the fine cloth to kiss his heels as it dropped to the floor behind him. Poentrikas smiled at the Prince, then, for the first time, bowed before him.

The old Master returned to his position at the fore.

Next came Haandos, who carried a silk pillow in the same Pathan colours, on it was a Pathan helmet, its beauty and prowess something to behold as it reflected in the yellow candlelight. Its blue plumage was shaved to the length of half a finger. Like all Pathans, this plumage would grow to reflect the measure of Cappa's deeds and become a symbol of earned merit and rank.

Haandos did not smile as he placed it on the young Prince's head, but his pride was evident as never before.

As the High Patruan withdrew, he reached down and took the apprentice's helmet, as was tradition. Its battered but well-maintained form was now his. He too then bowed before returning to the side of the Zarapathineon.

It was now the ruler's turn.

He unclipped the ceremonial sword strapped to his belt, perfect in almost every detail to the weapon passed down through the line of Kings.

The Sword of Princes.

He approached Cappa, pausing to present the sword before him. His smile beamed as he then strapped the weapon to his son's belt. The King collected the apprentice sword from the floor before returning to his position.

The choir stopped immediately as the Zarapathineon turned on his heels and boomed, "Armour!"

Poentrikas yelled in reply, "To protect the Pathan heart!"

"Helmet!" Thrusting an arm, Haandos held up the apprentice headgear, "To preserve a free Pathan mind!"

The stirring call of the surrounding Garpathan Monks then yelled out in unison, "Sword!"

The King held aloft the training weapon, "To safeguard the Pathan spirit!" He then smiled upon his son as he spoke in a softer tone, "And shield."

The room hushed.

Footsteps entered the now silent chamber as a newly anointed Pathan Knight walked in. He wore the helmet presented only hours before by his King and carried the sword presented by his father the High Patruan. The trailing blue of his cape rustled as he brought forth the huge round shield of a Pathan Warrior, its eagle emblazoned across the surface, its left talon holding the effigy of the sun.

As the Knight stood before Cappa, he bowed.

Laonardo then completed the ritual, presenting the shield with the measured words, "To Defend the Pathan Code. Shield all from tyranny and injustice."

Cappa took the heavy shield and swallowed hard as Laonardo's smile took hold. The Patruan stood alongside his future king, the two Knights facing their mentors.

The Zarapathineon then held out his hand in introduction, "Past, present and future unite, to protect, honour and obey. Hail this day as our great tradition moves forward!"

"Hail, Hail, Hail!" All present yelled the words as the choir broke into a song of celebration.

Both Cappa and Laonardo were lost within their emotions.

The two apprentices, who'd begun the day as boys, would welcome the night as Pathan.

*

With the inauguration complete, Cappa and Laonardo followed the Zarapathineon and High Patruan, who marched them at speed through myriad corridors of the Temple.

"I still don't understand," Cappa protested, "Why all the pretence over another two years of training still to come?"

"There is no pretence," the King replied without turning. "The training is four years. You and Laonardo simply advanced well enough before your time."

Haandos added, "This is not always the case. On occasion both King and Patruan have required the full four years, though I grant you such incidence is extremely rare."

"But to what end all this secrecy?" Cappa asked.

After yet another turn, the King finally led them into a room, Haandos remaining outside as the door closed. "Because of the reward that awaits." He smiled as he had the pair sit down.

"Reward?"

The King spoke in a hushed tone, "Yes, reward. A gift passed down to all Zarapathineon and Patruan heirs. The gift of true freedom, the essential finale to your apprenticeship."

Cappa was confused, though it was clear through Laonardo's expression, his Patruan had already been brought up to speed.

"The four years of training leading to the Pathantral is endured by all Pathan Warriors. However, both you and Laonardo, as future King and High Patruan, have been trained since childhood to be well ahead of the rest. You no doubt suspected this when separated from your peers during training. There is good reason for this. Because by completing your Pathantral early we are able to bestow upon you a great reward, and in doing so, pass down a tradition which has taught our two great households lessons you could never receive in any temple." The smile broadened, "What it is to be ordinary men. Men without privilege, without wealth and birth right."

This pricked Cappa's ears as he noted Laonardo's enthusiasm growing.

The Zarapathineon continued, "We were not always royal bloodlines, our people were not always free. So, to live as your people live, to know uncertainty, adventure, to experience hardship and the fear of the common man. These things are essential to our way of life. This is how we've maintained a thousand years of cohesion and peace. In this great tradition, both Prince and Patruan learn the need for one another. Learn to rely on each other totally while experiencing the real world and its dangers. This allows both heirs to appreciate the great position of honour and responsibility dealt them and ensures they never take each other, or any of their subjects, for granted." He clarified, "In order to truly appreciate, love, honour and defend your people, you must first become the people. That is the reward I offer you today."

Cappa was stunned. "But, where would we go, what would we do?"

Laonardo enthused, "Across the sea, to Ferenta."

"Ferenta?" Cappa was struggling. "What's in Ferenta?"

"Precisely," his father replied.

Ferenta was a vast, endless land of tribal territories and fiefdoms, a world of barren plains and unoccupied free zones, frequented by nomads. It was sparsely populated due its sheer size, infertile earth and disagreeable climate. Hot for months on end, with little to no rain, its water supplies guarded jealously by the tribes and sultans who owned them. Many early Thiazarran adventurers had travelled to the Ferentae Outlands, but all returned home with little love for the time spent there.

"It is a domain in which you may venture freely, a place to discover a new sense of self. Most speak a similar dialect to our Peninsoa tongue, and those that do not, speak Umarian. As you've completed your training you'll have two years of adventure, when upon completion you shall return ready to serve, to dedicate your life to the Pathan Code."

"Two years?"

"Believe me, not all are so lucky. For five generations the Patruan heirs found themselves held back slightly by the Zarapathineon bloodlines. Neither would know it of course. One can never complete the Pathantral without the other. Most only graduated in time for one year of free adventure, your grandfather had only six months." He smiled, "I'm happy to say, two years is becoming something of a tradition once again, as that's what Haandos and I both achieved during our own apprenticeship."

Laonardo cooed, "Imagine it, Cappa, what we've always dreamed of... adventure and freedom away from the watching eyes of the Kingdom."

"It wasn't so long ago I'd be in trouble for camping alone, a mere few miles away."

The King was stern, "But you shall not be alone, you will be together, as is our code. This is not a holiday, it's a tradition designed to build you up as worthy men. To illustrate to you the realities of life without privilege so you may govern fairly and with insight. There are rules that must be adhered to, oaths to be taken. You will be given a small purse to see you on your way. This will not last long. But no matter how hard things may be, and believe me there will be times of hardship, you must never rob, steal or murder in order to line your pocket. If things ever become so dire you can always make for home. Live by our Pathan Code, but never reveal yourself as Pathan unless dire emergency demands it."

The Zarapathineon paused, "We'll discuss such rules in a moment. As for the finer details of your own planning, well, you can study them to your hearts content over the ten-day voyage," the King laughed, "You sail before dawn."

"We leave tonight?" Cappa was struggling to keep up

"Under the guise of Thiazarran merchants," Laonardo said clearly pleased.

"The Reservoir Caves can be reached via a secret underground canal and tunnel system," the King said. "A boat and supplies are waiting for you there."

Cappa shook his head in disbelief.

The Zarapathineon smiled, "Now, let us discuss the laws which must be adhered to during your trip. Then we must go upstairs, your mothers are here to say goodbye."

CHAPTER 4

Several Garpathans led Cappa and Laonardo along two miles of narrow tunnel that connected the Temple to the hidden Reservoir Caves. Their entry into this secretly excavated pathway had been elaborate, the torch-lit burrow eventually opening into a deep underground fissure intersected by the dark waters of a canal.

Here, a further twenty Garpathans waited in the torchlight. Several of these guardians, known as the Harbour Brotherhood, slid a large stone disc across the access from which Cappa and Laonardo had entered. The disc was so precise and intricately carved it was difficult to tell the cave wall from the edges of the entrance the moment it was sealed. Foliage was then passed over the doorway until it appeared identical to the rest of the cave.

Cappa and Laonardo were then led to a waiting boat.

As they approached, they peered upstream with curious eyes. Somewhere, far in the darkness, this very underground river was fed by a deep-water spring, the catacombs of which sat directly beneath the palace walls of Prima itself.

They had recently learned it took a testing submerged swim to make it from the Palace to this underground channel, and it filled the pair with wonder to stand upon the banks of such a well-guarded secret.

Their boat had set off with the Garpathans rowing a steady pace and eventually, they left the gentle streams of the canal and entered the open water of a vast underground inlet.

The Garpathans rowed them onward until they entered an enormous cavern where an opening to the sea revealed itself in the distance. The cavern and waiting ocean stirred the senses, and when the boat eventually moored near the cave mouth a thick rope was connected to the bow. The rope ran out of the inlet and off into the dark rolling waters beyond where it was connected to their waiting ship already on the sea.

As they were towed out into the bright moonlight, Cappa and Laonardo once again marvelled at the Garpathan's ingenuity, as a combination of brute strength, pulleys and ropes saw a huge camouflaged plate slide over this entry also, sealing the cave from the world. Vines and foliage were dropped from the Inpenetra Fostra above, rolling down the cliffs until all was disguised.

The small ship awaiting them was named, the Kina, and she was built for cargo and speed.

They'd been informed that horses would be waiting on the other side of their crossing, and the only possessions Cappa and Laonardo carried aboard the boat were a roll of maps, a meagre purse and their newly granted Pathan attire.

The fine helmets, cloaks, armour and weapons would be carried throughout their adventure, but always hidden unless dire emergency dictated.

With their passage underway, Cappa reflected on the unbelievable events now in motion. His father had been most precise with the rules the two must adhere to, and Cappa had sworn to uphold them. His father instructed how travelling as Thiazarran citizens they would be granted free passage throughout Ferenta. However, he stressed that Cappa should be aware of the perils such unknown territories would hold, even for merchant travellers protected by the Royal Seal.

Cappa was at a loss as to how Zarrapathia's heirs could be risked in such a manner, but his father had simply reminded him how some risks were worth taking. He had hinted that some safety measures would be in place but refrained from giving any detail despite his son's best effort. He'd underlined Cappa never rely on the promise of rescue, as any help could be a long time coming. He had therefore asked for Cappa's vow he would depend only upon his wits, and on those of his Patruan, instructing how if all else failed the Pathan attire could be adorned - for as Pathan Knights they were untouchable, as few would risk incurring the wrath of the mighty Zarapathineon across the sea.

His father then presented the small amount of funds and several maps detailing the land, their allies and any dangers, before Cappa and Laonardo were taken to say goodbye to their mothers.

Even their brothers and sisters were kept in the dark.

Cappa sighed as he pondered recent events while lying on the deck, staring at the stars.

Laonardo returned from below, "Can you believe this is actually happening?"

Cappa smiled at his friend, "No, I cannot."

"At first light we should begin making plans. Study the maps in detail."

"And so we shall my friend," Cappa enjoyed Laonardo's enthusiasm. "So we shall."

*

Ten uneventful days at sea had seen Cappa and Laonardo plan the first months of their trip. When not studying maps, they took time to practice on the small deck with the weapons they'd been given as citizens of Zarrapathia.

All males within the kingdom were trained for possible entry into the Pathan Order, and as such most were capable fighters, but those who entered the Order trained with the specialist weapons of the Pathan Knight and Garpathan Warrior - Shield and spear, projectiles and dagger, until eventually concentrating solely on Thiakara, *the first sword*. Its blade measured from its owner's hip to ankle, this unique length utilised in the defence of its keeper.

So sharp, powerful and balanced was the steel it was as much a symbol of a Pathan Warrior as the shield and helmet, spear and eagle, as the blue shroud of his cape.

However, it would be the lesser arms of a citizen that would grace their horses and belts, and as land was spotted midway through the tenth day, both young warriors had reacquainted themselves fully with these more basic items of combat.

As the Ferentae coastline drew near, neither youth was able to conceal their excitement. It was the first time either of them had left the Peninsoola Sotra.

The Kina approached a desolate beach before turning slowly into a cove, bridged by a crude pontoon.

Beyond, the dark sand expanded from the shore into dunes as far as the eye could see.

The Garpathans were also disguised as merchants and the leader of their number, Velgarno, was the first to greet the pontoon master as the Kina moored.

They exchanged greetings and money for disembarkation.

Two of the pontoon-master's sons came to help but were waved away by Velgarno who tossed each of them a coin insisting the crew be left to manage their affairs.

Seven of the disguised Garpathans headed ashore, climbing the gentle slope of the dune to a stable at the rear of the pontoon master's lodge. Three strangers greeted them before leading them inside. Moments later two of the Garpathans returned, each riding a fine stallion with a pack pony in tow.

The four horses were steered to the pontoon and presented to Cappa and Laonardo by the riders. The two Garpathans then turned about and returned to the stable.

Soon after, the group exited the stables riding carmols, creatures that stored water inside humps on their backs, making them ideal for travel across desolate terrain.

Cappa and Laonardo watched as the group rode away.

Laonardo, as Patruan, had been given a little more detail by his father with regards certain options available during their trip. A discreet map placed in his care illustrated several locations where Garpathans could be found if assistance was needed. However, he'd been ordered to never disclose such information.

"Where do you think they're going?"

Laonardo shrugged, "There were too many on the boat to be sailors. Since they arrived disguised as merchants, I suppose they'd have little choice but to head inland to keep up the charade."

Cappa was not convinced. The Garpathan Brotherhood was notoriously clandestine. As well as being spiritual warriors, they were also highly trained infiltrators with a sophisticated spy and messenger network that gave the Pathan Order eyes and ears throughout the kingdoms and beyond.

"No doubt they're to become part of the vague safety measures my father spoke of," Cappa added.

They had of course discussed such matters during the voyage, but the Patruan kept his vow, the map showing the roads to possible reinforcements remaining hidden on his person. Laonardo turned to his friend, "Well, whatever they're up to, it has little to do with us now."

With their ponies loaded, Cappa and Laonardo took in the barren slope of the beach and the dusty dunes beyond. The landscape was hot and dry with a breeze that whipped up the whispering dirt and occasional reed.

The first impression of this land did not challenge why the Thiazarrans who had ventured here were happier when returning home to Zarrapathia.

Velgarno approached and spoke in hushed tones, "Remember, use the map against the sun and the stars for two days. This will take you to the plains. Head for the village and seek out Beronin the Blacksmith. He will give you food and re-supply you with water." The Garpathan smiled, "From there on my dear merchants, you will be on your own."

CHAPTER 5

Laonardo hadn't heard Cappa pull up on his horse, but he certainly heard him as he arrived at Petraisa's tent.

Cappa asked if she was decent before opening the canvas, "Excuse my brash entry *ma daya*," he said before entering.

Petraisa smiled. After two weeks travelling with this strange Thiazarran pair, she still got a kick out of being addressed as *my lady*. For as sweet and beautiful a woman as Petraisa was, one thing she most certainly was not, was a *daya*.

Cappa began gathering his belongings at the far side of the tent. His face was tanned, his chin graced with stubble. At twenty years of age, he was slightly broader in the shoulder, more confident in his manner. "Laonardo wake up."

His Patruan groaned and pulled one of Petraisa's pillows over his face.

"Laonardo!"

"I'm awake," he protested.

"Gather your things. I've managed to gain us employment with those genta herders."

This got his attention, "You have?"

He sat up before smiling wearily at his bed partner. Petraisa did not smile back. As fleeting as this affair with her younger man was to be, a part of her hoped these two gentlemen would stay with her a while longer.

"Hurry up, they leave shortly."

Laonardo let out a yawn. He too was tanned, his skin slightly more weathered. In the eighteen months of adventure since their arrival in these lands, the pair had seen and done many things - experienced highs and lows, been flush and broke.

However, at this stage of their travels they were certainly in the latter bracket. As such, even a miserable, lowly paid excursion herding a caravan of gentas - small, bearded creatures with an ability to survive just about anywhere while producing a seemingly endless supply of milk - was welcome.

Petraisa made a weak protest, "Dust-bowling? Come on, you can both find better."

Laonardo raised an eyebrow as he climbed out of the furs. "Better? I've but three bunpa on my person. That won't see us to the end of the week!" He smiled, "Don't worry, we'll be back through this way at some point." It was a feeble promise and he knew it, but Laonardo had never lied to this desert beauty, and she'd known this was to be a most casual affair.

He kissed her on the forehead then quickly began gathering his belongings.

*

The gentas numbered one hundred and thirty, a considerable herd. Khlamad, the livestock owner, had lost both his cousins to the desert in a terrible storm. As such, he'd been forced into hiring help. He'd already employed a young man named Trentach, and only planned on hiring one more. However, Cappa had told him he and Laonardo would work for a cut rate plus provide their own pack animals and tents.

Khlamad had instinctively liked Cappa and was reminded by Trentach that hiring Thiazarrans meant capable horsemen who would know how to fight if need arose.

Their caravan would be crossing bandit country, and although attacks on dustbowlers were rare, Khlamad and his aging carmol would be little use in protecting a scattered herd with only Trentach as his ally.

When welcoming Cappa and his young friend that morning, Khlamad knew he'd made the right decision.

Their stallions were in fine condition, even if their owners were not. The pack ponies had been equally well cared for. They carried supplies and tents, and Khlamad could not help but wonder why these young merchants were in the dustbowl.

At mid-morning the group ventured out, with Trentach and Laonardo marshalling the herd.

To their rear Khlamad and Cappa rode side by side.

"So, tell me young friend, how is it you come to need employment from one such as I?" He gestured to Cappa's fine horses.

"The desert takes a great many things. In our case we were fortunate to lose only our carmols and the merchandise they carried." It was the standard cover story, one they had used on countless occasions. "Luckily, we saved the horses. I've had Coba here since arriving in Ferenta." Cappa patted his fine stallion's charcoal neck with affection.

"But why remain here? Why not return home? Your animals would more than cover the costs of any such voyage."

Cappa smiled, "What, and return as beggars?"

Khlamad laughed, "Better beggars there than beggars here."

"In Thiazarra it would be easy to find our feet again. But only by returning to our families with our tails between our legs. This is our first adventure away from home. We're not ready to give it up just yet."

"Ah, the confidence of youth," the older man smiled, "And the time it grants you."

They paused their conversation to watch Laonardo and Trentach shepherd the lead gentas.

Khlamad's carmol grunted as he adjusted in his saddle. He stroked the animal's forward hump, "Easy, old girl."

Cappa turned to him, "And what about you, Khlamad. What will the future hold once you've taken the herd to market in Numbala?"

"I plan to sell seventy in number. From then on, I can manage with only one extra hand. I'll take the smaller caravan south and head back toward my homelands. I have family there who need to know the fate of those lost." He looked grim for a moment. "I'll be fifty years old next spring, but I have some adventure in me yet." He smiled.

"Will Trentach continue in your employ for this journey?"

"Trentach only wishes to go as far as Numbala."

"We've never travelled the outlands to Numbala before," Cappa enthused, "We've never been this far north. Perhaps there will be opportunity for two Thiazarrans also."

"There is always opportunity in Numbala. It's that sort of place. A typical oasis territory, ruled by a powerful water sultan known as Bunsaar."

"Can't say I've heard of him."

"If you've never been to the outlands there is no reason why you would, but rest assured, it's the only name you'll hear in Numbala, it is the capital of his territory."

Cappa nodded nonchalantly before noticing several stray gentas breaking away just ahead, "Well, if you will excuse me a moment, it appears I have work to do."

Khlamad laughed as the boy rode on to herd the drifting livestock and wondered if there had ever been such a courteous dustbowler.

CHAPTER 6

Nineteen days in the outlands meant the quartet were looking forward to some comforts in Numbala.

The dustbowlers had seen nothing of bandits or drama and, as they approached the township, Cappa and Laonardo were surprised at its size.

Khlamad explained how its inhabitants could number near seven thousand in the hot season but estimated it would be closer to four in this less harsh climate.

The herd was rounded into a holding area close to the market and counted. Trentach and Laonardo were then left to watch over the gentas and caravan as Khlamad and Cappa entered the busy township on foot to register the livestock.

It was a bustling place of simple buildings, marquees and tents, all crammed around one another in a labyrinth of clay-baked streets. The place was awash with nomads, merchants, dustbowlers and tribesmen. Stalls traded in all manner of goods, and music carried from every direction.

At its heart was a palace, simple and crude to Cappa, a marvel to the inhabitants of the Sultan Bunsaar's territory.

Within its ramparts was the Gurapass, or great well, a deep spring, which irrigated the town's waterholes. All within this trading post were taxed substantially; fees the Sultan could impose thanks to this natural, but precious, resource.

Khlamad found the market registrar's building and after ducking and weaving their way through a small crowd, the dustbowlers soon had what they'd come for.

Their seventy registered gentas would be sold that very afternoon.

*

Khlamad had little difficulty finding a new employee. His seventy gentas had brought a record price and as such he could offer his new dustbowler a good wage to manage his now modest herd. He'd also deemed it fit to pay Cappa, Laonardo and Trentach a little extra despite their protests.

They had made camp by the herd on the outskirts of town and celebrated their good fortune into the night.

As such, when it came to goodbyes the following morning, all were feeling a little worse for wear.

Khlamad's new employee was an experienced dustbowler with a reputation for being diligent and honest. He arrived after breakfast riding an athletic mare, pulling a tall carmol carrying supplies.

The gentas were quickly herded into lines, the dustbowlers ready to set off.

Cappa and Laonardo had grown accustomed to farewells. Some were naturally harder than others, but this parting pinched Cappa in a significant way. Khlamad had been more than just a companion; he'd been a mentor in many ways. His life was a hard one, not made any easier by his recent losses. Yet, he faced all in his path with a profound dignity and strength. He embraced the world and its teachings and had passed on much of this learning and wisdom during the course of their trip.

"I shall miss our conversations," Cappa declared with a smile.

Khlamad smiled. "As will I - I shall especially miss your manners. You make me feel like a lord even when asking to take a piss." The two embraced. "Remember, every day with the sun on your back is a blessing."

Cappa smiled, "But only water delivers you safely into night."

Khlamad was pleased, "You have the map I gave you?"

"Of course, it will never leave my person."

The dustbowler smiled, "Remember, some of those wells are known by only few. The tribesmen who reside by them will welcome you, but they guard these waterholes with suspicion. Say the words just spoken with blessings from Khlamad and you will be taken care of."

"Thank you," Cappa said, "For everything."

Laonardo and Trentach approached to say their own farewells.

The noble old dustbowler had touched them all.

Khlamad's new herdsman returned, "We are ready."

The old dustbowler stepped back and bowed to his three intrepid adventurers, "Good luck my young friends, and may blessings surround you." He laughed, "And I wish you every success in finding an employer as agreeable as I!"

More smiles followed and the trio were set to leave when Khlamad's new employee enquired, "You don't have work?" He'd presumed they were leaving for better employment.

"No," Laonardo replied. "Why, do you know of any?"

"Word has spread that a Torantum is to be held."

"Torantum?" Laonardo and Cappa were unfamiliar with the term.

"A tournament," Trentach explained, "An exhibition of horsemanship and combat, to select guards to protect caravans travelling the outlands."

The faces of both Cappa and Laonardo lit up.

"The Sultan Kirkoban travelled here several days ago, but his party was hit by a sandstorm. He lost many of his guards,"

Khlamad's new dustbowler added, "The Sultan Bunsaar, is to hold the games to select twenty men. I cannot guarantee such employ to be as gracious as Khlamad here, but the money will be good for those who know horse and combat." He turned about, "Ask around town. The Torantum is to be held in two days." He then rode away to settle the gentas yelling, "Good luck to you," as he went.

Khlamad prepared to depart. "The Sultan Kirkoban has a reputation for fairness, though equally for being short of both wits and funds. Good luck my friends, and if you enter this contest... Stay safe."

CHAPTER 7

It was a hot morning, and Cappa, Laonardo and Trentach were pleased they'd not awoken in the outlands on such a day.

Having never travelled the district, Cappa and Laonardo had quizzed Trentach on the traditions of which they were learning. He'd explained how it was not unusual in this region to hear of tragedy in the desert. For the most part it was simply barren, but the northern territories brought high risk of sandstorms together with powerful, unpredictable squalls on the salt flats to the east. As such, events like the Torantum were not uncommon, although Trentach emphasised it was unusual to see as many as twenty competitors employed at any one time. After further investigation, he'd confirmed how the best of these twenty could hope for more permanent employment. As Khlamad advised, this Sultan Kirkoban was far from flush and had few guards to call upon back in his own territory to replace those lost to the storm. Therefore, he would gladly take the best a Numbala Torantum had to offer, its population more diverse than in his own capital of Malbood.

Trentach had explained how the Great Sultan Clans formed a kind of co-operative.

The sultans were territory lords, their lands housing wells and oases that fed the populace.

Their lesser relations were Ward Sultans, canton lords whose smaller provinces offered fewer resources. Most were cousins or relatives of some description.

Under a strict code of conduct, they protected each other and their water supplies. As sultan, one such code was that of honouring one's commitments as host. Having personally invited Kirkoban to his region, the Sultan Bunsaar was obliged to offer assistance against Kirkoban's losses, misfortune incurred while making the journey.

To honour this, Bunsaar would help Kirkoban employ new soldiers and pay half the fee for any Mecdia mercenaries hired to protect the caravan during its return to Malbood – the rest would be paid on completion, at the other end by Kirkoban.

Trentach had also discovered that Bunsaar would be offering ten of his personal guards to assist the caravan until it reached the first of Kirkoban's territories, a small, fortified water outpost called Fraeda.

With Khlamad's recent ordeal and the misfortune of this Sultan Kirkoban, both Cappa and Laonardo wondered how anyone managed to get ahead in this northerly dustbowl.

The Torantum was but a few hours away.

The competition assessed equestrian ability and combat skills, just as Khlamad's herdsman had stated.

The games worked on a points system, which would eventually leave two finalists. The winner would be made Mecdia Captain, effectively the head of the mercenary guards, and the runner up would be his Lieutenant.

Both would receive a more substantial purse.

The remaining eighteen would make up the guards.

Rumour had it as many as ninety had put their names forward, but Cappa and Laonardo were quietly confident.

Trentach had since begun stretching his muscles and testing his sword arm.

Cappa and Laonardo refrained from such activity.

They would conserve their energy and take in plenty of water, happy in the knowledge both their muscles and sword arms were more than up to the task.

*

The arena chosen for the event wasn't actually an arena at all but the livestock market - and quite a crowd had gathered.

Staggered steps on three sides flanked a large, central dirt bowl with a knoll providing a viewpoint at its southern curve. The steps, frequented by traders, had been extended on the eastern face, with a box section reserved at its heart for the Sultan Bunsaar and his guests.

Although the dignitary's box was empty, the rest of the arena was awash with excitement; a united mass of yelling and cajoling as the crowd watched men from all walks of the outlands battle for a place on Kirkoban's desert guard.

The number of entrants had risen to one hundred and sixteen, but this reduced after the horse trials.

Both Pathans had excelled during this stage, Cappa riding Coba, Laonardo his own mount, Bolo.

Trentach had also eased through the round.

Now, as the third wave of fighting got underway, eighty remaining contestants would see their number dwindle to forty.

Cappa, Laonardo and Trentach had won their first rounds easily, though Trentach was having a harder time with his third opponent, Kombai, a skilled fighter from the north.

As he dodged yet another incoming blow from Kombai's leather-bound, blunted sword, both Cappa and Laonardo whispered to one another how they would have countered the strike and seen Kombai floored. Both had naturally refrained from exhibiting their true Pathan skills.

The duo had picked up several new fighting styles during their travels and could now amalgamate these in such a way as to hide their heritage.

That said, both Prince and Patruan had made easy work of their first opponents, and as they watched Trentach miss another glaring opportunity, they pondered over how they would have done the same to the brutish, somewhat predictable Kombai.

As their new friend was forced toward the competitor's pit, Laonardo found he could hold back no more, pushing through the bodies to the front barricade, "Trentach!" he yelled, "He dips his left shoulder before throwing a reverse swing. Side-step to force it then cut back and take-out his exposed neck!"

Trentach recognised the voice and remembered the same move being utilised by Laonardo earlier. Kombai had him on the back foot and was brutish enough to ignore the advice just shouted against him. So Trentach did as he was instructed and lured the ape closer.

Several exchanges rang out before the opportunity arose, and sure enough Kombai took the bait. Trentach imitated Laonardo's move and within moments every sinew and strained fibre sent his weapon crashing into Kombai's collarbone. It snapped and the only thing disguising the sound was Kombai's yelp as he crumpled to the floor.

Trentach had just successfully negotiated a path into the knockout rounds.

Several of the competitors passed nervous and ungracious stares Laonardo's way as he pushed back toward Cappa wearing a smile, impressed at Trentach's adaptability.

The two confident and capable youths were already on the shortlist of fighters the rest wished to avoid in the competition.

Within moments, Cappa's name was called.

"Good luck," Laonardo said as Cappa made his way out.

The crowd went wild as he entered the arena.

Cappa's adversary was a giant by the name of Duko, who'd destroyed his previous two opponents.

With the skills displayed by Cappa earlier in the contest, all were expecting a good fight.

In the cheers, and betting which followed their introductions, few noticed the two sultans, Bunsaar and Kirkoban, as they entered the dignitary's box. With Bunsaar was the first of his two wives together with his bodyguard, Vhlarm.

Accompanying Kirkoban was his daughter, Ruomaani-Skye, her face covered from the sun with a light silk scarf.

The Captain to Bunsaar's army - Vhlarm - was a hulk of a man. Though not quite as tall as the giant now in the centre of the ring, he nevertheless towered above most, with shoulders, arms and legs built for power. He was the ultimate fighter in the outlands with a reputation that preceded him.

Many in the crowd had not yet seen that the sultans had arrived, but the announcer most certainly had and as the cheers died away, he was quick to call honour on their host.

Bunsaar waved as the party took their seats, the crowd cheering their approval.

Bunsaar leaned toward Kirkoban. "This should be over quickly. Although size is not everything, I've seen this Duko before, he is a most capable warrior," he gestured toward his bodyguard, "Vhlarm tried to recruit him to my guard, but his wage demands were a little ambitious." He shrugged, "Not that I was offended. He earns a good income as a trader, and I tax him heavily for it."

Vhlarm sneered, "He's worth more to you trading than he is leaning against a palace gate."

Bunsaar laughed, "Indeed he is."

They turned to watch the fight. It seemed a mismatch to say the least. Duko's opponent appeared barely out of his teens.

Vhlarm however, instantly recognised the confidence to the youth's approach, as he began circling Duko slowly, with skilful footwork.

Ruomaani-Skye also took note of the athletic fighter, albeit for different reasons.

The makeshift stadium hushed as the tension began to build.

Neither man had yet committed to an attack. The giant Duko was known to be nimble and fast for a man of his size, but as the smaller, powerful looking youth continued to circle him, it was reminiscent of a mountain lion stalking larger prey.

Cappa would resist his more obvious Pathan training, but knew he'd have to defeat this brute quickly, and although Duko could not possibly know it, every twitch and eye movement gave his intentions away to the younger, superior warrior.

Duko finally committed, powering forward into a lunge.

The crowd gasped at the result.

Duko hadn't seen exactly how the smaller man avoided the attack, but he'd felt the excruciating pain as the back of his knee was taken out by blunted, leather-bound steel, and was quickly reminded of the sensation as the same weapon hit him immediately after, smashing the back of his neck with unbelievable speed, sending the tree crashing to the ground, gulping for air as the crowd became delirious.

He wanted to get up and make a fight of it, but the supremely quick youth was above him in an instant, warning in a calm but chilling tone, "Just stay down. I don't want to hurt you."

Usually such a threat would only serve to enrage Duko. However, as it was delivered from a man who'd just put him down without so much as breaking a sweat, he took note of the instruction.

On seeing Duko was not getting up, the young warrior backed away sending the mob into frenzy. He relaxed his posture and tilted respectfully to the crowd. On noticing the sultans and their entourage, he repeated the gesture, much to the delight of Bunsaar.

"Well, I was half right; the bout certainly didn't last very long."

Vhlarm didn't smile as he studied the skilled youth, but Kirkoban's ready laugh was more than adequate for the entire party.

His daughter's expression remained hidden by the silk of her scarf, which was fortunate, as it was a most enchanting smile she sent toward the young warrior.

*

Laonardo had also gone on to win his third fight with ease before making slightly harder work of it against a skilled opponent in the knockout stages. This ensured he was in the final twenty, guaranteeing him a position on the Sultan Kirkoban's staff. Cappa had joined him after defeating his next challenger, and both were pleased to see Trentach make the cut after scoring his own victory.

When Cappa next entered the arena, the crowd were on their feet. This time he was to fight Banteez Bayer, an older man of similar stature who'd shown great skill winning his previous fights. They approached one another with respect.

Cappa had already identified three weaknesses to the man's game, but he'd have to be careful. Both Thiazarrans desired the higher wage of a Mecdia Captain and Lieutenant, but neither wanted to stand out too much. Following the quick defeat of Duko and his last challenger, Cappa would have to hold back.

The announcer went into overdrive, as did the gambling odds behind the stands. All respected the capable Bayer, an outlander with a fighting pedigree, but the initially un-fancied stranger was now odds-on favourite.

Ruomaani-Skye's attention was keen behind the safety of her veil, and she watched with interest as the warriors made ready.

"This should be interesting," Bunsaar said. "Both are of similar stature and style."

Kirkoban agreed obediently though Vhlarm made no such gesture. The effective blows delivered to Duko were not fortuitous. Neither were the shots that dispatched the youth's last opponent with almost equal speed. All were clinical counterstrikes. The confident fighter was clearly a match beyond the skills available to Bayer, and Vhlarm was curious to see how this Cappa would choose to dispose of the outlander.

The fight began with Banteez Bayer the first to pounce, thrusting his sword forward.

Cappa was more than up to his defence and could have countered with a lethal blow but held back, a factor which did not go unnoticed by the accomplished Vhlarm.

Laonardo and Trentach watched as further exchanges saw the fighters move beneath the Sultan's box.

Cappa was intent on making a show of it. He could have broken his opponent's leg and right arm had he let loose.

As the young warrior came closer to the box, Vhlarm wondered if the youth was merely playing for the crowd.

The two fighters squared off once more, poised and ready.

As the crowd fell silent, Bayer flew into an attack that was met easily by Cappa - their swords clashing in time with a gust of wind that whistled through the arena.

In that moment, Ruomaani-Skye leaned forward to witness the spectacle below, the wind catching her scarf as she did, blowing it up into the air.

She broke into laughter as it left her face and quickly stood to make a grab for the silk. Her fingers almost touched as it floated beyond her reach, and as she bid the scarf farewell it was clear she was more than deserving of her name.

Ruomaani-Skye translated as 'Most Beautiful Sunset' in Ferentae, but the term seemed inadequate to describe her as she caught the young fighter's gaze below.

She was captivating, and as Cappa momentarily gave her his full attention, it wasn't just his heart that ached.

Bayer smashed his elbow into his bewitched opponent's mouth sending Cappa backwards.

As his frame met the dirt, he was struck a second time before Bayer pinned him down.

Ruomaani-Skye winced in time with the crowd's groan.

Cappa yielded and his victor pulled him to his feet, bloodied and bruised.

Cappa looked up to see the beauty return to her seat, and in that moment, he didn't remember defeat, nor feel injury. He didn't even feel the twinge at missing out on a Captain's pay.

CHAPTER 8

The contest reached its climax late in the afternoon with the winner and runner up presented before the cheering mob as Lieutenant and Captain of Kirkoban's hired guard.

As the crowd roared, the Sultan Bunsaar stood with Sultan Kirkoban to honour the victors and paid tribute to the eighteen who had won employ within the mercenary outfit.

After a short speech, he turned to his own champion and bodyguard Vhlarm. "We have a worthy winner in Banteez Bayer," he signalled to the newly appointed Mecdia Captain, "What say we lay a wager?"

Vhlarm stood on cue sending the crowd into a fresh frenzy.

Sultan Bunsaar signalled for silence. "I will wager fifteen silver pieces my man will defeat our new Torantum champion." He appreciated the look of reluctance that flashed across Bayer's face. "Loser takes five, the winner ten."

This was intended to make the proposition seem irresistible.

Bayer understood he had little choice but to fight, if he didn't, he would be humiliated out of his hard fought, newly appointed position. He looked up and nodded at Vhlarm who smiled darkly.

In the contestant's pit at the far side of the arena Laonardo turned to Trentach, "What is this? There was no mention of any wager."

Trentach shook his head. "He's sending a message. Having seen scrappers encamped within his township fight it out in the

Torantum, he's seizing the opportunity to remind all who holds real authority here, including his guest Kirkoban. Vhlarm is unmatched by any in the outlands and is certainly beyond the skills of Bayer. The crowd will witness a new champion being destroyed by the old one in Sultan Bunsaar's employ. A quick and effective show of power."

Laonardo turned to Cappa aghast, "Did you hear that?" Laonardo had thrown his last bout. As Patruan he must be at Cappa's side. A higher rank in Kirkoban's guard may see this goal hard to implement. As such, any possibility of Captain or Lieutenant had gone when his friend allowed himself to be distracted. "We could have been up there if you'd kept your eyes on the task at hand."

Cappa laughed, his mouth still swollen and sore.

"You think it funny? That's ten to fifteen pieces of silver we could have won. As much as they are paying up front for this entire enterprise!"

Trentach smiled at the confidence, "You are indeed a worthy fighter, Laonardo, but do not think Vhlarm in the same league as any who fought here today. He will break Banteez Bayer in two if he so wishes."

Laonardo turned to Cappa and raised an eyebrow, prompting Cappa to laugh once more.

Vhlarm donned his bull-horned helmet and entered the arena to a roar of approval.

Up in the dignitary's box Bunsaar turned to Kirkoban and grinned. Kirkoban smiled back at his powerful second cousin, aware of the game afoot. He only hoped Banteez Bayer would not be too badly hurt.

Ruomaani-Skye kept her focus on the warriors as they approached the centre of the ring, not wanting to attract the attention of her host Bunsaar, as silently she wished their new Mecdia Captain well.

*

It hadn't been a contest so much as a humiliation. Trentach was correct. Vhlarm was the very symbol of Bunsaar's army. To see him batter a newcomer who'd just beaten all put before him was a stark reminder of who held rule here.

It had also proved to be a spur for humility as far as Laonardo was concerned. He'd allowed his ego to blind him to the Pathan credo, *'No one man can outmatch all...'* believing himself invincible to all but Cappa in this contest. But as he'd watched Bayer dispatched so clinically by a combination of brute force and supreme skill, both young Pathans had to admit this Vhlarm certainly knew the art of combat.

His powerful metal spear was an unusual weapon. Unlike the graceful rod of their Pandral lance, this spear was broad with a long-styled dagger for a tip and a club for a base. From the mid-length of its pole two rods of opposing steel were welded, protruding out and down over the hand grip, acting as a shield to the fists which held it. These parallel rungs also enabled Vhlarm to slip his wrists through, allowing him to spin it round and about like a scythe attached to the ends of his arms. It was a devastating piece of equipment, which had it not been blunted and bound in leather, would have cut Bayer to pieces.

The crowd had loved the show, and Vhlarm milked the applause before casting his gaze toward the contestant's pit, hoping to locate the eye of the young warrior he'd hoped to fight - the boy Cappa who'd allowed himself to be so foolishly distracted by his master's new prize.

*

The following day Kirkoban's caravan was set to leave, and Cappa was bouncing with excitement - For his hopes of once again seeing the girl who'd stolen his heart at a glance, had been delivered.

Ruomaani-Skye, he'd been delighted to learn, was their new employer's daughter and would be travelling with the caravan under their protection.

Laonardo had never seen Cappa so besotted. He and Trentach laughed as Cappa prepared the horses in the sunshine with an exuberant spring in his step and whistle on his lips.

"Still," Laonardo mocked, "I bet you could have got closer to her had you made Mecdia Captain or Lieutenant."

"I doubt any of we mercenaries will be allowed audience with our employer or his daughter," Trentach laughed, "Whether Mecdia Captain or a General for that matter."

More laughter ensued before Laonardo caught glimpse of a soldier arriving on horseback, "Speaking of which…" It was the newly appointed Mecdia Lieutenant himself.

"You men there," he declared in a curt tone, "Hurry up and join the ranks. We leave shortly." He noted their fine animals, particularly the pack ponies loaded with covered bundles. "Present your animals to the Captain for use in the caravan," he stated haughtily, "Check your supplies into the guardsman itinerary, all will be returned to you on completion of this service." He held out his hand arrogantly, "Hand the reins of those ponies to me, I'll take them with me now."

Laonardo growled, "You will have to take them!" He stepped forward to protect the faithful ponies, Perii and Alto.

"While a part of Kirkoban's guard, you will obey my instructions!"

Cappa tried to pacify, "And so we shall in execution of our duties, but nothing was mentioned of surrendering property, this is but temporary employ, we are not sworn subordinates."

The Lieutenant was angry. "I ask you to hand over these ponies so they may be used during our passage. All will be returned on completion of this undertaking."

Laonardo laughed, "And I've told you these ponies are not open to negotiation."

57

The Lieutenant was nervous, he had of course seen these men fight and knew them to be more than capable, but he had advanced further than they and he was annoyed at the undermining of his new authority. "It seems you do not know your place!"

It was now Cappa who grew irritated, "No, I'm afraid it is you who does not. Order us to fetch and carry, to stand and fight and we will obey. Try to take advantage or mock our good nature and I'm afraid a different outcome awaits."

The Lieutenant was set to retort when another rider came clear of the tents.

"And that is something we should all seek to avoid, Juhmad."

The Lieutenant turned to see their new Mecdia Captain, Banteez Bayer, approach.

His newly issued attire and helmet did well to hide the bruising, though his slight lean betrayed the injured ribs.

"Captain, I was only…"

"These men are here to help keep us safe not give up their animals. We've more than enough to carry our caravan through the desert." Bayer smiled, "Go to the gates and have the party prepare for our departure."

Juhmad turned his horse about, stung by the disrespect. He glared at Laonardo as he spurred his horse forward, setting off to carry out his duty.

Bayer's smile remained as he eyed the trio. "Forgive our Lieutenant his lack of civility. He seems to believe we are a conscripted army, not a rag-tag bunch of mercenaries out to earn a purse."

Cappa smiled at the man responsible for his own swollen face. "Thank you, Captain. And rest assured… we are at your service."

"I'm glad to hear it." He pulled his horse around. "I am Banteez Bayer, and I'm no more a Captain than you are a dustbowler. But we can keep up pretences for such a trip I think. Just try not to kill Juhmad until after our work is done."

Bayer was no fool and he was more than aware of how events conspired to hand him victory over the supremely skilled youth. "Now, Cappa is it?"

Cappa nodded.

"I've a duty for which I think you'll prove suitably apt, a certain task to be carried out twice daily during our journey. A little demeaning, I'm afraid."

Cappa scowled and considered if Bayer was now toying with his good nature as the Lieutenant had done?

"I've been asked to select one in our number to assist with latrine duties. Transporting sewage barrels from the Sultan's 58aravan into the desert. The lowly ranked guard whose duty this fell to was one of the many lost to the storm." Bayer gestured to the distant collection of Bunsaar's soldiers, their dark robes flowing in the warm breeze, "And something tells me they won't be too keen to help." Bayer added, "Kirkoban only has his personal guard left, men of rank from his tribe. As such he deemed it more appropriate the job fall to one of our number, and since you've just openly disobeyed the Lieutenant's orders…" The Mecdia Captain fought hard not to laugh as he saw the anger build in Cappa. "Of course, the person selected will be expected to report to the Sultan's carriage. Therefore, he may also come into contact with his daughter from time to time." Bayer saw the realisation dawn upon the young warrior's face. "However, if such an occurrence were to arise, let me offer some advice, keep your eyes on the task at hand whenever she's near, you're less likely to run into trouble that way."

CHAPTER 9

They had journeyed the outlands for two days and still Cappa had seen nothing of the intoxicating Ruomaani-Skye, nor her elusive father for that matter.

At dawn and dusk he reported to the Sultan's carriage to transport the sealed barrels of waste beyond the perimeter of each new camp - so they could be emptied, and the contents buried as was customary. On each occasion Cappa saw and dealt only with Kirkoban's tribesmen.

The baked dustbowl clay would not give way to softer sand along the entire route of their caravan; only the equally firm salt flats of Kirkoban's territory lay ahead. Therefore, the carriage would be the only form of transport needed to carry the Sultan's daughter - and as the sun began to set on the second day, Cappa prayed he would see her again before they completed the passage.

He finished burying the swill before heading back to the tents, erected each day before sunset.

Cappa tethered his horse by the Sultan's marquee and coach, then rinsed the barrel in the water set out for him by the tribal guards. Usually, they watched him like a hawk, but on this occasion, there was none to be seen.

'*Perhaps they're getting used to me already,*' he thought. He placed the barrel under the carriage before washing his hands and then watched Bunsaar's mysterious soldiers for a moment as they set up camp.

Cappa was set to head back to his quarters when he heard a female voice inside the grand tent. He scanned around but saw nobody near, so decided to investigate in the hope of hearing the voice of his elusive dustbowl Princess.

He stood silently for a moment when he sensed movement behind him. He turned sharply, only to see Ruomaani-Skye staring back at him. Cappa's heart missed a beat as he took in her features. Her eyes were magnificent, her skin tanned and smooth, her lips full and dark. The light silks of her clothing swayed with the breeze.

He felt a lump rise in his throat and was set to speak when she asked, "Is there something I can help you with?" Her tone was somewhat cold, though her accent was alluring and exotic.

Cappa flushed but had little opportunity to form a reply.

"Because if you're struggling for things to do, I've carmols which require feeding."

Again, her tone was chilly, superior almost. Under normal circumstances, Cappa would have found her instantly dislikeable. However, he remained utterly captivated.

"Are you mute?" There was a different tone to this comment, one of mockery.

Before he could answer, three tribal guards came around the grand tent, the leader of whom looked angrily on Cappa, "My lady, I didn't know you were out here. You should have…"

She waved away Feldahd's protest, "Do not concern yourself, Feldahd. I'm merely passing instructions to our slop boy here."

Cappa raised an eyebrow at the rather demeaning term.

Feldahd was concerned, "My lady, you shouldn't be wondering the grounds unprotected. You must have an escort at all times until we reach Fraeda." He looked nervously to the distant gathering of Sultan Bunsaar's guard, but they paid no attention.

Ruomaani-Skye ordered him silent, "I hardly consider walking the perimeter of my own tent a dangerous pastime. If

I'm to be shadowed by an escort for the entire trip home, then I suggest you pay better attention to my movements." It was unfair, and she knew it. As always, she had sneaked away at the best possible moment and there was no way Feldahd, or any of her father's personal guard, could have noticed.

"Now, if you insist, I was just about to walk our slop boy here over to the feed coach, so he may tend to my animals."

Cappa was at a loss for words. Never had he stood in silence for so long while others talked around him as if he were not there. Never had he been so demeaned and disregarded, addressed in such a derogatory manner - *slop boy?*

It was so insulting the only reaction he could summon was stifled laughter seeing Ruomaani-Skye turn on him immediately, "And what is so funny?"

He shrugged, "Nothing at all… my lady."

"Ah, so he does speak." Her eyes sparkled as she continued, "Well, come on. These animals won't feed themselves."

*

Laonardo nearly fell from his chair, his wine spilling over. "She called you slop boy?"

It was too much, and he and Trentach laughed harder.

Cappa laughed with them as he poured himself a drink from the carafe.

Laonardo roared, "That is priceless, slop boy!" he snorted. "Then what happened?"

Cappa grinned, "She led me to the feed cart with this Feldahd in tow and demanded I feed her carmols."

Laonardo sniggered, "And that was it?"

"That was it."

"She dismissed you without a word?"

Cappa nodded, appreciating what this meant to Laonardo.

"And nothing more was said?" Trentach enquired.

"Not really, other than… put that there and fetch this here."

This finished it for Laonardo and he guffawed heartily,

"Ha hah... put it there slop boy, bring that here slop boy, kiss my Sultan-ess arse slop boy!"

Cappa laughed as Laonardo continued to mock.

"Still, I have the highest hopes for you. Perhaps next time she'll have you wipe her father's arse before carrying his slop." Laonardo managed to stem his laughter to maintain his wistful drama, "Could it be true? That you... a lowly slop boy, could one day rise to the dizzy heights of Royal Arse Wipe?" His performance was worthy of applause, but Laonardo settled for continuing laughter.

*

The wine had continued late into the night and as Cappa carried the barrel to the cesspit, his head felt a little fuzzy. It was his stomach however that was to suffer most as in his delicate nature he poured the pungent slops into the hole.

As he returned to the perimeter, those within the grounds were busy with breakfast before the dismantling of the camp would begin. He watched as a handful of Bunsaar's soldiers gathered their belongings nearby, as always never mixing with Kirkoban's rabble of hired men and tribal guards.

After returning the barrel to the Sultan's carriage, he let out an almighty yawn and felt the twinge of his headache once more.

"I see a slop boy's work is never done."

His heart thumped in his chest on hearing her voice, and Cappa realised at that moment he would always be happy to hear it, whether mocking him or not.

He turned and saw Ruomaani-Skye approach, Feldahd's glare not far behind her. The bodyguard was clearly displeased at this meeting and grunted to show this displeasure.

Ruomaani-Skye didn't turn to Feldahd as she quipped, "If your throat is dry Feldahd, get yourself some water." Her large brown eyes dazzled Cappa from beneath her silk headscarf, the dark waves of her hair just visible as they disappeared beneath woven finery.

"I will stay by your side as are my orders, my lady."

She smiled wickedly, "Then please try to do so without coughing on me like some dustbowl bear."

The bodyguard tried not to notice the smile this brought to Cappa's face. Ruomaani-Skye was quick to alter her offensive. "You find me amusing slop boy?"

"Only if you wish to be amusing, my lady." His answer was smooth and well spoken. None of the uncharacteristic stammers were present at this second opportunity.

Although she did not show it, this delighted Ruomaani-Skye. "The only wishes you need concern yourself with are those I instruct you to perform in my service."

Cappa bowed, "Serving you is an honour my lady, never a concern."

This time it was much harder for Ruomaani-Skye not to smile, but she managed it somehow. She looked at his bruised face and remembered the warrior in the Torantum.
Feldahd had heard quite enough and was set to step in when Juhmad, the Mecdia Lieutenant, pulled up on his horse.

He read the expression of annoyance on the bodyguard's face before tilting to the Sultan's daughter. "Forgive my intrusion, but is this boy bothering you?"

Feldahd was quick to air his frustration, "Lieutenant, kindly remind your people of their proper place within this caravan."

Juhmad was obedient, "Get back to your duties at once," he instructed. "When the caravan is ready to leave report to Captain Bayer - whereupon we shall discuss your manners!"

Juhmad delighted at Cappa's expression as Kirkoban's daughter was led away.

CHAPTER 10

Banteez Bayer understood Juhmad's strategy. Certain rules were put before those winning employment via the Torantum, and in being seen to enforce these rules with confidence, the Lieutenant could stake his claim to a more permanent position.

Bayer also appreciated Juhmad was one of those who thrived on such newly gained authority.

Banteez Bayer had no such ambition. He wanted a quick income, so he could head south through the Sultan Dreda's territory and on into the Ferentae Straights where he intended to seek his fortune mining silver. As such, Bayer had little time for Juhmad's latest spat with the young Thiazarran and had sent Cappa on his way with barely a slap on the wrist.

Bayer had then added a few words of caution to his Lieutenant on the wisdom of picking fights with the youth.

"You beat him!" Juhmad replied, clearly missing the point.

"I'm inclined to believe that may have been most fortunate on my part," Bayer had replied. "He, and his friend, are Thiazarran, and as such they've been trained to fight pretty much since the day they could crawl."

Juhmad had scoffed at the Captain, and as he'd gone on to help get the caravan underway, thought it a lack of leadership on Bayer's part not to add further punishment to the latrine duties already dished out.

*

As day four approached its climax, the caravan's attentions were drawn to the imminent arrival at the township, Fraeda.

As for Cappa, he'd seen nothing more of his desert Princess, though her father Kirkoban had grown much more self-assured. He'd made himself noticed several times since crossing the border into his own territory, both he and his stallion suddenly a predominant part of the caravan as the overnight stay in Fraeda approached.

As they'd journeyed on, the dark robed warriors of Bunsaar's private guard saw fit to continue at a healthy distance. Even Kirkoban seemed pretty much ignored by them for the most part, and Cappa, Laonardo and Trentach were at a loss as to whether this was just a soldiers' professionalism or simply a complete lack of interest.

Cappa was frustrated at gaining no further opportunity with Ruomaani-Skye, while Laonardo began harbouring private concerns over where such infatuation could lead.

*

The fourth day passed uneventfully, and so far it seemed guarding caravans was easy money. Fraeda was reached before sunset, its unimpressive turrets jutting out of the baked earth with little authority. It would have been swallowed whole within one quadrant of Numbala's citadel and had nothing of the bustling activity of Bunsaar's capital.

The walls protecting the township stood only twice an average person's height and showed signs of disrepair in places. The market close to the inner square was humble to say the least and the merchant stalls had little of the colour and vibrancy of those in the last town.

Fraeda was a water outpost, a border town close to the narrow strip of neutral ground between the two Sultans' territories.

Trentach informed Cappa and Laonardo to expect much of the same in Malbood, explaining how Kirkoban's capital offered little more than Fraeda other than being bigger and having a denser population.

Mounted in the saddle of his stallion, Sultan Kirkoban led the grand carriage into the small citadel at the town's heart, clearly pleased to be back in his homelands. Kirkoban's tribal guard followed together with Bunsaar's men, the Mecdia soldiers having been ordered to make camp in the market square outside.

With their tents erected and supplies unloaded, Laonardo had set off to see their horses into the designated paddock.

Cappa organised the supplies and luggage in the rear of their tent and was preparing to wash when Trentach returned after seeing his carmol fed and watered.

"You care for those bundles like your life depended on it," Trentach gestured to the concealed items and wrapped poles.

Cappa smiled, appreciating how his new friend had never pried into the contents of the bundles.

"They're cooking genta steaks at the far end of the market. I've also ordered wine from the merchant. He said to pick it up in a little while."

Cappa nodded and manoeuvred his back to Trentach, removing two throwing daggers from his belt, the only Pathan weapons he and Laonardo ever concealed on their person.

"Still dreaming of forbidden fruit?"

Cappa laughed, "Something like that." He wrapped the daggers in a towel.

"Well, there's going to be a dance tonight to take your mind off it. They're building a pyre in the central square, and I've just seen some musicians pitching up."

Laonardo appeared and gave Trentach a shove. "Did somebody mention a party?" He rubbed his hands. "You see, I told you this dust-hole had a certain understated charm."

*

The fire cracked as if sensing the change in tempo, spitting sparks into the air to accompany each musical note.

The baked earth fought hard against the dancers but as the night wore on it was turning quickly into sand - the town square of Fraeda a warm glow of dusty festivity.

The stars were out in force and the smell of cooked meat, smoke and wine lingered. Laughter fought with singing as the plucked strings battled against drums.

Kirkoban's sorry little town was sorry no longer.

Banteez Bayer danced a jig with Trentach, egged on by Laonardo who quaffed more wine.

The sight of an elegant brunette distracted Cappa, as he once again allowed himself to be fooled for a fleeting moment, that the Sultan's daughter had slipped out to play.

Laonardo leaned close, "She'll not be setting foot out here, even if she wanted to."

Cappa was a little embarrassed at being so transparent. He knew it of course, but his heart so wanted each chance to be the moment his commonsense was proved wrong.

On this occasion, the girl danced into a crowd of friends, and she looked even less like Ruomaani-Skye than the twenty previous candidates who he'd imagined might be her.

He sipped the wine and sighed.

Laonardo put his arm around him. "What say we take in the stars for a moment," he smiled at his friend, "Talk this through."

Cappa had known this was coming. As Patruan, Laonardo had a duty to ensure the wellbeing of his future King, and Cappa suspected the conversation would not be of aching hearts alone.

As they strolled into the night air, leaving the glow and warmth of the party behind, Laonardo was quick to prove Cappa's suspicion correct. "We need to discuss what's happening here," he said in a serious tone, "This isn't just another girl, is it?"

Cappa looked to his friend under the moonlight, "No. This is something else entirely."

Laonardo was not pleased. "And pray tell me, where do you see this thing going?"

Cappa shrugged, "I don't know. I haven't given it too much thought."

"Well maybe you should, because as an expatriate Thiazarran without a pot to piss in, you're not going to be allowed anywhere near that girl. If you keep pushing this flirtation, there could be serious consequences."

"I know."

"Consequences I have to seriously consider as your Patruan."

Cappa remained silent.

"As a dustbowl mercenary they'll cut your balls off if you make a play for a Sultan's daughter," he stopped Cappa from interrupting as he continued, "The only other option carries equally serious consequences, for the both of us."

Cappa sighed, "I appreciate what you're saying, of course I do. I'm fully aware of the potential dangers and complications." Cappa had thought long and hard on this over the past two days, when he'd seen no sign of his fantasy girl, "We're talking about someone I barely know." Cappa pressed his chest earnestly, "But I feel something so very real whenever I'm near her." He stopped and looked up at the stars. "I guess I'm just hoping for a moment, a meeting substantial enough so I can judge the situation better."

"The likes of which could put you in potential danger," Laonardo emphasised. "You've already got this Feldahd suspicious of you, a man who's had you taken before Bayer. Next time you may find yourself in front of somebody much less friendly to your cause." Laonardo added, "Then there's our brown-nosing Lieutenant just waiting in the wings."

"He's a fool."

"A fool he may be, but fools can stir a hornet's nest as easily as the cunning."

"But is it really so dangerous when compared to things we've done these past eighteen months?" Cappa pondered, "I mean these past days alone, dull yes, but we've just guarded a vagabond Sultan across four days of potential bandit country."

"I'm not saying the dangers are any more-or-less significant," Laonardo replied, "But it is my duty to inform you of a potential risk to your wellbeing. Although on the face of it this may seem trivial by comparison to many things we've done, it has the potential to put us in harm's way. And that is before we even consider the long-term complications that could arise if infatuation turns to something else entirely."

"I'll be careful." Cappa assured, "We have less than two days before we reach Malbood, then our service with this rabble is done if we so choose. Let's see what happens between now and then. See if fate steps in before we reassess the situation." Cappa smiled, "Who knows, maybe by then she'll be out of my system."

CHAPTER 11

The town's people of Fraeda began tidying the moment Kirkoban's convoy was packed and ready to go.

The Mecdia had risen early, most of them happy to help clear the mess left from the festivities. As they prepared to leave, the place had the feel of a carnival having been to town, and amidst goodbyes and groaning carmols, the procession headed for the main gate.

There was still no sign of Ruomaani-Skye, and as the caravan made its way to the town perimeter, Kirkoban opted for the fine stallion to make his exit, waving to the subjects he'd happily ignored the night before.

Kirkoban had reinforced the tribal contingent among his guards, taking ten of the thirty stationed in the township.

The dark collection of Bunsaar's guards paid tribute to Kirkoban before setting off back to Numbala, their duty to deliver the Sultan to his own territory fulfilled.

Riding at the rear, Cappa, Laonardo and Trentach watched as Bunsaar's troops rode away. "Those guys were a lot of fun." Trentach quipped. "I'm going to miss them."

Both Thiazarrans laughed.

Banteez Bayer dropped down the line, pulling his horse alongside, "Anyone else suffering a thick head? Or is it just me growing old?"

"Could be you getting old," Laonardo replied. "I feel fresh as spring flowers."

"I'm going to pretend you're lying to make myself feel better," Bayer watched Kirkoban as he rode alongside the carriage driven by Feldahd. "He's certainly a lot less shy when home."

"Let's hope he's as confident with his purse once we reach Malbood." The others agreed with Trentach.

Bayer's smile remained through squinted eyes, "We'll reach the Salt Canyon by noon. They can be a complex maze if you don't know them, but Feldahd knows a shorter route through that's wide enough for the coach. Reckons we'll reach the other side before sunset. We'll make camp in the caves then set off across the flats in order to reach Malbood by late afternoon tomorrow. Not long to figure out your next move."

The trio agreed but said little.

"The final leg should be pretty uneventful," Bayer added, "Though the ride across the valley-basin can be hazardous."

Trentach knew of this danger, "You're referring to the Grachk Plan-Nia?" he translated to his friends, "The Great White Noise."

The Mecdia Captain nodded.

"Great White Noise?" Laonardo asked.

Bayer explained, "Short but often severe storms. They slice through the valley we'll be crossing."

Trentach elaborated, "Gale force winds gather in the north and whip through a vast salt plain known as the Clamenta Basin. They travel south through the ravine we're to cross, picking up dirt from the cliffs on one side, throwing it together with the salt of the canyons opposite. The combination can be deadly as it builds up speed through the winding corridor."

Bayer informed, "We'll be headed for the narrow pass where the cliffs on Fraeda's side are low with gentler gradients. When the storms come, this topography creates a shrill whistle as powerful gusts pass overhead before the gales lash through the valley - a high pitched wind that warns of impending danger, hence the rather unimaginative name."

"And how regular are these storms?"

Trentach smiled at Laonardo, "Regular!"

"Great."

"Don't worry, the warning granted by the noise is usually sufficient to see caravans cross safely."

"You were going to mention this when?" Laonardo teased Trentach.

"I'm telling you now."

Laonardo shook his head, "How ironic it would be if our first danger as dustbowl mercenaries was to come courtesy of some mystical wind." He leaned on his saddle and addressed Cappa, "Deadly winds of salt and dirt, baked earth, bandits and no water. Remind me, why would anyone want to live here?"

The ensuing amusement gave way to Bayer's original query, "So, have you made any decision, on what your next move will be?"

A more disgruntled response followed on this occasion, a chorus of possibility without offering any real answer.

Cappa smiled, "We are awaiting divine intervention."

Bayer laughed, "Aren't we all my friends, aren't we all."

*

The noon sun seemed all the more relentless as the caravan reached the valley basin. The climb down had been a gradient of winding trails, but as the convoy traversed the lowland the baked earth succumbed to pallid salt, which reflected the heat more intensely.

Ahead loomed the impressive sight of the Salt Canyons.

Legend had it, the deep ravines carved through the towering cliffs were made by an ancient inland sea, long since taken by the sun. It once fed rivers and a lake the bed of which was rumoured to be the very floor on which they now walked. To the north, these deep chasms gave way to the colossal

Clamenta Cliffs, mountains of saline rock which towered over the Clamenta Basin, a plain of baked salt which reached as far west as Bunsaar's territory.

The caravan was halfway across with Trentach, Laonardo and Cappa keeping the rear, when a hot swirl picked up through the basin. Feldahd's instruction was relayed quickly down the line, "It's a gust, nothing more."

Cappa laughed at his Patruan's expression.

Laonardo grimaced, "You can taste the salt on the wind."

"Then keep your mouth closed and ears open," Cappa quipped, "I don't want to be caught out here if one of these storms hit."

"Oh, don't worry, I'm listening." Laonardo gestured to his following pack pony, "Perii broke wind several strides back and I nearly bolted for the other side."

Trentach laughed as he rode alongside Perii, patting her hind, "Always blaming you for his stench, eh girl?"

Laonardo turned, "Don't get her frisky, that's what sees her at her most productive."

The mood remained jovial, but such frivolity seemed misplaced suddenly, as once again the intensity of the wind picked up. The trio looked to one another with the first semblance of genuine concern. '*Surely the very thing so discussed and joked about wasn't actually set to happen.*'

With their senses pricked they turned their attention north through the ravine. There didn't seem to be anything out of the ordinary occurring, just the hot breeze picking up momentum.

Cappa turned his focus to the carriage. He still hadn't laid eyes on Ruomaani-Skye, and after the previous night's discussion found himself questioning his expectations once more. Again, he looked north to the distant face of the cliffs when he noticed something.

A number of carmols began lifting and dipping their heads. This was followed by disgruntled groans.

Cappa observed Trentach whose expression confirmed his alarm. "That is not a good sign," Trentach said frankly.

The tribal guards at the front of the line began bellowing instructions, which were now being relayed by Banteez Bayer.

The chain of yelled commands reached the three at the rear, "Quicken the pace! Kick in and quicken the pace!"

It seemed surreal to be faced with a danger that had been so casually discussed, but as the caravan picked up speed and the wind grew more aggressive, such thoughts of irony were no longer relevant.

The grunts and groans of their animals were mixed with yelled commands as the caravan accelerated. The Salt Canyons were close, but it was still a fair ride to reach them.

Cappa looked to the sound of a cracking whip followed by a yelled, "Yah!"

Feldahd was driving the carriage more keenly, the Sultan riding his stallion alongside it.

The trio upped their pace, Cappa and Laonardo towing their ponies, Trentach pulling his now grumbling carmol.

Another crack of the whip rang out.

Again, they glanced north, only this time a faint swirl could be seen turning into the ravine. The wind blew harder as a building haze interrupted the sunshine, its swirling momentum carried on the incoming gale, which now began whistling above their heads.

"The Grachk Plan-Nia," people began yelling as they kicked toward the canyons.

More whip-cracks followed as the carriage began to bounce over the salt flats toward the safety of the white ravines.

"Laonardo... Ruomaani-Skye's carriage!" Cappa yelled.

The two rode toward the tribal guards surrounding the coach, with Trentach quickly in tow.

They maintained a proper distance as the dust began to fly.

Another crack rang out, "Yah!"

They rode parallel to the guards as the wind picked up.

Cappa could see Feldahd driving the coach-horses hard. The carmols tethered to the rear kept the pace but it was clear the carriage would struggle to make the finish.

Kirkoban steered his stallion closer and began shouting instructions to Feldahd. His bodyguard immediately slowed the coach yelling several commands to the surrounding guards.

Cappa, Laonardo and Trentach maintained their distance, slowing in time with the coach. The wind howled with more intensity, the dust now whirling around them.

As Kirkoban moved to the rear of the carriage, Ruomaani-Skye appeared and within moments the Sultan plucked his daughter up and placed her behind him on his stallion.

The carriage ground to a halt and Feldahd headed into the coach as two guards vaulted in through the door at the rear. The two men reappeared carrying a heavy looking chest. Feldahd followed carrying a rigid-harness and woven cover. He attached the harness to the brace worn by one of the carmols tethered to the rear, and within moments, the guards heaved the chest into the mounting, before using the woven cover to conceal the trunk within.

Feldahd mounted a horse held by another waiting guard before claiming the reins of the carmol. He then set off at speed pulling the laden-carmol as he went.

On seeing the chest secure, Kirkoban set off with his daughter clutching his rear. The horses pulling the coach were slapped with another loud, "Yah!" to see if they could make the caves under their own speed. The whole transfer had taken moments and it was clear this was a sequence that had been well rehearsed.

The guards surrounded the Sultan and Feldahd as the race for the safety of the canyons was on once again.

Cappa and the others, unnoticed throughout this entire process, were snapping at their heels, maintaining a safe distance so as not to panic the tribal soldiers.

As the canyons drew closer a sense of chaos ensued, the wind turning to something else entirely. The dust and salt blasted around them as stones and debris hurtled through the air.

The commotion began to build, the dirt whipping their faces, the visibility dropping dramatically as Feldahd called out, "Aim for the cave directly ahead!"

Through the hail and swirl the black mouth of a cavern was just visible, most of the convoy already heading directly for it.

The poor horses pulling the heavy coach were left behind as the sprint took the group closer to safety.

The intensity of the wind increased, as did the volume, as more debris was sent flying through the air seeing riders duck low while clenching their reins as they rode through the mayhem.

Cappa made an attempt to see if Ruomaani-Skye was safe when he saw Feldahd suddenly struck by a shard of rock.

Feldahd yelped as it punched his forehead, knocking him from his horse. He hit the floor with a crunch, but the convoy rode on oblivious.

"Laonardo," Cappa yelled, "Feldahd is down!"

Through the sting of dirt and salt, they could see him on the floor clinging to the reins of both his horse and the cargo-laden carmol, both animals agitated as Feldahd desperately tried to pull himself up.

Laonardo dismounted and handed his reins to Cappa before pulling the concussed Feldahd to his feet. Cappa steered Coba alongside and took control of Feldahd's mounts when suddenly Kirkoban came into view, Ruomaani-Skye still clutching his back.

The Sultan yelled for his daughter to take charge of their stallion as he pulled to a stop. Ruomaani-Skye did so, as her father leapt to Laonardo's side.

Kirkoban offered no assistance and instead mounted Feldahd's horse, snatching the reins from Cappa to take control of both the steed and the cargo-laden carmol.

Kirkoban held firm for a moment, but as the tempest intensified, he kicked his heels yelling, "Head for the caves!"

Laonardo hauled Feldahd over his shoulder and struggled through the swirling dirt. He hoisted the fallen guard over the bundles on his pack-pony's rear, before mounting his stallion. Both he and Cappa could hear Trentach yelling for them to hurry but could no longer see him through the howling storm.

More debris began lashing the air as the Sultan began his ride for the cave, his daughter now in pursuit once she'd seen Feldahd placed safely on the pony. They too disappeared into the storm with Cappa and Laonardo chasing.

"Follow my voice!" Trentach kept yelling at the top of his lungs. They obeyed, catching sight once again of the carmol carrying the chest as it bounded through the swirling storm.

More debris lashed their faces when the darkness of the cave mouth came into view. Suddenly, the shadows of the great salt cliffs were above and around them and through the swirling madness Cappa and Laonardo could see riders from their convoy welcoming the Sultan into the safety of the vast cave entrance.

The two followed, pulling their mounts to a stop, the whinnying snorts of their steeds blending with the echoes of the other recent arrivals to the large cavern.

The dark calm of their natural fortress seemed surreal after the stinging gales, and both men turned to witness the passing bedlam through the safety of the cave window.

Several tribal guards began fussing over the Sultan, mortified at having unintentionally left him behind.

More came to the aid of Feldahd as Laonardo dismounted, pulling him down with the help of a very relieved looking Trentach.

In the melee nobody seemed to share Cappa's concern.

He flashed his gaze across the cave a third time, "Where is Ruomaani-Skye?"

Before any could answer, the cries of the Sultan's daughter were heard as she struggled through the storm.

On realising she was still outside, Cappa cut the tie tethering his pony to Coba and dug in his heels.

Laonardo shouted, but as he laid Feldahd to the ground it was too late, his friend had bolted out of the cave back into the storm.

Other animals crowded Laonardo's horse, and he began shooing them away, so he could go to Cappa's aid.

This only added to the confusion as Kirkoban realised what was transpiring. "Ruomaani?" he yelled over and over.

She answered, clearly not far from the entrance, but as several guards and Laonardo prepared to exit, they were relieved to hear Cappa call out, "Stay in there, I have her!"

In the violence of the storm he had caught sight of her wandering without the stallion. He rode to her, pulling her quickly up onto Coba, shouting, "Hold tight!"

A wall of wind struck them. Coba whinnied and reared, but Cappa controlled him well.

Ruomaani-Skye held on as Cappa then kicked them forward, the stallion grunting as he fought the storm.

The cave entrance was suddenly in view, "Don't come out!" Cappa yelled, "We're coming in!"

Cappa had Coba leap for the cave just as the real storm rallied, the Great White Noise now truly present. It blasted them sideways and up into the air but just as they prepared for the worst, they were back within the safety of the hollow.

Cappa pulled them to a stop, Coba grunting and spinning. They panted as the storm blasted past the entrance, the pair slouching forward in relief. However, this respite quickly turned to confusion as Cappa flashed his focus around their surroundings.

This was not the same cave.

CHAPTER 12

Ruomaani-Skye was under no illusion how close they had just come to death. The power of the wind, which struck as they entered the cave, was incredible.

She dismounted and turned to Cappa, "Thank you," she breathed heavily. "Thank you for coming back. I never would have made it."

Cappa jumped off his horse, "It was lucky you were close by." He began calming Coba. "Are you injured? What happened to your horse?"

"I was thrown from the saddle," she explained. "But no, I'm fine." Ruomaani-Skye turned to watch the storm as it raged across the narrow entrance. "Where are the others?"

Her alluring accent enchanted despite the storm's efforts, "They must be in the cave next to us."

She observed the easy light inside the cavern, then pointed upwards, "This is no cave… Look."

Cappa followed her gaze up the salt rock that ascended in a jagged vertical passage. High above through a narrow opening they could make out the stormy sky.

Ruomaani-Skye was right; this wasn't a cave it was a deep ravine, one of the cavernous alleyways that sliced through the peaks to make the Salt Canyons.

Cappa's gaze fell back on the desert beauty as she watched the tempest above. Her scarf had been blown away; her dark hair dishevelled. Her skin was stimulated by the stinging storm, her eyes dark and wide. The silks of her attire suffered the full effects of the squall, yet it only served to make her more intensifying.

He caught his breath; aware it was not just the adrenaline forcing him to do so.

Ruomaani-Skye could feel his eyes on her, but she allowed him his moment before looking to him, "What?" she asked.

A moment passed between them, when even the storm seemed to fade momentarily.

The man staring back at her was no stumbling slop boy.

She breathed slowly, her chest heaving.

Cappa broke the spell by allowing a huge grin to appear.

This made Ruomaani-Skye smile as she enquired of him once more, "What?"

Cappa laughed, "How close did we just come? Did you feel the wind as we jumped for the entrance? I thought we were heading up into the air."

Ruomaani-Skye grinned, "My heart stopped," she placed her palm across her chest, "I'm not certain it's even started again." She laughed, both of them indulging the powerful sensation of relief.

Cappa turned to his grumbling horse, "Oh I know we shouldn't laugh, Coba." He patted the stallion's neck as if to apologise for placing him in such danger, checking him once more for signs of injury.

The more sombre reality returned, as Ruomaani-Skye enquired, "Did my father make it back? And your friend with Feldahd?"

"They're fine. I think most people made it to the cave." She appeared relieved. They fell silent once more and watched the storm, its raging torrents suddenly more conspicuous as it whipped the entrance. Eventually she turned to him, "Where do you think we are in relation to the others?"

"I'm guessing they are over there," he pointed at the wall, "Maybe fifty strides? It's hard to say, the storm was so intense."

She nodded.

"We'll just sit it out. They can't be far away. How long do these storms last?"

"This is only the third I've witnessed. On both prior occasions they were fairly brief."

"Only the third?" Cappa smiled, "There was me thinking storms are all you people know."

Ruomaani-Skye was set to reply when she noticed a stream of dust fall from above. She frowned and looked up to see a broad shadow forming rapidly above them. She stared for a moment, as if her brain was not prepared to process the information, but then the realisation struck, "Look out!"

He turned just as Ruomaani-Skye hit him at speed, tackling him to safety as an avalanche of earth and rubble fell - missing them by inches. As they hit the floor, Coba bolted to safety, the melee crashing and cascading all around them.

Where there had been humour and concourse, there was now blackness and salty dust. The cavern walls hissed under the crumbling dirt, until eventually the commotion settled.

Cappa protected her head under his arms as she lay on top of him. He felt her cough into his chest, "Are you alright?"

She pulled clear of his embrace, "I'm fine, you?"

"I'm okay."

She coughed again, the polluted air aggravating her throat.

Their faces almost touched; their eyes close enough to just see the glimmer of those staring back at them.

They wriggled clear of the debris, helping each other up before brushing themselves down. "You sure you're okay?" Cappa asked as she coughed again.

"It's just dust in my throat," she reassured.

They squinted to take in their surroundings. Where the canyon entrance had stood only moments before was now a wall of fallen rubble, the window to the storm outside now a curtain plunging them into near darkness.

It took a moment for their vision to readjust.

They looked up to see the slither of stormy sky still there.

Only the entry had collapsed.

It looked like the storm was beginning to abate, the noise of the tempest now distant through the rubble cutting them off from the outside world. The darkness eased another shade as they adjusted to the new conditions.

Cappa turned to Ruomaani-Skye, "I guess that makes us even."

"We'd better get out of here in case there's another landslide," she gestured to the barricade, "We won't be able to climb our way out. It's too unstable." She pointed along the open roof of the winding crevasse. "This fissure may well cut through to the other side of the canyons."

He looked to where Ruomaani-Skye indicated as more debris crumbled to the ground at the entrance.

They heard Coba whinny and caught a glimpse of his eye reflected in the shadows. Cappa headed to him, relieved to see his mount had survived unscathed.

After a moment of fussing, Cappa paused, not certain if he'd just heard something. He concentrated, noticing several thin cracks in the walls of the passage, "Listen."

As they investigated, they could feel a draught on their faces as faint yelling could be heard through several fractures. "There it is again," Cappa said. "It must be the others."

They both began shouting through the gaps. It took several attempts until eventually they got the faintest of replies. "Ruomaani, is that you?"

It was her father, though he sounded far away.

"It's me, I'm alright. We got to safety just before the storm hit."

"Where are you?"

"We entered a narrow catacomb, but the entrance has collapsed, and we're trapped."

"The storm is breaking; we'll come and dig you out."

"It's too unstable. You'll only bury yourselves if you try. We're going to follow the canyon until we reach the other side. The gorge appears to slice all the way through."

A brief silence followed.

"Let us at least try to get through to you first."

More dirt and dust hissed down the walls, "Believe me it will be far less dangerous for us to travel through the canyon. The whole place could come crashing down any moment." Another silence followed. "Father, we have a horse, and the corridor appears wide enough for us to ride. We'll meet you on the other side. It's the only option."

A weak protest followed as Ruomaani moved away from the communication hole. She looked to Cappa, "Well, are you up for trying to make it through?"

He returned his attention to the crack, "Laonardo?"

After a moment his Patruan's voice could be heard. "I'm here."

"Follow Feldahd's trail. Once you reach the other side, light signal fires. As soon as we are through, we'll head to you."

Laonardo agreed and though neither could know it, at that moment both Patruan and Prince shared exactly the same thought, '*Perhaps fate was stepping in after all.*'

CHAPTER 13

Laonardo had been most relieved to hear Cappa's voice through the fracture. He'd feared the worst when Cappa fled the safety of the cave to aid Ruomaani-Skye.

He had managed to clear a path to go after him as those around him dithered, but he and his stallion were struck by the awesome power of the storm as they attempted to venture out. It blasted them backward, throwing Laonardo from his saddle.

From that moment his world was in danger of collapsing, until two of the mercenaries heard yelled replies emanating from the walls of the cave just as the storm began to cease.

The relief was almost too much to bear.

Later he would chastise Cappa, but for the moment Laonardo was jubilant his friend was alive and well.

As he checked the ropes linking the pack ponies, Laonardo acknowledged the quirk of fate once more, how Cappa and the girl of his dreams, were now alone together... a girl whose cowardly father had just summoned Laonardo to report.

Laonardo turned to Trentach as he mounted, "Ready?"

Trentach was already in the saddle with his grumbling carmol at the rear. He nodded with a smile.

The Sultan and his guards were still inspecting the landfall at the mouth of the blocked ravine. Laonardo had examined it the moment the storm abated, quickly ascertaining that nobody would be getting through such a blockade any time soon. He had smiled despite the situation, understanding once again how happy his friend would be at the position he found himself in.

The pair approached the tribal guards surrounding Kirkoban, who continued to aimlessly scrutinize the mountain of dirt sealing him from his daughter. Feldahd was laid on a stretcher tethered to the rear of a horse. His deputy rode toward them, "The Sultan will see you alone."

Trentach shrugged indifferently, "I'll wait here."

The sun had returned - the skies now clear as if nothing had happened. There was little to no debris on the plain, as the Great White Noise had ejected the evidence far and wide.

Had it not been for the enormous rock fall one could be forgiven for believing there had been no storm. Even the fine carriage and the horses pulling it had vanished without trace, so powerful was the visiting tempest.

Seeing Laonardo approach, the Sultan turned his horse about and headed his way. "Ride with me," he said as the two met head on.

Laonardo pulled alongside Kirkoban, keeping the gentle pace of the Sultan's mount.

Kirkoban was apprehensive, "Your friend, Cappa. How long have you known him?"

Laonardo understood where this was going, "All of my life."

Kirkoban nodded. "He is a good man? An honourable man?"

Laonardo cut to the chase, "You want to know if you can trust him with your daughter?"

"Can I?" Kirkoban appreciated the thrust.

"You can." Laonardo looked over his shoulder to see Feldahd's deputy following slowly.

Kirkoban continued, "You must understand why I have to ask. My daughter is very precious to me. As is her reputation."

Laonardo stared at him, "You could not have placed her in better care had you planned it. Believe me, both your daughter and her reputation will remain safe."

The Sultan appeared reassured. "You and this, Cappa... you are Thiazarran, yes?"

Laonardo nodded.

"Traders, who lost their goods to the storms?"

"Yes."

Again, he seemed a little more at ease. "You are a noble people."

It was more of an enquiry than a statement of fact.

"Noble enough to face danger in order to help others," Laonardo stated firmly, "Cappa was the first to turn back for your bodyguard, the first out of the cave to aid your daughter."

Kirkoban pursed his lips then grunted his satisfaction. He turned his horse, steering them back toward the group waiting by the canyons. "You will both be rewarded. Cappa for saving my daughter... you for saving Feldahd."

"We require no reward."

The Sultan turned to him with a raised eyebrow, "A foolish statement, and you are clearly not a fool." He gestured to the crowd just a short trot away, "We lost two to the storm. One of them was Juhmad your Lieutenant. I will be promoting you to take his post. Cappa likewise once he has reunited me with my daughter. I'm sure Banteez Bayer will appreciate having two worthy deputies for the remainder of our short trip. Once we are in Malbood, we shall discuss a more fitting tribute."

*

Cappa led Coba on foot with Ruomaani-Skye perched in the saddle. The ravine had at first narrowed to little more than a passage as they left the blocked entrance behind, but had since opened into a broad corridor, much to the relief of the stallion.

Ruomaani-Skye had proved keen to proceed, showing little interest in awaiting her father's attempts at finding a route through. A factor picked up on by Cappa, who wondered if the opportunity for adventure was instantly appealing to her.

'*Perhaps this was her best chance to escape the constraints of normal life, even if just for a day?*' Naturally, Cappa understood this more than she could possibly know.

The sky was bright overhead, though the towering walls of the gorge ensured any heat wishing to penetrate the depths had little success. A welcome factor during the day, though Cappa was concerned at the possible drop in temperature come night. They couldn't be certain of this jagged canyon's path and as such, could not predict how long they may be held within its walls.

As they continued down the ravine, Cappa noticed some fallen foliage ahead. He brought the stallion to a stop before bending down to inspect the remains.

Ruomaani-Skye watched as he pulled twine from one of his saddlebags. He then set about gathering the brushwood and wrapping it into a bundle. "For a fire should we be forced to spend the night here," he said as he looked to her. "Feldahd's route through was to see the caravan reach the caves on the other side by sundown. We have no way of knowing if this path will do the same. It feels to me like we are already curving away from our intended course. It will be cold down here at night." As he began snapping the coarser wood Ruomaani-Skye jumped down to offer assistance. Cappa protested, "Please, don't trouble…"

"If there's any chance we are staying down here tonight," she interrupted, "Then I want a decent fire." She wondered if the excitement she was trying to conceal was obvious to Cappa. To be free of her watchful father for an entire night was an exciting prospect to say the least. To be spending it with the handsome and intriguing Thiazarran was a thrill beyond imagining.

Once they'd tied the wood, Cappa pondered how best to strap it to the horse.

"I'll walk," Ruomaani-Skye instructed, "That way we can tether the bundles across the saddle."

Cappa agreed and the two set about binding the wood to the leather seat before setting off once more.

After a few steps she asked, "Your name is, Cappa?"

"Yes."

"A nickname - or is there more to your title?" she smiled.

"Just Cappa." He returned her smile.

She tilted, "My name is Ruomaani-Skye," she of course knew he was aware, "Though you may call me Ruomaani."

He acknowledged the privilege, "It is nice to meet you, Ruomaani."

The informality thrilled her, though Ruomaani did her best to conceal the fact. "So, you are Thiazarran?"

"Is it so obvious?"

She smiled, "I heard it mentioned somewhere."

"Heard it mentioned? I wasn't aware I was of such interest."

She flushed a little, "Feldahd spoke of it to my father."

Cappa joked, "The Thiazarran slop boy."

She laughed.

"The very nerve of him talking to my daughter!" Cappa impersonated a stern father.

"Indeed." She looked at him enjoying his humour.

"Yet, if I was one to split hairs, it was actually you who first addressed me." He added.

"Yes, because I caught you snooping around my tent."

"I was hardly snooping."

"Then what were you doing?" Her eyes dazzled him.

"Oh, you know… slop boy stuff." She laughed as Cappa continued, "You may mock, but I'll have you know there's far more to being a slop boy than people think."

"Really?"

"Really."

"Such as?"

Cappa shrugged. "I'm not prepared to divulge the secrets of my trade. If I was to tell all of the complexities then anyone could become a slop boy, and where would that leave me?"

She smiled, "Something tells me you'd get by. You seem a little too, cultured shall we say, to rely on such a vocation."

"Nothing is beneath you when you need food in your belly."

"I meant no offence."

He smiled, "And none was taken."

"I merely meant you appear educated."

"I can write my own name," he said mockingly.

"And you can also fight, which can only lead me to believe your slop boy duties were perhaps a punishment of some kind?"

"Why presume it a punishment?"

"Need I really go into it?" Her manner was hugely disarming.

Cappa kept his focus on the trail ahead as he responded, "Such duties have their benefits."

She blushed at the implication as an awkward but intoxicating silence followed.

"So, what did you do?" Ruomaani asked intuitively as the moment passed.

He grinned, "I was insubordinate."

"Ooh, the unruly sort?" she teased. "And in my father's employ."

"It's to be expected under such recruitment methods."

"I see. I take it a Torantum would feature less prominently in Thiazarran society?"

"It wouldn't feature at all. Recruitment to such a cause is achieved somewhat differently where I come from."

This tweaked her interest, "Hmm. Different, better... or different worse?"

"Different... different."

She pursed her lips. "Your tone suggests you disapprove."

"Hardly," he replied, "without such a custom I'd still be tending gentas."

"As opposed to emptying sewage."

"Precisely," he laughed.

"If I'm honest, I find it difficult to see you doing either."
The transparency to her compliment was intended.

"As I said, we all need to make a living."

"I find it intriguing. Zarrapathia is a most prosperous place is
it not and Thiazarra its most prominent realm? So why would
an educated Thiazarran find himself emptying slops in the
outlands of Ferenta?"

"My friend Laonardo and I are merchants. We came here to
sell ploona."

"Thiazarran silk?"

"You know of it?"

"You could say that... I'm wearing some."

"Really?" He quickly studied her outfit, "Where?"

The red tinge to her cheeks returned. "Just trust me on it."

"Oh," he laughed at the impropriety, "Well, then you'll
know of its value."

"So, what happened?" she was happy to move the
conversation on.

"We lost our supplies to the desert. Everything but our
stallions and pack ponies."

"Why didn't you just return home?"

"Money, pride," he looked at her knowing she would
understand his next statement, "Freedom."

She nodded.

He went on, "Out here we can make our own adventure.
Neither of us is quite ready to give that up. Back home certain
responsibilities await - Here they do not."

Ruomaani-Skye understood this all too well. "Would these
responsibilities stem from your family by any chance?"

"Yes," Cappa replied. "But more than that. It's
complicated."

Ruomaani noted how his tone remained upbeat, cheerful
almost, despite the resignation to such a fate. This she
understood less well. "Most intriguing." She said before
offering an empty smile, "Commitments put on you by family

can be a heavy burden." She remained silent for a moment. "So, what commitments await this educated slop boy once he's returned home? The family business? An arranged marriage? The girl of his dreams?"

Cappa smiled, "Like I said, it's complicated."

Her interest was tweaked further, "A young man of mystery."

"It's not my intention."

She grinned, "Oh come now, Cappa, yes it is, and a fine ploy it is to play. Mystery can be very…" she contemplated.

"Mysterious?"

Ruomaani laughed, "Precisely." She was warming to her companion. "I'm told some girls would find such an attribute most intoxicating."

"Really?" Cappa smiled, "and you?"

"I am the daughter of a Sultan - I've little time for such indulgence."

"If the amount of time you spent hiding in that carriage is anything to go by, I'd have thought time is a luxury you do have."

His humour was well intended but she was clearly put out. The last thing she wanted to discuss during this briefest gift of liberty was the restrictions of her desert coach.

Cappa decided to offer up some insight to reignite her fun, "No girl of my dreams, and thankfully, no arranged marriage awaits. As for the family business, let's just say I have a certain role to play and leave it at that."

She was clearly happier with this direction.

"And what about you?" He asked with an air of caution.

The empty smile returned, "I also have a certain role to play," the smile warmed as she looked at him, "Let us leave it at that."

Cappa stared into her dark eyes and bristled. Her rich accent was like music pulling him to his knees, her beauty so alluring it was like a sweet poison that left him numb.

She was aware of his longing, enjoyed it. Cappa, like all men, was clearly captivated by her, but she sensed something so much more in the young Thiazarran.

Her smile grew into a broader grin, "How is your lip?"

The choice of words employed to break the brief spell threw Cappa at first, but then he remembered the swelling left courtesy of Banteez Bayer. "Oh," he stumbled, "Fine."

"I'd wager such a blow hurt greatly at the time?"

"An elbow clean in the face does tend to smart a little. But it's only bruised."

"Like your ego?" she continued to tease.

"I have no ego when fighting. It clouds judgement, distracts from the clarity required."

She was delighted. "So, you are never distracted during such moments?"

He remembered the scarf sailing on the breeze, revisited the moment he first saw the beauty now tormenting him. Only now she was but a few short paces from his embrace - he was but a brave moment from feeling her lips in a warm kiss. He dared himself to act but instead found himself blushing at her observation.

She decided to provide an escape route, "I suspect Vhlarm was more disappointed."

"Vhlarm?"

"The Sultan Bunsaar's bodyguard."

"Ah yes, the bull with the horns who battered Bayer in the Torantum."

"Humiliated, would be a more apt description." She clearly held no affection for Bunsaar's Captain, "I saw his reaction to you. I think he would have preferred to meet you in the arena rather than Bayer." Though she would not admit it, a small part of her would have liked to see the same spectacle.

"Then I can count myself fortunate Bayer saved me from such an ordeal."

Another short silence took hold as they headed deeper into the ravine.

"Do all Thiazarrans know how to fight?"

"Yes."

"Even the merchants?"

"Especially the merchants."

Her smile returned. "And are all Thiazarran's so eloquent and brave?" The compliment was spoken with warmth. She knew she should steer away from such indulgence, but she couldn't help herself. Ruomaani had never met anyone like Cappa before. Their paths had crossed several times in the past few days, and she'd felt each moment most profoundly, not least when he'd ventured back into the storm to save her life.

"When speaking of or fighting for those we care about," Cappa turned to her, "Yes."

She turned from his piercing stare and chastised herself for her foolish flirtation. She was getting the answers she desired, but in doing so was only making matters worse.

Cappa witnessed her withdrawal and understood the need for retreat. "I have some bread, cheese and water in the saddle bag. We should take a moment to eat and drink something. We've some ground to cover and we'll need our strength."

Ruomaani stood silently as he set about fetching the supplies and discreetly admired the strength in his calf as he reached into the bag. She turned away and sighed, a part of her wishing the freedom of this ravine could go on forever.

*

Laonardo observed the rich red sunset from the mouth of the small cavern he and Trentach had chosen as their dwelling for the evening. Feldahd's route had seen them almost through to the other side of the Salt Canyons and, although behind schedule, the deep cut of the ravine was already giving way to easier landscape.

He sighed as he thought of Cappa and Ruomaani-Skye, the natural dose of mixed emotions affecting his mood.

He could see several guards lighting a pyre in one of the larger caves, the wood still in abundance despite losing one of their fuel carrying carmols to the storm.

With Trentach tending to the animals in the makeshift paddock, Laonardo pulled himself away from the majestic sky to set about building a more humble fire.

As he crouched to prepare more kindling, he heard the fall of a footstep. He turned to see Feldahd approach, wearing a large diagonal bandage to comfort the bloodstain above his temple.

Laonardo gestured to the evening glory, "A desolate place this may be, but I swear the sunsets here are greater than anywhere I've seen." Feldahd was clearly still uncomfortable from his wound. "Should you be up walking?" Laonardo asked, "That was some blow to the head you took."

Feldahd smiled, "I won't deny I've seen easier evenings, but I'm past the worst I think."

"Dizziness, nausea or just a headache?"

Feldahd's smile remained, "Just a headache."

Laonardo pursed his lips before stacking more of the kindling, "So, what brings the Captain of the Guards to my dwelling?"

"I think you know."

Laonardo raised an eyebrow. "I've already explained things to the Sultan. His daughter will be safe with Cappa." He stared at Feldahd, "Safer than with anyone you could put forward here."

The old guard returned the resolute gaze, "It's not his credentials that concern me. The Sultan is perhaps less observant than you or I. We both know how they look at one another."

"My companion admires her beauty as any man alive would. However, being aware of her looks is one thing, acting on impulse is something else entirely. We Thiazarrans are bred to believe in honour above all else."

Feldahd appreciated the candour. "A factor I would never normally question, but he is young, and she, is Ruomaani-Skye."

"Stunning as she may be, believe this, her virtue could not be under safer protection."

They both turned and saw Trentach returning.

Feldahd bowed his head in goodbye. "Then I will bid you a good evening." He turned to walk away nodding to Trentach as he passed. After only several more paces, Feldahd stopped and turned back to the confident youth building his fire, "Laonardo," Feldahd looked most sincere, "Thank you for saving my life."

Laonardo acknowledged the gesture with a tilt of his head then watched as Feldahd hobbled away.

CHAPTER 14

As expected, the darkness had brought with it a chill.

Cappa placed more wood on the fire but kept the blaze small. They'd picked up a little more foliage during the journey that afternoon, but not enough to see them through the night unless used sparingly.

He poked at the embers to stir them some more.

They had found themselves a little alcove on a ledge cut into the canyon wall and set up camp.

A modest portion of the cheese and bread had been eaten, the water warmed in a metal cup and sipped in measures.

During the day a new liquid source had come courtesy of the only vegetation growing in the canyon, a wiry bush of thorns called flontac. Ruomaani had demonstrated how they could suck the roots for their moisture.

Cappa gave as much of their water as could be spared to his horse, but he knew this was little more than a spoonful as far as his animal was concerned.

The deep cut of the canyon spared them the sun's attention for the most part, reducing their need to drink, but he knew he needed to keep an eye on the situation. Their meagre food supply was enough for another day, but Cappa was aware how different the water situation could become once the ravine opened into broader, more exposed valley.

The fire cracked sending a new dance of shadow and sparks against the illuminated walls around them.

Beyond the sanctity of their shelter, was a cold black void.

Ruomaani leaned into the backrest provided by the saddle and huddled under the blanket.

Cappa did likewise beneath the cover of his tattered cape.

As a Pathan he'd been trained to endure such conditions and he was keen not to let her see the chill affecting him.

"Are you warm enough?" he asked.

"All things considered I'm no too bad," she replied. "How about you?"

He leaned in close to the fire. "I'm alright."

They both turned as Coba grunted, the stallion just a few paces from their position, yet invisible to them in the darkness.

"Are you sure your cape is enough of a blanket?"

"Honestly, I'm fine." It was a small lie and one he forced himself to question. To share her blanket would be nourishing in more ways than one. He smiled, "Well, I bet you didn't think you'd be out here with me when you woke up this morning."

She laughed but like Cappa withheld her true feelings on such a notion. She was quite happy to be here with the young Thiazarran, cold or not.

Their journey throughout the afternoon had continued in pretty much the same vein, with a touch of flirting and humour interlacing their questions and curiosities.

Both were well accustomed at not allowing their emotions to dictate their actions, but if either had truly known what the other was thinking at times, their situation would be in danger of becoming a lot more complicated.

"So, tell me," Ruomaani enquired, "Is Zarrapathia as beautiful as our traders say?"

He smiled as he thought of home. "Yes. It has forest teeming with game, rivers and seas filled with fish. There are dense swamps and golden desert intertwined with miles upon miles of fertile plains. The west is protected by the ocean, the north by a vast fortification, the remainder kept secure by the dramatic mountain ranges which surround her borders." He pulled the cape a little tighter, "There are great walled cities awash with people of every walk of life, from merchants to magicians, farmers to entertainers."

She grinned, "Oh, I love to be entertained by performers."

"Then you should visit. We could take in a show in one of the amphitheatres. Afterwards you could dance the night away at one of our town festivals."

"How I would love that." Her smile seemed empty again.

He sensed the sadness in her, wanted to enquire as to its source, but once again his usual boldness evaded him.

She had bewitched him.

"When will you and your friend return home?"

"A few months from now."

"Back to reality?"

He smiled, "Yes, but in truth it is a fine reality."

She rubbed her arms beneath the coarse blanket. "It sounds distinctly more appealing than the outlands, of that there can be little argument."

He looked into her eyes, "Then it's beyond question. You must come and visit."

She laughed, "Then visit I shall."

Although Cappa understood the game, the sadness at realising this was a promise she would never keep wounded him. At that moment he wanted to steal her away and make her his own. To show her Prima during its midsummer carnival, the Early Moon Circus of Zegunda, or the Pathan Commemoration Festival in the capital, Preminenta. He steered away from such empty thoughts, returning instead to humour for comfort, "You could bring your father, and Feldahd," he quipped. "I'm certain he likes me."

Once again, she laughed. "I fear Feldahd may prove a little serious for fairs and carnivals. As for my father," she looked distant momentarily, "Well, where would a Sultan be without his Kingdom in the dust?"

"As I said, we have deserts of our own. We could dump your father and Feldahd out there while we take in a festival or two."

"That could work," she replied happy again. "Though they would need a well to squabble and barter over. Just to keep them out of mischief."

"Consider it done."

Another short silence followed.

"Is that what happens out here?" Cappa asked after a moment, "People squabble over wells and water?"

She showed no reluctance in offering her reply, "Water, pride, territory and money. The same as in most places, I would imagine." A dark smile appeared, "Though the order may vary depending on circumstance."

He looked at her, "What about the love of a woman?"

She raised an eyebrow, "I think that comes under the definition of pride out here… perhaps territory, often money."

"Meaning?" His flirting had clearly struck an unintended nerve.

"Meaning women, like everything else, are commodities."

"To be traded like water and territory?"

She found his response naïve. "Surely such practices are the same the world over. Women are as much a status symbol as an oasis, or a chest stuffed with gold."

He found her response prejudiced, "As you said, I think you'll find the order may vary depending on circumstance."

She acknowledged his riposte with a warmer smile.

He added another branch to the fire, causing further hot sparks to snap into the air. He was cautious as he continued, "So is that what was in the chest Feldahd and your father were so desperate to retrieve?" their eyes met in a piercing hold. "Bartered for gold that takes many men to guard?"

Her smile remained, though Ruomaani's response was a while in coming, "My father is not as fortunate as the Sultan

Bunsaar. The money in the chest is a loan. Money needed to keep my father's territory in order."

Cappa thought back to the disrepair witnessed in Fraeda. To the various comments made with regards to Kirkoban's financial status, "And the interest on such a loan?"

Her gaze was sharp as a hawk, "High," she said simply.

Another long pause followed. There was so much Cappa wanted to say and ask, but once again he sensed it would be better to hold his tongue for the time being.

"I hope the other Torantum winners are not so observant," she gave him a measured look. "The chest was never intended for a mercenary's eye. Not when they outnumber tribals two to one."

The cold chill seemed to pick up a degree and Cappa hunched a little closer to the fire. "Only my two companions saw anything. We can be trusted."

"Of that I've little doubt." Her tone was soft again, her expression sincere. "Which is why I must insist you come and share this blanket," she smiled, "For as much as I appreciate your gallant shivering, you'll be of little use to me dying of a fever."

*

A damp bite lingered on the chilly outland morning. Cappa had risen at first light and set about rekindling the small fire. A section of foliage sparked into flame, the crack stirring Ruomaani who remained huddled under the blanket.

She yawned as she peered at him. "I didn't hear you get up."

"You did but decided on more sleep. You spoke to me as I left to tend the fire."

"Did I? I don't remember."

"Don't worry you made little sense. One might even describe it as gibberish."

Ruomaani stretched. "You must be mistaken." Another yawn followed. "It's cold."

"Come closer to the fire." He passed her a cup of warm water. "Are you hungry?"

Ruomaani nodded as she moved closer, the blanket wrapped around her tightly.

Cappa pulled two pieces of bread from a hot stone. On one he placed a small portion of cheese. He wedged the portions together and passed her the sandwich.

She took a tentative bite. "Oh, that's good. Camp fire cheese and toasted bread, who would have thought it could taste so utterly divine?"

He smiled.

"Are you not having any?"

"I had my share a moment ago." It was the whitest of lies. No cheese had accompanied his meagre breakfast. "While you were sleeping."

"How ungracious of me. Next, you'll be telling me I snore."

"Well, now that you mention it."

She enjoyed the moment and ate some more of the simple food. She glanced across to the small pile close to the horse. "Is that the last of the wood?"

"I'm afraid so. We'll have to make this the last piece we burn, just in case."

She nodded. They expected to reach the other side of the canyon while there was still daylight, however nothing could be taken for granted. It was clear their route had taken them well away from the intended course. "I'll soon warm up once we are underway."

Cappa stood and headed past her to collect the saddle before preparing Coba.

Ruomaani watched him as she finished her food. The smell of the fire and the sensation of waking outdoors, easing her chill. She'd never woken alone with a man, never felt the warmth of a male body close to her own under a blanket through the night.

She was exhilarated by the situation and more so by him. Ruomaani observed the athletic curves of his legs, the power in the arms as he set about saddling his fine horse.

She sipped the water, chewed the last morsel of bread and felt touched by his morning efforts. '*Oh, how delightful life might be with such a beautiful man.*'

The thought didn't cheer Ruomaani… it only served to remind her of how this short adventure was all but done.

*

Laonardo watched as the tribal guards lit two large pyres. He stared into the distance and wondered if Cappa and Ruomaani-Skye would see the smoke. The rag-tag caravan had a plentiful wood supply, but certainly not enough to light too many furnaces such as these. He pondered on the ramifications of all that was happening, concerned at what might lie ahead.

They had left the canyons behind and made camp on the baked flats by noon. Laonardo and Bayer had the mercenaries fortify a light perimeter before overseeing the construction of the signal fires. The tribal guards had then doused the wood in fragrant oil that saw the smoke burn black.

For the time being, all they could do was wait.

Laonardo turned to see Trentach approach.

"Still no sign?"

"None."

"They're unlikely to miss us once out of the canyon. The gorges fade into plains at a similar axis along the basin," he smiled, "If nothing else they should smell our location."

Laonardo saw the Sultan in the distance. "Anyone mention the chest?"

Trentach shook his head. "Nobody saw it but us. I'm convinced of it. There was so much confusion," he followed

Laonardo's gaze. "Whatever it is, they've got it hidden away again." He patted Laonardo on the back, "Come, I've prepared a little food."

Laonardo turned and followed Trentach, his concern for his friend still lingering. He would be a damn sight happier when Cappa and this desert princess were back safe and sound.

He would then concern himself with what could follow.

CHAPTER 15

Ruomaani watched as Cappa reached the top of the steep slope. "Can you see anything?" Her voice echoed through the gorge.

Above, Cappa observed the plateau stretching out before him. "It looks like the other path will still lead us out. Although it will certainly mean a wider detour!"

A short time earlier their canyon trail had hit a dead end, so Cappa decided to scale the canyon to weigh up the alternatives. There had been a fork in the valley a little way back and as Cappa now studied this fissure from the cliff-top above, it appeared to wind back in a similar direction to their intended route.

He began the journey down.

As he drew closer, he informed Ruomaani of what he'd seen, "If we head back to the fork, the alternate pathway actually circles back and appears to follow a similar route. It will take longer, but as long as we don't encounter more blockages we should make it out okay." He made the path and headed back to her, "Our main concern will be water. It doesn't seem to be the greatest of detours, but I'd estimate it might mean another night out here. With the walls of the ravine abating we'll be more exposed to the…" He stopped speaking as he read the concerned expression on her face.

"That may prove the least of our troubles for the time being," she whispered slowly.

He followed her gaze to the rocks in the distance.

"Do you see her?"

Cappa focussed.

"On the triangular rock there, just where the shadow strikes?"

His senses were sharp as he plugged into her trepidation.

"A mataba," she announced, "A white mountain lion."

Cappa spotted the long frame of the big-cat and took the sword from Ruomaani's grasp. "And these matabas, do they hunt in prides, or alone?" His voice was analytical. The strategies required playing through his brain... defence, attack... retreat.

Ruomaani held Coba close on the rein, the stallion grunting into a dance, sensing the large predator in the distance. "They live and hunt alone - very solitary creatures. But they are relentless stalkers once their prey has been sighted."

"Do they ever commit to open attack?"

"It's rare for them to attack people. They're more likely to make a play for a caravan's animals. Striking in darkness, returning later for the carcass if disturbed. It's unusual to see one so far south. There's little food here. Usually, they stalk the northern valley for wild gentas." Ruomaani studied the beast as it observed them from distance, its stare cold and calculating, "She's big but lean, bordering on thin."

"That suggests hungry." He unfastened the shield from his stallion. "Steer Coba slowly about, head for the fork in the gorge. I'll cover the rear... keep our new friend in sight."

*

Cappa and Ruomaani had made good progress along the new path. Its gorge was broad to begin with, but had since narrowed, the walls casting heavy shade around them.

Sometime back they'd discovered an abundant flontac bush, its wiry vegetation providing much appreciated fluid.

The taste was foul, but it meant they could avoid breaking into their precious water supply.

Both were mindful of the mataba, and although the white feline had not been seen for a time, Cappa still had Ruomaani lead Coba as he scanned all angles, his sword and shield at the ready. His two throwing knives were hidden discreetly within his belt, but what he truly longed for was his Pandral spear. He checked the shadows to their rear once more.

"Anything?" she asked.

"Still no sign."

"She'll be out there; you can count on it. She'll probably wait until dark."

Cappa looked at the sky. "Night can't be too far away; we've been travelling this path for some time now. We should keep an eye out for a cavern big enough to house Coba. That way we can defend both the stallion and us in one position."

She agreed.

They continued on and after a time, the canyon walls eased back into opposing slopes, though at the base the path narrowed. A flood of sunlight washed clean over the trail. Just beyond this warm light was another section of heavy shade, cast over the path courtesy of a large rocky stack.

Ruomaani studied the new terrain with suspicion as their route returned them to sunshine.

Cappa, still at the rear, scowled as he thought he heard something. He focussed, staring into the shade they had just left behind, as he too now entered the bright sunlight.

'Was that the flash of the mataba's eye?'

Coba grunted and Ruomaani tightened her grip on the rein, her senses bristling with caution. "You may want to look at the terrain ahead." Her eyes scanned the shadows beneath the stack.

His tone was equally hushed, "Hold on a moment," he crouched slightly, concentrating his eye into the changing light.

He tensed immediately as his suspicions were confirmed, his focus catching the eyes of the stalking mataba, the imposing cat cloaked by the blanket of shade. As Cappa's eyes met those of the beast he didn't notice Ruomaani's own concern as he announced, "I have her. She's behind us."

"Then we have a real problem." Ruomaani said softly.

He turned as she brought Coba to a halt and saw quickly the cause to her concern. For there, ahead of them, was another mataba, skulking in the shade directly ahead.

"So much for them being solitary," she whispered.

"Clever. They've waited until now to pounce." He passed Ruomaani his shield. "If they're smart enough to trap us here then they'll be smart enough to attack as a pair."

She took the shield, it was heavy, forcing her to readjust her stance. "They're almost certainly hoping to startle us, see us give up the horse and run."

"When the attack comes, get behind the shield and dig in." He ordered. "Don't look up, just get your body between the shield and Coba at your rear."

"What are you going to do?"

"I'll be right by your side. Just stay low when I give the signal."

In the opposing distances the two felines stared upon the prey. They'd gone many days without food and were happy to see the prospect of such a tantalising meal.
The bigger of the large females licked her lips.

Ruomaani could feel her heart beating in her chest as she struggled to hold both the shield and the jittery stallion's reins.

Cappa stabbed his sword into the dirt and took a central stance. His eyes flashed from one mataba to the other as the two pale cats stalked into full view.

He focussed, thought out his plan then quickly checked the terrain once more to ensure there were no more of these mountain cats. As he flashed his gaze at the mataba nearest him, he saw the white of her jowls tense, the intent in her eyes dazzle. "Remember, get behind the shield - don't worry about your rear."

She gulped and wanted to answer, but then, it happened.

The first mountain cat lunged into the hunt, quickly moving from a gentle prowl into an all-out sprint. Her heavy paws played a terrifying dance as she covered the terrain toward Ruomaani. The horse panicked, but somehow, she held Coba firm as she yelled, "Cappa!"

"Hold your position," he boomed as he too prepared for the full flight of his own, now incoming, predator.

The mountain cats were masters at this game and timed their attacks to perfection.

Cappa switched his gaze toward Ruomaani's attacker before switching back to see the bounding strides and cold intent of his own aggressor, *'This will be close.'*

The horse whinnied and again Ruomaani did well to hold on. She could hear the cat's stride as it approached.

"Ruomaani, brace for the impact. Whatever happens, stay low behind that defence!"

Cappa then leapt into action.

He pulled the throwing daggers from his belt and squatted into his aim. His mataba was almost upon him, her jaws opening as she prepared to deal with the small creature guarding her main course. Her muscles primed from tail to toe as she readied the transformation from run to attack.

Cappa launched the first dagger, striking the mataba's shoulder. It only wounded the beast, and her determination pushed her on.

 He launched the second projectile, this time scoring a lethal hit as it tore into the mataba's skull. The animal lost all control as it collapsed to the floor in a howl of forward momentum.

Cappa pulled his sword from the dirt in a sweeping turn, hearing the crash of the second mataba as it struck against the shield accompanied by Ruomaani's shriek. Coba reared but

Ruomaani managed to keep him, her firm stance having done enough to see the creature repelled by the defence.

The mataba scrambled, its vicious paws striking out, slicing Ruomaani's right tricep as she fought the creature off.

This action was met by the first strike of Cappa's sword.

The mataba roared in agony but was not about to give up so easily. It jumped away from Ruomaani and squared up to the attacker who now drew her into the open.

"Whatever you hear," Cappa said, "Do not come out from under that shield!" His tone was strangely calm, his form without fear.

Cappa and the cat circled one another for a moment, its paws jabbing out at him but not yet ready to attack. Its growls and hissing fury were terrifying, but Cappa stared the beast down, his left hand stretched in front of his face, his right holding out the sword ready to strike. The moment seemed to last an eternity, when suddenly the cat made its move.

She was fast and powerful even when injured, and her claws ripped at Cappa's forearm.

He lunged low and swung his sword into her forward leg, chopping a great chunk out of her. The mataba squealed onto her back and tried to bolt upright, but Cappa was clinical with his killing blow, the sword slicing into her neck.

The mountain cat whimpered and slouched as the Pathan warrior quickly ended the death-match, sending the sword down into the base of her magnificent skull.

Cappa staggered back, the wound to his arm not as bad as he'd thought. He turned to see Ruomaani still under the shield, Coba still held in her determined hand.

"It's over," he said calmly.

Ruomaani lifted the shield and loosened her grip allowing Coba to bolt, bucking and snorting his protest until content the cats were in a permanent sleep.

She was bleeding from a wound similar to that suffered by the man standing before her. Behind him lay the two slain matabas. She stared in silence for a moment then asked, "Are you alright?"

"It's just a flesh wound. You?"

"Scratched, but I'm okay." She dropped the shield and felt the sting in her injured arm grow as she approached Cappa slowly... Then without a thought, the pair embraced.

*

Ruomaani and Cappa had ventured a little further along the gorge before setting up camp, but even in the short distance covered it was clear they were close to exiting the Canyons.

They'd found a cave spacious enough to house Coba and lit a small fire at its mouth before darkness could claim them.

Cappa had skilfully skinned the two matabas, throwing the hides over the saddle. He'd butchered steaks from their flesh and these had been cooked over their fire. Although bitter and tough, the meat was somehow better than any Ruomaani had eaten before.

With their meal finished the fire had reached its lowest flame. They'd found little by way of extra fuel and with the towering walls abating the night came in cold.

A clear sky allowed a bright moon to light the cave mouth and as Cappa and Ruomaani huddled close to the humble blaze, their faces were a mixture of flickering orange and moonlit grey.

He winced as she caught the scratches on his arm with her elbow. "I'm sorry." She couldn't help but laugh, it was the third time she'd hit the wound.

Cappa shook his head, "I don't know what's worse, you or the matabas."

Her laughter continued.

They'd cleaned the wounds with a little hot water heated in Cappa's metal cup then patched each other up using torn cloth. With the adrenaline long since gone, the skin around their scratches felt tight and uncomfortable, but Cappa and Ruomaani had spoken little of such discomfort.

He pulled clear of the shared blanket and poked at the fire once more. As he did, Ruomaani noticed blood seeping from the bandaged wound. "Oh, it's bleeding again."

He glanced at it, "Really, I wonder why?"

She reached for clean bandages.

"It's fine," he protested.

Ruomaani ignored the remark and turned back to him holding the new piece of cloth. "Hold your arm out in the moonlight." She set about undressing the wound. "Hold still," she said as she took a firm grip on his arm.

"I am holding still."

"No - You're cowering away from me."

"Cowering?"

"Flinching."

"Is there any wonder with such a gentle nurse?"

Ruomaani pulled the old bandage away. As she applied a new dressing over the fresh cuts she shivered at the thought of the mataba claws.

He winced as she pulled the dressing tighter.

"Don't be such a baby," she teased.

As she finished the knot he turned to her in the half-light, "You, would be in the belly of one of those solitary, rarely attack people matabas, had it not been for this, baby." He gave a defiant thumb toward himself to add weight to his protest.

She laughed again, "I had everything under control."

"So it seemed."

"Besides, had it been up to me I'd have left Coba there to fend for himself. Then there would have been no need for our little spat with the matabas."

He feigned shock and quickly turned to his horse, "Coba, cover your ears. She doesn't mean it."

They both laughed some more.

As he turned back he caught the top of her trailing arm, this time causing her to wince. He showed genuine remorse, "Oh, I'm so sorry, really I am." He then announced to Coba, "There you go boy, I got her for you, right where it hurts."

She rubbed near the wound and called him a few choice names.

He turned his attention to the scratches, his manner more serious this time around.

"Stay away from me you dustbowl oaf," she joked.

"I'm sorry, really, let me see."

She allowed him to lean in close.

"It's not bleeding."

He pulled her arm into the light and examined it.

She shivered as her eyes caught his, the teasing quickly ceasing in both of them. They held each other's gaze for a long, binding moment, and it was difficult to pinpoint just who it was that instigated the kiss - but kiss they did.

It was a long, full kiss.

At first their embrace was gentle, as if the two understood this was not a path they should venture. However, such forbidden promise only increased their passion as they ignored the sting of their wounds. The intensity increased until Cappa found himself on top of her, holding his weight off as she pulled him in closer.

Cappa kissed her lips and neck until Ruomaani implored, "Please, do not take me. I must remain a virgin."

He looked into her eyes, deep as midnight pools, "I would never do such a thing without your consent."

His reassurance was met with another kiss before she eventually turned away from the moment. "Please, just hold me if you can bear the frustration." She manoeuvred until her back was turned to him, uncertain she could trust herself.

He eased his passion, embracing her as she had asked.

"Just hold me by our fire," she echoed.

There they remained for a long time until the heat eventually drained from the moment.

Cappa kissed the back of her head and breathed in Ruomaani's hair until eventually the exertions of the day took a hold, coaxing him toward slumber.

Ruomaani spoke gently to him as he succumbed and did her best to ensure he remained unaware of her tears as they reflected the illumination of their fire and the moon.

CHAPTER 16

Despite the warmth of the new day, Cappa had awoken to a somewhat frosty Ruomaani-Skye. Her conversation remained pleasant enough, as did the smile, which greeted him at dawn, but as they'd sat down to a breakfast of dried meat and water Cappa was certain of the change in her character.

He'd enquired if she felt awkward about events the previous night only to be told firmly, that the episode should never be spoken of again.

Cappa tried to have her open up about it, but she'd been adamant and had remained so as they started their journey.

With their wood supply gone, he'd insisted she ride in the saddle and soon the Salt Canyons had diminished, gradually giving way to the basin on the other side.

The hot sun was high as they altered their course, travelling alongside the last remnants of the canyons in search of the others. The once mighty cliff walls were reduced to an occasional stack or jagged hillside. However, as a taller section of slope was reached, Cappa decided to check on Coba while making good use of the much-needed shade.

Ruomaani jumped down from the horse, "I'll walk from here on. Coba doesn't need to be carrying me in this heat. The others can't be too far away."

Cappa could see his horse would fare better without the added weight. He poured a little water into his helmet and had Coba take a drink. "We're running dangerously low."

They took small sips of their own.

As Ruomaani handed back the water her eyes caught his. She looked away, peering into the distance. "Perhaps we should wait here a while, let Coba cool down."

"Ruomaani…"

"Even with the detours we can't be too far away from my father."

"Ruomaani!" for the first time Cappa was forceful, "Why are you being like this?"

She smiled, "Being like what?"

"You know full well. You've barely spoken to me since we left the cave."

"You're being too sensitive," again she tried to make light of his drama.

"Too sensitive?" he was angry at the comment. "Last night we shared an incredible moment, this morning you can barely look me in the eye. Have I offended you?"

"Of course not," she was struggling, "But last night was only…"

"Only what?" he interrupted. "A mistake?"

"I never said it was a mistake… only that we should never speak of it."

"To each other?" he said incredulously. He gestured to the barren terrain. "Look around you, there's nobody to hear. I understand the need for discretion, but must we pretend it never happened even as we stand here alone?"

She was dismayed, "We must, and it begins right here, right now, with the two of us."

"Why?" he implored, "What happened last night was no lustful sin. There is something between us. You and I both know it. I felt it the moment I first laid eyes on you, when your scarf was taken by the wind."

Ruomaani appeared deeply troubled.

"Why do you deny it now? Is it because of my position? Because if my lowly standing makes you fear such a course let me tell you… you could not be more wrong."

"Don't speak like this," she pleaded with him.

"You have to tell me what's happening here. I can't just switch this off and…"

"I'm engaged to be married!"

He was stunned, "What?"

She sighed, as if resigned to an unwanted fate. "I'm engaged to be married," she repeated, immediately ashamed at her actions the night before. She pinched the bridge of her nose and closed her eyes, hating the silence that now engulfed them. "To the Sultan Bunsaar," she announced sounding utterly defeated. "That's why we were in Numbala. I'm to become his wife."

"I thought he was married." There was an empty desperation to his comment.

"I'm to be his third wife," she said shaking her head.

Cappa looked at her crestfallen. "But you do not want this?"

"Want it?" She fired a furious look at him, "It's not about what I want!"

He saw a momentary window of hope, "But of course it is," Cappa's heart filled with purpose, certain his words could save them all over again, just as his sword had saved them from the matabas, "If you only knew…"

She interrupted him, "Cappa, I've taken what is known as the inzraba, the sacred oath. It's a vow made before our gods; a promise written - sworn in front of witnesses. I am betrothed, the property of Bunsaar." She hated the expression now settling across his face. "In our custom, the future bride travels to her husband in-waiting and takes the inzraba. A dowry is then paid to the bride's father. She then returns home and begins the puraka, a nine-day waiting period. Her last days of innocence before her purity is surrendered to her husband."

She looked utterly devastated, his continued silence crushing her. "My father, as you've no doubt ascertained, is not a wealthy man. Sultan yes, but not rich. He has squandered the wealth of our tribe. Fortunately, I'm deemed beautiful enough to save both my father and our family from ruin. Many of the Sultans have made enquiries in order to obtain my hand. Bunsaar's was by far the most generous."

"You've been sold?" Cappa was disgusted. The concept went against his every belief.

"A dowry has been paid for my hand in marriage!" She corrected, defending her position.

He shook his head, unable to accept what he was hearing. "So that's what is in the chest, why your father needed so many guards. You've been purchased, like a slave."

"I'm to be third wife to the most powerful Sultan in the country," she said instantly annoyed, "And as is our custom a significant dowry has been paid to my father. A dowry that will secure my tribe's future." She hated him at that moment. "How dare you judge me, scorn our traditions, customs which have stood for centuries."

He immediately regretted upsetting her. "Ruomaani, I don't mean to offend. But you must understand how shocking this is to me, as a Thiazarran I…"

"As a Thiazarran you are in my country, working for my father." She stared angrily at him, the gallant hero from yesterday now only making her feel cheap. "You would do well to remember you're not at home now. How dare you make me feel so below your high Thiazarran values." Her eyes glistened, "If I were from your world do you believe I'd choose Bunsaar over you?"

She looked on him with disdain, "Of course I have felt the things you feel. I've been captivated by you since the moment I first laid eyes on you. Fate saw fit to see us placed together out here in the desert… To test my faculty… And I have failed. You're everything I would wish for if I had the right to choose." Her anger turned to frustration, "But I do not have a choice. As such I must turn away from my moment of weakness and remember only my duty."

He felt her pain, hated himself for his superior reaction. He saw the woman he was falling in love with trapped. It choked him to see her this way and he reached out for her.

"No," she insisted, "Haven't you listened to a word I've said?" Tears threatened. "This cannot go on any further. It ends here. It ends now."

He was desperate. "But there are so many things you do not know. My family, we are more powerful than any of your Sultans here. I can speak to your father…"

She looked at him mortified, "And tell him what, that our impropriety has seen us fall for one another? Demand his daughter break her sacred vow. Her solemn oath that if broken would see my entire family destroyed? It doesn't matter who or what you are. My shame would see Bunsaar and the Sultan clans destroy us all."

"But Ruomaani," he implored, "You don't know what I could do. I could pay Bunsaar back his dowry a thousand times over."

She shook her head, her face incredulous, "Don't you understand? Bunsaar wants me, and he has gone to great lengths to ensure he gets me. I'm sworn to him now. Nothing can break a vow made before the gods. If either of us were to renege on this pact we'd be destroying ourselves, everything our traditions are built upon."

He reached for her hands, "But if you only knew."

Ruomaani pulled away from him quickly. She looked shocked suddenly and gestured to his rear. She wiped her eyes and began composing herself.

Cappa turned to see what had forced her to act in such a manner and was dejected at what he saw. For out of the heat ripples and dust, five riders were approaching.

Three wore Kirkoban's colours; with them were Laonardo and Trentach.

He could sense time slipping away, the urgency of which made him realise what he needed to say before it was too late, "Ruomaani, forgive my earlier reaction. It's just… I'm falling in love with you…"

Ruomaani interrupted him with sorrowful eyes, "There is nothing either of us can do about such feelings. Not for all the money in the world. I must fulfil my duty."

As the group approached, Cappa's heart sank, distraught that he and Ruomaani would never again share such precious moments like those experienced in the wilderness.

CHAPTER 17

As Laonardo, Trentach and the tribals arrived, Cappa played the game required, following her lead as best he could. He'd embraced his Patruan, apologising for his rash departure from the cave. He'd made a similar show of it with Trentach, informing his comrades how he and Ruomaani-Skye were both fine, but for a few cuts and bruises.

Laonardo strongly suspected, however, his friend was anything but fine. During the short ride back, Laonardo informed Cappa of Juhmad's disappearance and how they were now Lieutenants in Kirkoban's rag-tag mob.

Cappa tried his best to appear interested, if only to ensure the guards who surrounded Ruomaani-Skye during the ride back were given no cause for suspicion. Much of the same was to follow when she was finally reunited with the Sultan.

During the emotional reunion, Kirkoban expressed his deep gratitude to Cappa and made promises to reward the Thiazarran, guaranteeing the newly promoted Lieutenant a private audience as soon as they were back in Malbood.

After the fuss, Cappa and Ruomaani-Skye found themselves back within the bosom of the group making passage for the Sultan's capital, which they reached by early evening.

Ruomaani-Skye had been wrapped like a delicate doll for the remaining short trip, her features hidden from all as she was delivered to Malbood on the back of a carmol. It was tearing Cappa apart and he struggled to decide his next move.

As at Fraeda, Kirkoban staged a magnificent return, strutting around on his stallion to much cheering and bravado.

Malbood had a central citadel at its heart, the walls taller and a little more grandiose than the previous outpost. For the most part however, Kirkoban's capital was exactly as Trentach said it would be... Fraeda - only bigger.

The market was closing as they arrived, and the large square and side streets were depleted of any real bustle as a result.

Even so, the crowd gathered made quite a fuss, and they followed the caravan all the way to the large wooden gate, which sealed the central palace from the township.

Following protocol, Kirkoban and the tribal guards headed through with Ruomaani-Skye, as the mercenary guards were ordered to make camp in the square. On this occasion, however, Feldahd's deputy rode over to Cappa and Laonardo.

"The Sultan Kirkoban wishes the two of you to enter the palace with me. He will request your presence shortly. Bring clean clothes, you'll be given quarters in which to freshen up." He then rode toward Banteez Bayer, informing the Captain he too would be called upon, but not until nightfall.

Laonardo turned to Trentach, "Where will you make camp?"

Trentach pointed.

Laonardo smiled, "Save us a spot, just in case."

Trentach agreed then watched as Cappa and Laonardo followed the tribals into the humble palace perimeter, their pack ponies trotting behind.

*

Their quarters within the palace grounds were on the second floor of the three-storey structure. The room was clean and vibrantly furbished. Lamps burned scented oil in each alcove, providing a warm and fragrant glow throughout the chamber.

The plush curtains on the tall window framed a net of finely spun cotton secured to the frame to keep away the insects, while the far corner played host to a large floor mattress, the bedspread a mass of different coloured cushions.

Adjoining the room was a parlour of mosaic tiles, housing a bath filled with hot water. After bathing, Cappa whispered his tale to Laonardo. When the hushed story ended, Laonardo sat back and sighed, his eyes once again checking their surroundings... the door, the window, the ceiling.

After a moment, he leaned in close, his voice a near silent purr. "Cappa, we must tread carefully. This is a most dangerous game. If anyone was to suspect something you'd be in serious danger." He was most concerned, "It seems to me there is little you can do. You say Ruomaani-Skye has taken a vow before her gods, done so before witnesses, in the binding tradition of her people... then there appears no tangible way out, for either of you."

"But if these people learned of my true identity."

"What difference would it make?" Laonardo was quick to retort. "She said all the money in the world could and would not undo this sacred oath. That suggests a pretty strong vow to me. It would be like trying to buy you or I out of our Pathan oath. No money could achieve such a thing."

It was Cappa's turn to sigh, "I cannot sit back and do nothing."

"You said fate would decide. Indeed, fate played you an incredible hand. A precious moment to be with her," he looked on his brother with regret. "But you cannot deny, fate has equally shown how the two of you cannot be together."

"I can't believe fate would allow me to love her, only to see her snatched away by a scenario so utterly beyond my control."

"As our fathers told us before allowing this great adventure, the purpose of this trip is to teach us humility. To illustrate how we, living as ordinary men, cannot always obtain what we want. Perhaps fate is illustrating this to you now in the cruellest of ways."

"How is breaking my heart and leaving me embittered, supposed to help me rule with greater wisdom and parity?"

Laonardo looked at his friend earnestly, "I cannot say. The future is yet to be written. You have to admit this is not a scenario you'd face if back home. That in itself means it is a lesson to be heeded."

Cappa exhaled a long breath, "Laonardo, I know it must sound like I simply want my own way. And yes, of course that's true, but I feel in my very bones I'm supposed to be with this girl. I feel something beyond infatuation. It's like she's a missing part of me. That she is the real destiny to come out of my being here."

Laonardo's eyes bolted toward the door as approaching footsteps were followed by a light knock against the woodwork. "Masters Cappa and Laonardo," It was the servant who'd shown them to their quarters, "The Sultan will receive you soon. You have a little longer, but I'll return shortly to collect you."

Laonardo waited until his footsteps faded, "Then it's to be as I said... a most dangerous game." He warned Cappa, "If you wish to wait a little longer then so be it. If you believe fate will illustrate an escape for you both, I'm prepared to wait for this sign to appear. But I must insist you do nothing without consulting me first." He emphasised, "I mean it, Cappa. You must not act until you have discussed all with me beforehand."

Laonardo looked stern. "Whatever happens, we must leave before this Sultan Bunsaar comes to claim his bride," he determined, "if fate has not stepped in by then, lesson learned."

CHAPTER 18

The servant led Cappa and Laonardo to Kirkoban's court.

As they approached the open arch entry, he held out a stiff arm, "We must wait here a moment."

They followed the servant's gaze through the archway.

Ahead seated on a throne, was Kirkoban, to his left was Ruomaani-Skye and to his right a man of similar age to Cappa and Laonardo. The trio were splendidly dressed in silks, their chairs elevated on a rostrum lifting them clear of the patterned floor. A conversation was taking place with others they could not yet see, but as Kirkoban saw the Thiazarrans waiting he announced, "Ah, here are the two brave men of whom we speak."

This was the servant's cue and he led Cappa and Laonardo to the Sultan before making his exit.

The duo took in their surroundings.

They were inside a large, ornate room graced with hanging silk swathes, warm lanterns and carved features burning incense. To their right stood a small gathering, one of whom was a bandaged Feldahd.

The pair scanned the faces of the dignitaries before returning their attention to the trio at the fore. They both bowed, Cappa taking a fleeting look at Ruomaani-Skye.

"Welcome our brave Thiazarrans from across the sea." The Sultan was as theatrical at court as he was when riding his stallion into townships. "My daughter, you already know," he gestured to Ruomaani with an open palm, "This is my son and heir, Zuda," he said gesturing with his other. "The man closest to you is my nephew, Menka. Next to him is Luucar, my second cousin and Chief Counsel." Kirkoban beamed, "While the rather splendid gentlemen at his side, is the Sultan Dreda, my greatest friend and ally, hanouri to my daughter."

The white-haired Sultan of the Southlands smiled before taking over the introduction, "This is my first wife, Maerkoola." The beautiful lady tilted; her mature features dignified, her eyes sharp as a hawk. "And my eldest daughter, Sooramena." The charming girl followed her mother's lead.

Kirkoban added, "Of course, you already know my military Commander and bodyguard." Feldahd smiled on queue.

With the introductions made, Dreda was the first to speak, "You may or may not know, but *hanouri* in our custom means honorary father, an oath of guardianship taken soon after a child's birth," he gestured to Ruomaani-Skye. "Which means you saved the life of my own daughter as far as I'm concerned. Therefore, I am also deeply indebted to you, Cappa." His smile was genuine, his sentiments sincere.

Ruomaani-Skye looked at her beloved hanouri and smiled.

It was now the turn of Luucar, who like Kirkoban, was theatrical to say the least. "As for life without Feldahd!" he gestured to the old soldier, "Why, it would leave us empty - not to mention less secure in our beds."

Laonardo sensed unease lingering behind Luucar's façade of appreciation, but he took the gratitude with good grace.

Kirkoban continued, "We owe you both a great debt, and I'd like to first honour you with an offer of permanent employment as Mecdia Lieutenants." He held up his hands, "You do not need to decide now, sleep on your decision if you wish. I should also like to reward the two of you for your courage." The Sultan clapped his hands and the servant returned carrying a small chest.

"One hundred pieces of silver, plus water rights to all the wells in my territory." Kirkoban seemed most pleased with his own generosity.

Dreda spoke softly, "You can add the rights to any of my wells also." His tone lacked the drama and was the more genuine as a result.

Kirkoban was delighted, turning the gesture into more theatre, "How gracious, Dreda," he looked to the two Thiazarrans, "That allows free access to you, and all who travel with you, to wells stretching over two great territories."

Despite her best efforts, Ruomaani could not resist glancing toward Cappa; catching his eyes on the occasions he too looked her way.

"Great Sultans, you are too kind," Laonardo bowed, "Our only true reward is in seeing your loved ones here safe. You honour us both with such generosity."

This delighted the court, the Thiazarrans living up to expectations. Brief enquiries of their Thiazarran roots followed prompting Cappa and Laonardo to divulge modest details of their well-rehearsed cover stories.

The discussion soon ventured toward the severity of the Great White Noise and of the high toll such natural events placed on their society each year. They talked of Feldahd and Ruomaani-Skye's rescue, and how she has in turn saved Cappa from the landslide - until eventually they turned their attention to the finale, the dramatic slaying of the two matabas.

Ruomaani employed all of her willpower as she recollected events, desperate to maintain a cool emotional distance.

Her audience gasped as she spoke, particularly when, at the behest of her brother, she displayed the freshly clawed scars.

Laonardo listened with his own private reservations brewing. He thought of the similar wound he'd just redressed on Cappa's arm, of the mataba skin his friend presented him as a trophy, of the further trouble this love interest could bring.

More praise followed until eventually, Cappa decided to play a hand of his own, when quite unexpectedly, he took a knee before Kirkoban. "Generous Sultan, please allow me to honour your family in the same manner you honour us. During our time in the Salt Canyon I learned of your daughter's impending marriage," he reached into his pocket and pulled out a polished hooked-claw almost the size of his little finger, "Do not think me too forward, but I have a wedding gift for Ruomaani-Skye, in recognition of her bravery when using the shield to protect me from the second mataba attack," he held it aloft, "We Thiazarrans respect courage and honour above all else." Cappa looked to Ruomaani then back to Kirkoban, "Your daughter makes you proud on all counts." He offered the claw allowing the Sultan to take it from his grasp. "A memento to always reassert how the scars inflicted, were merely the cost of a brave and noble victory."

Kirkoban smiled and held it for all to see, the celebration which followed a most fitting end to this audience with the Thiazarran heroes.

*

Laonardo was furious. "Is that what you call including me on your every move?"

Cappa was defensive, "I promised I would not act without speaking to you first."

"So how would you describe your gesture with the mataba claw?"

"As precisely that... a gesture."

"Don't play games with me. I need you to start thinking clearly."

Cappa held up his hands, "You're right, it was impetuous. But I want her to be thinking of our time together. Besides, you saw how both Sultans loved the performance."

Laonardo said nothing more as footsteps could be heard approaching their apartment. He held up his finger for silence.

The knock striking the woodwork was heavier than the gentle hand of the servant.

Cappa opened the door to reveal Kirkoban's chief advisor, Luucar, with his bodyguard, Seban, who loitered in the shadows to his rear. "Hello again. May I speak with you both for a moment?"

"Of course," Cappa stepped aside to allow access.

As Luucar entered, Seban remained silent in the corridor.

Luucar walked to the centre of the apartment, wearing a smile, "I trust the room is adequate?" He pointed to the large mattress dressed in cushions. "I'm sorry there's only one bed, I hope it will suffice." He answered his own query, "Better than sleeping in a tent no doubt."

Cappa disliked his condescending tone.

"Well, let me cut to the chase. Banteez Bayer has just refused further employment. He is heading to mine silver in the Ferentae Straights. Damn foolish errand in my opinion, but each man to his own path. In light of this, and of course recent events, it's been decided you should be offered the position of Mecdia Captain and Laonardo here your First Lieutenant. You may also appoint a second. Bayer led me to believe your companion, Trentach, would be suitable?" The over familiar smile grew, "We are most grateful for all you've done and recognise the importance of employing capable men to our ranks. There'll be a modest increase to your pay. Together with the silver and water rights granted, this would make you our most prosperous employees by some margin, should you choose to accept?"

Cappa looked to Laonardo, who nodded his consent.

Cappa was pleased, "It would be an honour."

"Excellent," Luucar's smile widened. "With agreement to your new employment, there are other matters I wish to discuss. Firstly, with regards a more sensitive issue," his smile narrowed, "As you well know our good lady, Ruomaani-Skye, is set to marry the Sultan Bunsaar, a union of great importance to our families. As such, may I request your assistance?" He looked to Cappa, "The Sultan Bunsaar is a most reasonable man. However, for the sake of all concerned, may I ask for discretion with regards your recent adventure? We are in a most delicate position. I'm sure you understand. For as reasonable as the Sultan Bunsaar may be, I'm not certain how he'd react if he knew Ruomaani-Skye was alone in the desert with a handsome stranger."

The compliment covering the veiled insinuation only served to make Cappa's skin crawl.

"For similar reasons can I ask the same rule be applied to our earlier meeting in court? Ruomaani-Skye is supposed to be observing the puraka, a ritual sealing her from men's eyes until her husband comes to claim her. Under the circumstances we deemed an exception could be made. We thought it proper she be present as the man who saved her life was rewarded. However, since two days of this tradition have already been lost in the canyons, I'm sure you can see how silence will be the best policy for all involved."

Once again both Thiazarrans agreed before Luucar divulged, "Come tomorrow the Mecdia troop will assist in guarding a caravan heading to our water outposts of Ninkal and Razh. They'll be gone for eleven days. Naturally this will benefit our current situation." A difficult smile then announced, "However, the Sultan Kirkoban wants you stationed here."

Both Thiazarrans felt certain Luucar did not share his master's desire. Cappa swallowed his distaste. "You have our word, nothing will be said."

"Good. May I also ask for the same discretion in regard to anything discussed with Ruomaani-Skye while out in the canyons?"

Cappa scowled, "Discussed?"

"Details of the dowry, any losses we incurred during our first trip to Numbala."

"The only things spoken of were storms, building fires, desert cats and Zarrapathia."

"I meant no offence. I just want to make sure we all pull together on this. My only purpose is to deter any possibility for misunderstandings."

Cappa looked to Laonardo, clearly at a loss as to his exact meaning.

Luucar seemed happy with this reaction. "Well, I'll leave the two of you to rest, but before I go, I should tell you of a duty I wish you to perform come the morning." He elaborated, "I want you to assist a small welcoming party I must send to our south western border. To meet an incoming Ward Sultan who is to attend the wedding. It's but one day's ride," his ensuing false laughter was irritating. "So, don't get too accustomed to that bed." Luucar headed for the door.

Before he went Cappa asked casually, "Is this Ward Sultan to be brought back to Malbood directly. I understand the wedding is still five days from now?"

Luucar turned, "Ward Sultan Binka is to attend the agmanta." Luucar appreciated the blank expressions, "The husband claims his bride on the ninth day. Prior to this, the daughter's family receives the husband-to-be for three days of feasting and festivities. By the time you return this will be almost upon us." A touch of disdain coloured Luucar's tone as he added, "Ward Sultan Binka is, as always, arriving early." Luucar then bid them farewell before turning to make his exit.

Laonardo closed the door and listened to the fading footsteps, "Kirkoban may deem us a reasonable risk, but if I were to hazard a guess, I'd say our new friend is as keen to see us out of the way as he is the rest of the Mecdia troop."

*

As the lady-in-waiting finished her duties, Ruomaani-Skye was finally left alone in her room. She was glad of the solitude, happy to no longer keep up the charade, though the welcome silence did nothing to end her torment.

She pulled the mataba claw from her handkerchief and glanced at her forearm, the lion's stinging memento blazing beneath the dressing. She sighed and stared for a long while at the curving polished talon.

Ruomaani-Skye had often dreamed of romance and adventure. As a little girl her mother would regale her with the most wonderful bedtime stories, colouring Ruomaani's mind as she fell asleep to the sweet melody of her mother's voice.

A welcome distraction from the reality of her situation, also instilled from an early age.

For, in reality, Ruomaani-Skye would grow into womanhood with only one destiny, to be selected by the finest of suitors and become his bride. This was her fate, her purpose.

She had always accepted this destiny and despite youthful dreams of faraway lands with love before duty, she saw these whims as precisely that, romantic dreams and fantasy.

At least, she had until her time in the canyons with the hypnotic Thiazarran.

Ruomaani shivered as she remembered his touch, closed her eyes to breathe him in through her memory. She focussed on the claw once more, *'Oh mother, what would you think if you could see me now. Dreaming of another during my puraka?'*

She felt so alone.

When Cappa presented the tooth a part of her had died inside, that last part which dared to dream of a mother's long-ago tales. To greet him in such a formal manner was more difficult than she'd expected, but she had to remain cold in order to protect him. If any suspected the slightest transgression he'd be dealt with in the worst possible way, wealthy Thiazarran or not.

She drifted back into her memories, thought of his claim to pay her dowry a thousand times over, a delicious promise to tempt her from her most solemn vows.

She tried not to think on such words any longer. Things were already dangerous enough without this distraction.

Her father had decided to lie to Bunsaar about the bandit attack. An assault inflicted while on home territory, which resulted in them having to travel to Numbala so depleted in numbers. The men supposedly lost to the storm had actually died by the sword when en route to meet Bunsaar.

Her father knew what the other Sultan's reaction would be. No Sultan was so weak that bandits would dare raid their caravans while travelling within their own homelands. If the Sultan clans were to get wind of such a thing, Kirkoban's already fragile position would be close to untenable.

Although Ruomaani agreed they should stage the story of the storm instead, she was mortified to learn of her father's intention to lie about the real number lost to it. He'd insisted it was to appear stronger than they actually were. Ruomaani suspected however, her father simply wanted to dupe a little extra out of Bunsaar, knowing the powerful Sultan would be obliged to host a Torantum and pay half toward replacing the numbers lost while making passage across the outlands under his invitation. Her father was playing a most dangerous game.

A gentle knock at the door disturbed her ponderings, "Yes?"

It opened gingerly and a smiling face peered around the upright. It was Menka.

She covered the claw, "Menka, what are you doing? You shouldn't be here." She whispered as he entered.

"I know, cousin, but I just wanted to make sure you were alright. I'll not see you again after tonight until you're married, and I was worried about you."

Menka and Ruomaani were born but three weeks apart and had been inseparable since childhood, their affection for one another so strong it became a concern to Kirkoban during his daughter's adolescent years. Ruomaani was so beautiful, and he felt she should be shielded from the desires of men. The situation had become precarious until Ruomaani's mother stepped in to dispel concern, explaining how the two had been raised as brother and sister, and should be seen as such.

Ruomaani was concerned, "I'm supposed to be observing my puraka."

"What's a moment more when you've misspent half of it already? Besides... it's me."

"I don't think my father would recognise such exception."

"Well, I don't care too much of what your father thinks, as well you know."

She smiled, but it was an empty effort.

"What's wrong my sweet Ruomaani?"

"Nothing," another sigh escaped her, "I was just thinking about my mother."

"She's with you always, you know that."

Ruomaani wondered once again what her beloved mother would have made of events in the Salt Canyons.

"You seem so sad since you've returned."

"Am I so transparent. I thought I was making a decent show of it?"

"To all but me, yes." He looked at her for a long moment. "Did things not go to your liking with Bunsaar?"

"The Sultan Bunsaar will make a fine husband."

"Yes, we both know the mantra, but did it go well?"

She looked at him at a loss. "It went as it should."

"You don't want to talk about it?"

"Not really. I'm supposed to be up here concentrating on how to please my soon to be husband, not..." she didn't complete her sentence.

"Not what?" he asked. "Not thinking of adventures with a certain Thiazarran?"

She hushed him furiously, "Menka lower your tone. Have you lost your mind?"

"I don't think so. Have you lost yours?" He smiled, "I seem to have struck a chord."

"The only thing you've struck is your own over active imagination. That kind of talk can only lead to trouble - the kind of trouble this family does not need."

"Ruomaani," he placated, "I'm only teasing. I meant no offence."

"Whether you meant it or not is irrelevant. You cannot say such things, and you cannot be here." Her face flushed.

"I'm sorry," he said defensively, "I didn't mean to cause you distress. You just didn't seem yourself and I wanted to make sure you were alright."

She hated wounding him. "I apologise if I'm being tetchy. I know you care for my wellbeing." She gave him a hug, "But you really should go."

He squeezed her gently, "I shall, as soon as you tell me you're going to be alright."

She was set to answer when a sudden knock struck the door, quickly followed by an impertinent Luucar entering her chamber with a startled looking Feldahd in tow.

Ruomaani-Skye pulled out of the embrace stating furiously, "I did not tell you to come in!"

Luucar glared at the pair disapprovingly. "I'm sorry, my lady, I thought you said to enter." It was a lie. "Menka, we have come to remove you from our lady's presence - what in the names of our gods are you doing in here?"

Menka scowled, "It is not I barging into a lady's chamber unannounced. And it most certainly is not I who answers to you!"

Feldahd interrupted before the usual spat could begin. "Menka, your cousin is right. You cannot be in here." He was quick to emphasise, "I appreciate you love Ruomaani-Skye as a sister, but this doesn't see you exempt from the rules."

Menka flushed. "I am saying my goodbyes before she gives herself to wedlock."

"Menka was just leaving," Ruomaani stated, "Circumstance prevented us any personal farewell." She glared at Luucar, "And as inappropriate such a goodbye may be, it does not authorise you to storm my chamber without consent to enter!"

Luucar bowed, "I'm sorry, my lady. I was certain I heard you speak such permission. It must have been one of the maids I heard, further down the hall."

Feldahd was clearly embarrassed. "Come, Menka, our lady must begin what is left of her puraka," he looked to Ruomaani-Skye earnestly, "And please forgive this intrusion."

The three left her presence.

As they marched, Feldahd chastised both men, "Menka, you know better. And Luucar, what were you thinking entering Ruomaani-Skye's chambers like that? We were not certain Menka was even in there!"

"I could have sworn I heard her say enter." As third in line, Luucar would usually take a moment to remind Feldahd of his place and tone, however under current circumstance he remained silent, letting this transgression go with the narrowest of smiles.

CHAPTER 19

Laonardo woke to find Cappa perched in a chair staring out of the window. The sun had barely risen but it was enough to see the sky brighten with swirls of yellow signifying the dawn.

He yawned before enquiring softly, "Are you alright?"

Cappa looked over his shoulder and answered in a hushed tone, "I'm fine."

"You sure?"

"I dreamed of her last night." Cappa stared back at the sunrise, "I dreamed she was the most important Queen of Zarrapathia."

Laonardo sighed, "Hardly surprising all things considered."

Cappa shook his head, "It felt so real."

"I've never seen you like this."

"I've never felt like this. For the first time in my life, I feel at a complete loss as to what my next move should be."

"Well, you know my feelings," he urged Cappa once again to see sense and rethink his position. "In accepting Luucar's errand you won't even be here for two days, two days which take her further away from you. Perhaps it is time to accept that the outcome cannot justify the danger. Let's just take the money and get out of here."

Cappa was unrelenting, "I promise I'll leave before Bunsaar arrives. But I must return before he does, allow for the possibility of one final sign, one last opportunity."

"But why?"

"I have to, Laonardo, all within my being tells me to do so."

"It's infatuation." Laonardo spoke the words, but deep down he knew better.

Cappa looked at him, "No… I'm falling in love with her. But I also sense something bigger. It's as if there's more at stake than she or I." Cappa added, "We have both been trained to focus our acuity, to hone our intuition. Well, each time I do, the only answer to come back at me is her. I'm well aware of my responsibility. You have my word I shall not force the issue, but I must see this through in the hope of a suitable opening presenting itself."

Laonardo dipped his head in compliance, knowing only too well the keenness of his future King's intuition, it had served the Prince well throughout his life. Cappa was determined to see events run their course, and since Laonardo could say nothing to sway him, he would back him all the way.

*

Cappa and Laonardo made their way to the market square to check on Trentach and their supplies.

They found him already up and finishing his breakfast.

As always, he was in good spirits.

"Well, if it isn't the high and mighty making a return," Trentach laughed and gestured to the morning meal of fruit and sweetbread, "Are you hungry?"

"I could eat something." Laonardo helped himself seeing Cappa follow suit.

"Do they not feed you up there in high society?"

Laonardo grinned, "They tried, but it was all silk sandwiches and incense soup."

"Sounds horrendous."

"It was. And they made us share a bed."

Trentach raised an eyebrow. "In fairness, I always suspected that of the two of you."

Cappa smiled as he ate the bread.

"So, did you see anything of your desert princess?"

"Not really."

"We do have news though," Laonardo was quick to interrupt.

"As do I," Trentach replied. "But please, you go first."

"Cappa was promoted to Mecdia Captain as Banteez Bayer is hanging up his spurs."

"I spoke with Bayer last night," Trentach smiled. "We had a feeling the job may swing your way after saving the Sultan's daughter." Trentach pointed to Bayer's tent at the far side of the square, "He hasn't left yet. He's to head out this morning."

"I'm glad we'll have opportunity to see him before he leaves," Cappa added before Laonardo continued his bulletin.

"Apparently, I'm now First Lieutenant," Laonardo informed, "While you my friend, have been made Second Lieutenant. Don't ask me what the difference is because I've no idea. In all honesty, I suspect there isn't one, that in reality I'm the only one here not being promoted." Laonardo smiled mockingly, "Trentach, do you accept this high honour?"

"Is there an increase in pay?"

"Modest," Laonardo replied.

"Do I get a uniform?"

"Probably not."

"Then I accept."

The three laughed.

Cappa informed Trentach of their assignment, "We've been asked to accompany a welcoming party. We're to meet a Ward Sultan named Binka at a place known as the Boodan Bowl, a day's ride to the southwest. Do you know of it?"

"A natural basin where the salt flats are reclaimed by hills of baked earth. A pretty uninspiring place."

"And this, Binka?" Laonardo asked.

"Not much. I know he's small fry. He holds a tiny territory between Kirkoban's southern region and the northerly tip of the Sultan Dreda's lands."

"We met Dreda last night," Cappa said.

"I had heard he was here," Trentach replied, "How many are accompanying you to meet this, Binka?"

"Three tribals."

Trentach laughed, "Is that it?"

"And you of course. But Cappa is going to suggest you be left here to organise a few things ready for our return. You know, rest the horses, sort out more lasting accommodation."

"You mean keep an eye on events here," Trentach said shrewdly, "While the two of you are kicked out of harm's way on a carmol-shit mission for two days?"

Laonardo smiled at his astute friend.

"Will they go for me remaining here? If they're keen to send the two of you to meet Binka, why would they not send me?"

Cappa said, "I'm hoping if they wanted you out of the way they'd have sent you with the rest of the Mecdia who are heading to the water outposts of Ninkal and Razh."

"Well, you know me," Trentach shrugged, "Always happy to play along."

The duo smiled at Trentach. On finishing their breakfast Cappa asked, "You said you have news also?"

"Not so much news - more information. I thought you'd appreciate some understanding into all that's going on here. A who's who and what's what so to speak," he added, "Though I'm guessing you may have learned much of this yourselves."

Cappa encouraged him to divulge all he'd learned.

"Well, let's start with our benefactor. As we know, not the wealthiest of Sultans. He has one son, Zuda, and of course a daughter, Ruomaani-Skye. Both conceived by his first wife, who died some years ago. Apparently, Kirkoban never recovered. He has two other wives, as is tradition with the Sultans, but I'm told he has little love or time for either. The children produced by these other women have proven sickly at birth and died soon after." Trentach continued, "From what I can gather, Zuda is very much his father's son and I suspect some are concerned over the tribe's future under his stewardship. Zuda and Ruomaani-Skye have a first cousin called Menka. He's second in line to Kirkoban's seat, a most colourful character by all accounts."

Cappa and Laonardo thought back to their meeting in court as the impressive Trentach continued his dissection.

"Then there's Luucar, second cousin and third in line. He's regarded as the brains of the outfit, a shrewd operator by all accounts. He has his eye on the Sultan Dreda's daughter, Sooramena, but rumour has it he lacks the funds to take her in marriage. I'm guessing if you met Dreda last night, you met these people also?"

They nodded but encouraged him to continue.

"Dreda is a powerful and influential Sultan with lands to the south and west of here. He is an old friend of Kirkoban, cousin to his first wife. He is what's known as Ruomaani-Skye's hanouri, or honorary father, if you like."

Cappa explained how they'd discovered this fact.

"Dreda is in town early, probably to ensure Kirkoban doesn't mess everything up. Evidently, he worships Ruomaani-Skye and treats her as if his natural daughter," Trentach smiled. "That's all I've learned for the moment."

Laonardo shook his head, "I don't know what's more worrying. The fact you so often know of such information, or the thought of how you go about getting it."

"People have loose tongues once alcohol passes their lips."

"Remind me to never drink with this man again." Laonardo said with a laugh, slapping Trentach on the shoulder.

The trio then cleared away the breakfast pots.

CHAPTER 20

Luucar had refused the new Mecdia Captain's request and insisted Trentach go along for the ride. It left Cappa in little doubt this exercise was as much to get them all out of the way as it was for the benefit of any incoming dignitary.

This suspicion was only amplified when Cappa met the three tribals picked to lead them to Binka's camp. The clan escorts were clearly inexperienced and lowly ranked.

By the time Cappa returned with them to the square, Laonardo and Trentach had finished packing the supplies and readying their animals. Banteez Bayer had offered to ride south with the group on his way to the Ferentae Straights, his own horse and newly purchased carmol also prepared for the journey. The tribal trio offered little resistance, and so they'd set off at a pace to make their rendezvous before nightfall.

By late afternoon, they were already close to their destination, the three junior tribals clearly keen to make an impression with an early arrival.

Not for the first time Trentach and Bayer aired their concerns to the new Mecdia Captain.

"We should slow the pace in this heat," Bayer declared.

"We're well ahead of schedule," Trentach added in support.

Cappa rode to the three tribals leading the procession. "I appreciate you want to arrive in good time, but we shouldn't be punishing the animals like this. Not in the peak of afternoon. Trentach tells me we're close to the Boodan Bowl already, so what say we ease down a notch?"

The higher ranked of the three was no older than Cappa, his lack of leadership and experience evident throughout the day. At one stage he and his two subordinates had begun bickering over when to stop to water the animals. The other two were marginally older and clearly had little faith in their younger leader. However, when Cappa and the others had tried to mediate, it had become clear the only thing they held more disdain for than each other were dustbowl mercenaries interfering with tribal business.

The young tribal did not even look Cappa's way. "The animals are fine. They had plenty of water on our last stop." For a lowly desert guard, he had a wonderful knack for sounding superior.

Cappa patted Coba's neck, "That may be, but horses aren't cut out for speed in such conditions. If it's a sprint you wanted, you should have used carmols alone."

"The Boodan Bowl offers shade. The animals will have ample opportunity to cool down, drink and rest once we reach the Sultan's camp."

"The Bowl will be there regardless. It's senseless pushing the animals like this."

The clan soldier looked to Cappa for the first time, "Either keep up or be left behind, Mecdia Captain."

And that was that.

Cappa dropped back to the others.

"What did he say?" Bayer asked.

"He said, of course, Captain, we value your input, Captain. Thank you for bringing this somewhat obvious fact to our attention, Captain."

Bayer and the others laughed.

"You know it's to your credit," Bayer smiled. "You've been in the job but a day and already you've improved the balance between tribal and Mecdia significantly. Never have I seen such cohesion across the ranks. I don't know what I was doing wrong. I do know the Mecdia tradition will speak your name with reverence for years to come."

Again, they all laughed. The group were pleased Bayer had offered to detour his course slightly, to assist and remain with the group a while longer.

Trentach pointed, "The three little shits have actually upped their pace."

More laughter followed before Laonardo asked, "Do either of you know the exact location of our rendezvous?"

"Pretty much," Trentach replied, "However, I wouldn't recommend losing track of our tribal escort just in case."

"Then keep up we shall," Cappa declared, "Although, how about we maintain this respectable distance? That way I'll avoid any growing temptation to bury the three of them out here."

*

The night was coming in quickly as Cappa approached the three tribals. The trio had insisted on building a large fire of their own, maintaining a healthy distance between clan soldier and Mecdia. The heat of the flames licked Cappa's arms and face as he stepped into their circle, "It would be better to share a fire." It was the second time he'd expressed such concern, only now as darkness loomed his disquiet was more sincere. "For whatever reason, Ward Sultan Binka is not going to arrive before nightfall. As such it makes little sense splitting our group." Cappa glanced back at his own discreet fire some thirty strides away, Bayer and Laonardo keeping guard, as Trentach prepared some supper. He looked back to the tribals and pointed to the flagon of wine, "Perhaps it would be a better idea to lay off the drink too."

"Perhaps, Mecdia, it would serve you better to mind your own affairs." The middle-ranked tribal scorned.

Cappa sucked in a breath, "With respect, your safety is my affair."

"Our safety?" the younger leader snorted, "You need not concern yourself with anyone's safety but your own."

Cappa looked at the three despairingly, "We should stay within the same perimeter. Soon there'll be next to no visibility away from the flames and the cloud cover suggests little moonlight will be on offer."

The elder of the three took a turn, "Afraid of the dark, Mecdia?"

Cappa shook his head, "Both Bayer and Trentach inform me it's not unheard of for bandits to attack this far south."

"Bandits?" the leader was incredulous, "On tribal land? I think your friends are a little fanciful. Now, why don't you go back to them, reassure them of their safety." Another skin of wine was opened, followed by more derogatory laughter.

Cappa headed back to his friends, "Idiots, plain and simple."

No jokes surfaced this time.

Cappa sat as Bayer and Laonardo continued their vigil.

Bayer looked to him, "Even lower order tribals are distant relatives of the Sultans by some dilution. This gives them an illusion of rank. Unfortunately, it guarantees little else."

"Don't take it personally," Trentach added, "They're fools."

"I'm not taking it personally. I couldn't care less about any of them, but we find ourselves in unexpected circumstances. As such, even a fool knows a defensive perimeter should be set up - Particularly if you intend to advertise your position with a bonfire in the open - while seven makes for a better defence than four."

Trentach passed around some of the food.

"You maintain there's nothing unusual in this Sultan's no-show?" Laonardo reiterated.

"You've seen for yourself what these dustbowls can bring. Any number of things, from storms to bandits." Bayer's dagger took away a sliver of meat.

"I thought storms were rare in this more southerly region?"
Bayer offered a cold smile, "They are."

The group looked over as the tribals made a fresh assault on
the wine, their volume and cackling increasing. Their camp
was clumsy and exposed, their pyre too high. Unlike the
Mecdia effort, which saw weapons on hand, their animals set
around them as an early warning alarm and all within a
perimeter of scrounged thorn bushes and piled saddles.

Cappa looked once again to the darkening heavens, the
blanket of cloud blocking any input from the moon and stars.

He scanned the terrain.

Upon their arrival, they'd been surprised to find no Ward
Sultan Binka and his caravan awaiting them. It made Cappa
nervous. He sighed and took more of the meat on offer, his
prickly senses suggesting he was in for a long night.

*

Ruomaani leaned in close. It was strange to see her wearing
the ceremonial garbs of Prima. *'And I love you,'* she kissed
Cappa sweetly, *'But the kingdom must always come first,'* she
stroked her abdomen, *'This is far bigger than you or I.'*

Cappa's eyes snapped open, his nostrils reminding him of
his place by the campfire.

He reached for his sword, aware of movement as Laonardo
whispered, "There's somebody out there."

Cappa snatched himself from the dream and bolted upright.

Trentach stirred Bayer from his slumber.

It was dark, and it felt like the depth of night.

"How many?" Cappa whispered.

"I'm not sure, but there's definitely someone there."

Cappa took in his surroundings. The embers of their fire
gave a warm glow within the pit. The cloud cover was
breaking allowing intermittent stars to twinkle but the moon

was still hidden. Cappa was suddenly aware of the snoring from the tribals, their fire still licking with sporadic flame.

Bayer was now up and ready as Trentach placed a bucket of water close to the hot coals.

The movement had only been detected moments prior during Laonardo and Trentach's shift.

"It's definitely not one of the tribals." Laonardo said, as if reading Cappa's thoughts, "You can see them laid by the fire."

Cappa focused on the tribal camp to see Laonardo was right. The four crouched low with weapons and shields drawn. Trentach placed his foot close to the bucket as he prepared. Bayer scowled, allowing his eyes to adjust to the darkness. The two Pathans employed their breathing techniques, calming themselves, making ready for the possible fight.

"Somebody should wake them," Bayer whispered.

"They're drunk, you'd have to kick them out of their beds, and that's not an option right now." Trentach declared, as suddenly, their animals began to grumble…

And then it happened.

The three snoring tribals were slain in their beds by a mass of shadowy devils pouncing on them from the darkness.

The attack was swift and deadly.

The four had little time to concern themselves as their animals became more agitated. They all heard the movement, felt the threat, but they could see little.

Then it came.

Suddenly the camp was alive with the attack but, as the devils moved in, Trentach kicked the water bucket onto the hot pit, engulfing the four defenders in thick white smoke.

What followed was an orgy of sound.

Swords clashing and thrusting, shields striking, men yelling, the deadly chaos a chorus of killing. Suddenly, as more cloud broke, the moon came into play, lighting their surroundings through the diluting smoke.

A shadow, fast and strong flew in toward Cappa but the Thiazarran was more than up to the challenge. Seeing the lunge, Cappa leaned back onto his hind leg allowing the thrust of the blade to pass. As the attacking arm extended Cappa battered down with his shield almost snapping his aggressor's neck. He moved forward chopping his sword into the lower back, kicking his foe out of the arena as he turned to meet the next attack with the same smooth motion.

The next devil fared no better, Cappa swiftly altering his position, his bodyline slicing through the dissipating smoke as he butchered his next opponent.

To his right, Laonardo had despatched three already, his instincts spurring him through his aggressors like a jungle cat. Every muscle and sinew trained since childhood for such moments powered him forward. He ducked, weaved and spun like a gladiator, destroying the shadows moving in on him.

Wails and screams were now friends of the smoky moonlight as Bayer narrowly avoided having his right arm removed by an incoming blow. His shield crashed against his aggressor sending Bayer into a stumble, but as the attacker moved in for the kill a swifter shadow interrupted proceedings.

Bayer witnessed the movement, appreciated the kill, as Trentach flashed across his view. Bayer was up on his feet in an instant and back in the fight.

Trentach didn't wait for gratitude, and moved head on into the attacking shadows, his shield circled his form at lightning speed, an impenetrable fortress of moving steel - his sword whipping out with deadly accuracy as more screams and groans followed.

As the smoke cleared, the moon came into full force and Cappa caught a glimpse of Trentach's fighting display as he skilfully eliminated two more predators.

His attention was soon brought back to his own affairs, as Cappa was forced into slaying another dark devil that moved in on him. To his right, Laonardo was lethal, slaughtering two more assassins with brutal efficiency.

Cappa drove into another full attack. Now standing at the perimeter of the thorn bushes, his movement was so deadly it could be described as poetic, each kill blending into a motion of defence and countermeasure. His shield reflected the moon as his death dance orchestrated the end for three more assailants - when as suddenly as it had begun - it was over.

Nobody moved at first, their stances defiant as they heard scattering footfalls. In the distance they heard horses leaving but the moon refused to illustrate their number or direction.

Their heavy breathing took over, sweat salting their eyes, their throats dried by the smoke. As the adrenaline passed the cuts and bruises introduced their presence, as did their animals, sensing it was now safe to renew their complaints.

There were no groans from the injured, so deadly had their resistance proved.

The four looked to one another, panting, suspicious, still ready for the fight, but their attackers had gone.

CHAPTER 21

As dawn finally broke, the four warriors had remained free from further attack. The darkness had seemed to last an eternity, but as it lifted, Bayer was startled by the number of dead. Including their own unfortunate tribals, the body count numbered twenty-three, a devastating testimony to their killing prowess. Bayer took in some water, astounded at the final count. He was certain he'd slain three at best. He looked to his three companions, "Who are you people?"

Laonardo smiled, "Oh come now, don't be modest. You sent at least three to the afterlife."

He raised an eyebrow, "That leaves six a piece for each of you." He turned to Trentach, "And thank you, I'd be dead if it were not for you."

Trentach scanned the bodies. "You don't owe me a thing."

"To the contrary, I owe you everything, and since I'm still talking and breathing it's a debt I'm happy to be in."

"Your gratitude is more than enough." Trentach replied.

Laonardo looked across at their friend, he too having witnessed Trentach's ruthless skill. "Nevertheless, that was quite a display. Much more accomplished than anything you put together during the Torantum."

"I could say the same about the two of you," Trentach said.

Cappa paid little attention, instead concentrating on the bodies, "Are they bandits?"

Bayer didn't appear convinced as he and Trentach began examining them in the dawn light. "Their clothing is what you'd expect of a bandit, as are their weapons."

"But?" Laonardo asked.

Bayer crouched over one of the fallen and pulled away the chest section of his cuirass. He then tore open the tunic beneath. Trentach followed suit, until they'd exposed several more of their dead attackers.

Laonardo and Cappa looked on patiently.

"None have painted skin," Bayer said suspiciously. He looked to Trentach.

"Nor have any of these."

"Meaning?" Laonardo enquired.

"It's by no means infallible, but I'd expect to see tattoos on these bodies," Bayer replied. "Bandits tend to decorate themselves with symbols affiliating them to a certain group, a particular heritage. They see themselves as freedom fighters, resisting the iron rule of the Sultan clans. These marks tell the stories of their deeds against such oppression."

Cappa scowled, "What made you suspect these bodies would be clean?"

"Only the suspicion all is not as it seems," Bayer replied.

"Based upon?"

Trentach took over, "Based on the fact they kept coming." He stood and looked to his comrades. "Look around you." He gestured to the mass of corpses. "All this to attack two small camp fires guarding little to no possessions?" He pointed to their animals, "They didn't even steal our horses or carmols. Yet they kept on coming."

Bayer agreed, "Even taking into account the darkness and confusion, I'd never expect bandits to sacrifice so many for so little. Especially not on Sultan territory."

"They can expect richer pickings in the outlands with far less risk." Trentach added with concern, "Unless of course, they knew about the cask of silver you were rewarded?"

"So, what are we suspecting?" Laonardo asked feeling he already had the answer.

"A set up," they looked to Cappa as he made the timely intervention. "These men were clearly following orders. Luucar wants us gone."

Bayer scowled, "If Luucar wants you gone he relieves you of service, he doesn't promote you."

"He didn't - Kirkoban did." Cappa looked to Trentach, "You stated Luucar is the brains of the outfit. He sees me as a threat to Ruomaani-Skye's impending marriage. He essentially said it himself when he asked Laonardo and I to show discretion."

Bayer was unaware of the incident, but asked, "But doesn't that make Kirkoban just as likely a suspect?"

Laonardo shook his head. "When Kirkoban gave us our reward he was genuinely thankful, as was this Dreda. It was Luucar who appeared uneasy by our presence."

Bayer was confused. "Then why not send you away with the rest of the Mecdia?"

"He likely tried. It was Kirkoban who wanted us to remain," Cappa speculated, "Kirkoban's new wealth may place him under a different threat - the ambitions of those closest to him. Maybe Kirkoban sees us as outsiders, honourable Thiazarrans, useful in a fight, useful in protecting him. Fighting merchants with royal seals he may one day exploit." Cappa ascertained, "No, this is not the work of our benefactor - either keeping us around is too great a risk as far as the more cautious Luucar is concerned, or he wants us out of the way for an entirely different reason."

Bayer frowned, "But to go to trouble such as this?"

"I suspect something else is at play here, something less obvious, something more sinister - certainly something bigger than stealing back a hundred pieces of silver." Cappa added with gravitas, "And all my instincts tell me it is Luucar."

"And what about this, Binka?" Bayer was struggling.

"Probably nowhere near here," Cappa replied.

Trentach's expression darkened. "Kirkoban's clan doesn't have a wealth of soldiers. Therefore, if we are in agreement Luucar is the likely suspect, he too will be short of men loyal to his cause." He pointed at the bodies, "Which suggests hired men. How could Luucar cover such expense and mobilise a hired force so quickly?" He added, "Why engage such risk?"

"He didn't believe it was a risk," Laonardo stated. "Bayer's reaction said it all, twenty-plus against four fighters and three fools. Good odds, with an added bonus of a small trunk of silver," Laonardo now wore a dark expression of his own, "But you are right, these men must have been ready to move at short notice from a location close to Malbood." He looked to Cappa, "If this is indeed the work of Luucar, this means he has a paid-for group of fighters ready to do his bidding."

"Which backs up the notion there is another, larger play at hand," Cappa pondered.

"Or another player!" Laonardo agreed. "Which indeed suggests a plot - a strategy which requires hidden forces such as these on hand and ready to act. A game we've clearly stumbled into." He looked to Trentach, "Any suggestions?"

Trentach took a long moment, "This is all conjecture," he declared. "Compelling, yes - credible, very much so, but assumption all the same. All that really matters here and now, is what you intend to do." His gaze returned to Cappa.

The certainty of Cappa's next statement choked Laonardo before it was even said.

"I'm going to head back to Malbood."

Laonardo looked to the heavens as Bayer asked, "Why?"

"Because I believe my destiny is with Ruomaani-Skye."

Trentach glared, "Ruomaani-Skye is set to marry Bunsaar before the week is out."

Laonardo noted the growing gravity to Trentach's concern.

"I know."

"Then why consider returning?" Trentach pointed at the bodies, "Risk crossing a person responsible for this, whoever that may be? Go up against one such as Luucar on his own territory, even Bunsaar if he learns of your time alone with her?"

"I have no desire to cross anyone, simply to return. If Luucar had the confidence to deal with me openly in Malbood then we would not be standing here. By returning, having survived a bandit attack, nothing will have changed. So long as he believes I do not suspect him in any way responsible."

"And you wish to return solely on the whim you may have a chance with this, girl?" Trentach was incredulous, "This woman already betrothed to another? She cannot betray her vow!"

"I've been raised in a tradition which pays heed to omens and destiny. I believe I've found mine. I also believe this destiny will one day benefit the future of my people."

Laonardo stepped forward to remind his friend of the required discretion, "Cappa."

"Your people?" Bayer was growing all the more confused.

"Cappa!" Laonardo echoed.

"And this destiny?" Trentach was a little too interested for Laonardo's liking, "How could it possibly benefit anyone but yourself? Surely, it's your own desire you wish to see fulfilled."

"I believe it is much more than that," Cappa retorted.

Laonardo was firm, "Cappa, now is not the time."

"Not the time for what?" Bayer scowled.

"And why would you believe such a thing?" Trentach demanded. "Why would you believe risking your life for this woman could possibly aid anyone but yourself?"

Laonardo stepped forward. He did not like Trentach's increasingly antagonistic tone.

Cappa stared at Trentach, "I feel it."

"Feel?" Trentach scorned, "To feel is not enough. Only focus and revelation can bring enlightenment."

"You, my friend, seem to know an awful lot of what my actions and processes should be," Cappa replied.

"And you should know better than to place yourself at risk on a fool's errand!" Trentach said stepping forward a little too aggressively, seeing Laonardo grip the hilt of his weapon.

"Then rest assured this is no foolish errand, no impulsive response to infatuation. I believe this girl is destined to be Queen, perhaps the greatest Queen," he pointed to the dead. "I also fear this conspiracy is to involve Ruomaani-Skye, which could place her in grave danger. This alone would be enough."

Bayer was at a complete loss as Trentach turned to Laonardo, "So tell me, what is your take on this, Patruan?"

The realisation struck. Trentach's fighting ability the previous night, his continual willing to back them throughout their adventures - his unlimited knowledge of the area and the people with whom they associated. Laonardo thought of the secret map given to him, of the Garpathans who'd ridden into the desert on their first arrival in Ferenta.

He relaxed his weapon as he looked on Trentach with fresh eyes... eyes that now recognised one of his own, that now saw Trentach the Garpathan.

*

Trentach demanded Bayer swear a solemn oath of secrecy before another word was spoken. Bayer did so, albeit increasingly confused at events now transpiring.

"How many of you have made our acquaintance during our travels?" Cappa enquired.

"Let's just say wherever possible we like to keep an eye on things."

Laonardo thought back over their time in Ferenta, to the strangers and friends who had helped and guided them over the past year and a half, a list of possible Garpathan candidates quickly forming in his mind, "Wlako?"

"Wlako was one of us yes."

"NikoLindo the stargazer?"

"An old friend," Trentach agreed.

"LoPaule the acrobat, or Khlamad?"

"LoPaule is not known to me. Khlamad was simply a wise and likable dustbowler."

Laonardo shook his head, "Then why all the secrecy with regards the map if you were to be among us throughout our journey regardless?"

"Map?" Cappa scowled, "What map?"

Laonardo looked apologetic, "I'm sorry, Cappa, before we left my father gave me a map. On it were locations of hidden Garpathans who could assist us if need arose. I had to take a solemn vow never to reveal it unless dire emergency demanded. A promise all Patruans must make before these adventures are allowed to take place."

Trentach tried to placate his companions, "As you no doubt suspected, risking the future of our nation is not something we take lightly. The two of you are bred to serve, rule and protect. The final part of that training is the gift of freedom that you are living right now. You have learned to be ordinary men and, as you well know, this is a practice deemed worthy of risk, a vital ingredient, one that has helped sustain our way of life for centuries. For such a practice to succeed a small section of the Garpathan Brotherhood is trained to take up the task of protecting our rulers during this rite of passage, to hide in the shadows, watch from a distance. Many never get the chance to meet you, some are acquaintances for a day or so. However, on occasion fate steps in, allowing a rare few to spend time with those they protect, to perhaps even become friends."

He smiled graciously and tilted before his future rulers, "As for the map, it is of vital importance. No matter how organised and prepared we are fate can never be second-guessed with absolute accuracy. A left turn instead of a right, the periods when the two of you are inevitably alone, a desert storm.

There will always be occasion when we are further behind than we would like. For this reason, it is essential, Patruan, that you also know how to reach us. Since the most important part of this adventure is to teach the two of you the values of ordinary life, the map can only be a failsafe. The rest must remain as much a mystery to you, Laonardo, as it does to Cappa here - so the two of you may utilise these experiences in order to rule with equality and wisdom."

"But tracking us all this time?" Cappa queried in disbelief.

"Believe me it is not easy, but we have a thorough network of spies." He smiled, "As I've said, despite this, we certainly lose you from time to time."

Bayer looked on spellbound.

Trentach turned to him, "Banteez Bayer, I must reiterate the importance of your vow. These practices must never be spoken of. You will be paid handsomely for such discretion."

Bayer looked annoyed, "I've given my word which is sacred. I owe you my life, and I happen to take that quite seriously too."

"Still," Cappa smiled before delivering his next line with impeccable timing, "A title and a trunk load of treasure wouldn't be too much to ask for under the circumstances. Save a lot of time and effort mining silver."

The four looked to one another and burst into laughter.

The moment broke the enormity of the situation, allowing them to take stock.

Eventually Laonardo asked, "So, does this network have any idea what's happening here. If this Luucar is responsible, and if so, who he may be in league with and why?"

"The Garpathans awaiting my instruction know only what I told them when I sent word at Fraeda." Trentach looked sombre, "However, if I were to guess, only another Sultan would have the means to make such a move, or indeed to back Luucar in such a manner."

CHAPTER 22

It had been a morning of revelation.

Banteez Bayer regarded himself a worldly man, but this was beyond his comprehension, and as he listened to Cappa go into greater detail of his recent dreams of Ruomaani-Skye, he couldn't quite grasp the magnitude of what he'd stumbled into.

Bayer had known from the beginning there was something profoundly different about the two Thiazarrans, but he certainly hadn't suspected them to be two of the most powerful men in the known world.

He sat silently as Trentach dissected the interpretations Cappa had taken from recent dreams and events.

"You must understand the vow to marriage here is a solemn one. If broken, the repercussions are terrible. Therefore, however much you may believe Ruomaani-Skye will be delivered to you, it cannot be without danger. Your desire may well be infecting your intuition." Trentach spoke thoughtfully, his affiliation to the Garpathan Brotherhood ensuring a broad depth to the more spiritual ways of the Pathan Code.

"I appreciate the path seems obscured, but I believe it to be the correct one." Cappa reiterated, "If nothing else, I sense the danger she is in, and I cannot stand idly by."

Trentach pondered, "No matter how pure our intent, no matter how able we are to remove ourselves in order to gain objectivity, interpretation remains precisely that. As such, we can only hope our integrity, intelligence and instinct will help show the way." Trentach looked into Cappa's eyes, "My superiors inform me you are one of their greatest students, that your ability to focus your intuition could one day match even Poentrikas." He noted the surprise such a statement brought to Cappa's face. "As such, I will trust your judgement. I am your servant. I will obey your instruction to the letter."

"You are my friend, Trentach," Cappa smiled, "I thank you for your support."

Trentach tilted, acknowledging the honour.

Cappa turned to Banteez Bayer who smiled, "I'm in way over my head, but a title and a trunk load of treasure sounds pretty good to me."

The following laughter was welcome.

The Prince's gaze then fell upon Laonardo.

"I am your Patruan," he declared, "If you are so certain Ruomaani-Skye is to be your Queen, then she is to be my Queen also. I will give my life to her as I would to you. But if we are to follow this through, we need to formulate a plan. We need to know who our enemies are, sooner rather than later."

Cappa was pleased.

"First, we need to establish your intention," Laonardo continued. "Such as, do you intend on making a play for Ruomaani-Skye whatever the cost? Do you intend to reveal your true identity in the hope you may bail her out of this sacred commitment? Or do you maintain your original course? That you'll return as Mecdia Captain, await a sign, and if nothing is forthcoming, leave Malbood before the wedding?"

Cappa's response was swift, "So confident am I fate will step in, my intention is to return to Malbood as Mecdia Captain, nothing else. As promised, I will not force the issue purely for my own gain, nor will I reveal myself simply to see her delivered to me. As weak as these Sultans may be, I will not spit on their traditions."

Both Laonardo and Trentach seemed pleased.

"Nevertheless, the sooner we have reinforcements nearby the better - just in case." Laonardo pointed to his long-hidden map. "If my calculations are correct, the nearest Garpathan camp is four days to the northeast of here." He looked to Trentach.

"Closer to five days, though a company of our men are actually a day and a half east of Malbood. Back in Fraeda I sent word to have a posse move closer over the coming days."

Laonardo looked to him admiringly, "How many men?"

"Twenty. More than enough to hold off a force five times the size of anything these Sultans have to throw at us, Bunsaar being the possible exception." He noted the query etched on both Cappa and Laonardo's faces. "Bunsaar's tribal army numbers almost two hundred fully mobilised, all trained by their Captain, Vhlarm. They're disciplined and can be backed up by further Mecdia at short notice. Since it is Bunsaar you may end up tangling with one way or another, these are factors of which you should familiarise yourself."

Bayer added, "Vhlarm certainly shouldn't be underestimated. I've paid testimony to that."

"No, he should not," Trentach echoed. "He is a mighty opponent, schooled in war." He added, "There is also the unknown factor of the mercenaries who attacked us in the night, whoever their allegiance is to - All potential enemies need to be considered."

Laonardo's concern returned, "With the twenty close to Malbood, how many does that leave at the Garpathan camp?"

"Eighteen, but they are over three more days from the advanced group." He added, "I will need to go to my brothers to deliver word of our situation."

"I was prepared to risk this strategy without knowledge of such reinforcements available to me. And I am grateful for them." Cappa reassured, "However, despite the obvious danger in seeing this through, it is not my intention to pick a fight. I have given you my word I will not force the issue with

Ruomaani-Skye. Such a thing has never been my intention, otherwise I would have revealed my identity in Malbood."
"But perhaps that's your best course of action," Bayer interjected. "I mean - you keep talking of signs and opportunities. Seems to me the best chance you have of winning her is to step in as future King of Zarrapathia. These Sultans are greedy, intent on gaining more wealth. Perhaps stepping up and offering them such fortune is the best hand you can play."

Trentach disagreed, "For any Sultan to renege on public vows made before their gods would spell disaster. As ragtag as they may be most adhere to a strict code of conduct. I doubt simply riding into town as second in line to Zarrapathia will work. You'd have to buy off every Sultan in the territory, see each of them desecrate their position before their gods, which could weaken their long-term rule over their people. Even if some of the Sultan clans agreed you'd be sparking a potential tinderbox with those that refused."

Cappa agreed, "I have faith Ruomaani will be delivered without need for such action. I return to Malbood as Mecdia Captain. I will await the signs. If none are forthcoming, I'll accept desire has clearly clouded my judgement and leave."
He looked to Laonardo, "Lesson learned."

*

Ruomaani suffered a restless sleep, haunted by dreams of matabas and dangers in the desert night. She'd risen at dawn and paid homage to the sun god, thanking all of heaven for her fortune in marriage. The prayers were spoken aloud, but they felt empty, spoken more for the benefit of her lady-in-waiting whom she held little trust or affection for.

Ruomaani hated being locked away like this but felt no real desire to be free of her prison if it meant the bedchamber of the Sultan Bunsaar. She entered the bathing room, her lady-in-waiting removing Ruomaani's gown before leaving her.

Ruomaani walked into the sunken pool and sighed as she submerged into the soothing hot waters of the fragrant bath.

She closed her eyes, only to see Cappa's face smiling down on her. She removed the image, tried to focus on how she was saving her father, her sweet brother Zuda. As her thoughts drifted toward Menka, she tried desperately to remind herself of her duty, to turn away from the temptation to take flight.

*

Possible conspirators had been discussed throughout the morning ride, with some interesting theories arising as a result. At the halfway stage Trentach said his farewells and headed to rendezvous with the advance company of Garpathans. Once located, he would have a rider return to the main camp in order to see the remaining eighteen warriors mobilise - Trentach would then lead the advance troop to the outskirts of Malbood. Cappa had agreed another messenger should head for the coast and make passage to Kiniphul, his mission to return quickly with a Pathan fleet, just in case anything unforeseen was to unfold.

They had estimated it would take thirty days to see an army arrive at Malbood. A situation they hoped would never arise.

Cappa remained convinced Luucar was central to the conspiracy, and that Kirkoban's advisor would not act directly against them.

Upon his return, the Mecdia Captain would simply detail a victory against an audacious bandit attack, while enquiring over the safety and whereabouts of Ward Sultan Binka.

Laonardo understood his belief but was nervous of what their opponent may conjure up, or who else could be involved.

Events were moving quickly and as he, Bayer and Cappa saw the thin silhouette of Malbood in the late afternoon sun, a sense of foreboding made a return to the Patruan's psyche.

It was busy as they approached the main gate, with traders and merchants yelling toward a newly arriving caravan, a sturdy coach being towed at its heart.

Cappa, Laonardo and Bayer tagged onto the end of the convoy as it entered the township. The square was alive with the last throws of the market and they approached the inner citadel with the desert caravan at the fore.

The gates to the sanctum remained sealed as a guard set about checking the credentials of the procession. "Open the gates for Ward Sultan Binka!" the guard yelled. The order was echoed, "Ward Sultan Binka arrives, open the gates!"

Cappa, Laonardo and Bayer looked to one another in stunned silence, the coincidence almost too much to acknowledge - for unwittingly, the three were set to enter the palace with the very convoy they'd been sent to escort.

Bayer leaned close to his companions, "Well, if that isn't one of your omens, I don't know what is."

As the caravan began moving into the citadel square, several tribal guards acknowledged the trio at its rear.

The three measured the incoming stares for signs of surprise or suspicion. None were forthcoming.

The convoy came to a halt by the main entrance.

Luucar emerged and was heading quickly down the steps toward the visitors. As he came, he noted the three Mecdia, his face confirming to Cappa all he needed to know.

*

As Cappa knelt before Kirkoban, Luucar's expression indicated he'd have preferred a more private consultation.

Unfortunately for the third in line, events had moved quickly.

Binka had been furious upon his arrival and demanded to know why no honourable escort had been sent to greet his small desert procession. On hearing of Cappa's return, Kirkoban had the Mecdias brought before him to answer for their failures in the presence of the disgruntled Binka.

Laonardo and Bayer remained kneeling at the rear of the room, their heads lowered as Cappa spoke, "Great Sultans, I can only beg your forgiveness. We followed our tribal escort to the Boodan Bowl as instructed, but could find no trace…"

Binka barked at the court, "Boodan Bowl? I was never at the Boodan Bowl." He looked to Kirkoban who immediately turned toward the Sultan Dreda, and then to Luucar.

Luucar handled it well, bowing low, "Forgive me, Ward Sultan Binka, but I was led to believe this was your chosen place of rendezvous."

"The Bowl was mentioned, but it was disregarded in favour of the Alcimar Pass."

Luucar looked mortified, "Then the burden for humiliation is mine, Ward Sultan, for I sent these men with tribal escorts to the Boodan Bowl."

"And where are these escorts?" Binka demanded, "I only see Mecdia before me!"

"Dead, Ward Sultan," Cappa responded.

"Dead?"

Cappa turned to Kirkoban, "Killed in the night by unseen attackers. I also lost my Second Lieutenant, Trentach. Cut off during the fight. We fear the worst. I re-deputised Banteez Bayer here after he volunteered to help see us back to Malbood. He fought most bravely."

Kirkoban flushed at the account, his gaze crossing the room to the Sultan Dreda.

Cappa looked to Luucar and noted a momentary flash of pleasure play over his eyes before the sorrowful act continued.

"Ward Sultan Binka, I can only beg your forgiveness."
Luucar stepped forward, "The messenger sent with your
invitation returned with instructions to meet you at the Bowl."

Binka was swift to pour scorn, "Then this messenger is a
fool, the Boodan Bowl was clearly disregarded. Where is this
man so he may answer for his stupidity?"

Luucar looked to the floor sadly, "I regret, Ward Sultan, he
was one of the tribals sent out with the three Mecdia here."

Binka's self-absorption blinded him to the true gravity of the
situation. For Kirkoban's men to be attacked while operating
within the Sultan's own territory was shameful.

"I can only state my relief at not having followed such a
route," Binka eyed Kirkoban, "How many did you lose in this
misguided venture to see my caravan protected?"

Without thinking Kirkoban blurted out, "We sent six tribals
and six Mecdia."

Binka was suitably honoured at the number.

Cappa and the others remained silent, their heads bowed.

Luucar had to utilise all of his willpower to stop himself
sneering, despite his understanding of his Sultan's logic.

If Kirkoban admitted to sending only three tribals and three
Mecdia, Binka would be mortified after hearing of such an
attack. Even a low-ranking Ward Sultan was entitled honour
and protection. However, as was his rash nature, Kirkoban had
now lied to another Sultan directly in front of Dreda, who
knew the real number sent.

Dreda was quick to begin damage limitation, "Ward Sultan
Binka. Clearly the messenger sent back to Luucar has made a
foolish error. This foolishness has been punished in the worst
possible way. May we praise the gods for seeing you make
safe passage to Malbood and pray you have the noble grace to
forgive such incompetence."

Dreda gestured toward Kirkoban who stuttered into action,
"Yes, yes, please forgive our mistake. Allow me to honour you

with two hundred pieces of silver and a twenty-strong guard led by Feldahd to return you home after the festivities."

To any other of the Sultan brethren, such a gesture would be an insult. To one as lowly as Binka, it was extravagant - and with such an act, Kirkoban had managed to buy off the one Sultan more foolish than he.

*

With the pleasantries and repair work done, the Sultans removed themselves from court to prepare for the festivities set to honour the arrival of Binka.

Kirkoban was in his quarters when Feldahd announced Dreda's presence. As Dreda entered the chambers, he was clearly annoyed. "What were you thinking?"

Kirkoban was rueful, "I'm sorry. The circumstances forced me to panic. I couldn't risk Binka thinking I'd not sent sufficient protection. Not after news of an attack."

"But in saying you sent more suggests a larger bandit party, one with the stones to attack your guard while in their own territory."

"I appreciate that, but what would you have me do? If I'd said three tribals and three Mecdia he'd have been doubly offended and less likely to be bought off so swiftly."

For once Dreda had some sympathy with Kirkoban's situation. He loved him like a brother but despaired of his rash judgements and lack of control over his own court. He knew only too well the dangers surrounding Kirkoban - dangers Dreda hoped would finally be averted once the marriage of his *hanouri* had gone ahead to Bunsaar.

In his heart he hated that his beloved Ruomaani-Skye would become third wife to such a tyrant, but Bunsaar had offered triple what any other suitor could afford. His beautiful hanouri meant the world to him, and Dreda felt great pride in the strength she had shown, in her noble ability to understand and embrace her duty to the tribal clan. He sighed as he thought of her mother, "Well, fortunately, it is Binka we're talking about here. We'll get him drunk tonight then have Zuda take him out with his hawks tomorrow. You know how Binka loves Zuda's birds. In the meantime, have the Mecdia involved redirected on where *we* say the attack happened. We'll have them testify it took place beyond the southern reach of the Bowl. At least that's closer to the outland border." He paused, "How many did this Cappa and his Mecdia kill?"

Kirkoban sighed, "They reported slaying twenty."

Dreda acknowledged the statistic, "Well, at least you now have men capable of scoring such victories. This is the third bandit attack in as many months." Dreda shook his head and sighed, "Let's just make sure our mataba slayer is enlightened as to where and how we say the incident took place."

CHAPTER 23

The room set aside for the Mecdia Captain and his Lieutenants was at the rear of the palace compound above the blacksmith's shop and stable. The quarters were large with baked clay walls painted white. Three plush bedrolls had been set out in each corner and a private wash area graced the landing below. They'd joked of their relief at not having found themselves sharing three to a bed before discussing the events within court in greater detail.

The trio had quickly agreed to remove Binka from their list of potential conspirators, and concurred that Dreda was clearly in Kirkoban's corner. Their discussions had continued into the night, until they could resist the pull of sleep no longer. The exertions in the Bowl had taken a toll and despite the looming uncertainty, the trio were surprised at how well they'd slept.

The three had risen soon after dawn.

Luucar had given them the morning off, a gesture that made Cappa suspicious rather than grateful, and as he washed in the wet-room, Cappa wondered what lay ahead.

He had only one more dawn before Bunsaar's arrival for the agmanta. The Sultan's marriage to Ruomaani-Skye would come three short days later. Cappa emptied the used water into the drain before returning to their room to find Laonardo and Bayer staring out of the window.

"Something's definitely going on," Laonardo said.

"What's happening?" Cappa asked as he closed the door.

"I'm not sure. It's not exactly a prime view, but that's the third time I've seen senior high ranking tribals running to the main chamber like their lives depended on it." Laonardo tensed suddenly, "Hello, four are headed our way." He watched them approach, "Arm yourselves."

The senior tribals entered at the side of the blacksmith's shop. The Mecdia trio stood ready as they heard the rumble of approaching feet on the stairs.

The door was struck aggressively. "Mecdia, open the door."

Cappa lifted the latch.

"We have orders to search your room."

"Search the room, what before the gods do you expect to find?"

"Step aside, the order comes from Sultan Kirkoban."

They did as they were asked as the ranking tribals made quick work of the apartment. "Check the wet-room then the smith-house and stables below. Don't forget the forge and store in the basement," the leader barked, sending two guards quickly on their way. "You three, get dressed and report to the Sultan with me."

"Of course," Bayer said. "May we ask what is happening?"

The brash, impetuous tribal responded, "The Sultan's daughter, she's missing."

*

The morning turned into frenzy with a dozen senior tribals combing the citadel. Feldahd and Seban had seen the palace sealed to all but essential staff.

Kirkoban had the three Mecdia report due to a suspicion Cappa may have influenced or even fled with his daughter. On seeing the Mecdia Captain at a loss with clear concern for her wellbeing, Kirkoban, Dreda and Feldahd had instead pulled Cappa aside to question him on his time spent with Ruomaani-Skye in the wilderness. "Did she say anything to you about fleeing? Did she discuss her feelings toward the marriage? Did you sense she was going to attempt something rash?"

The queries came thick and fast, Cappa's same reply only succeeding to crush their line of enquiry. "No!"

Cappa and his Lieutenants were ordered not to leave the palace grounds and as Luucar began barking fresh orders, the three Mecdia were pushed into the court corridor as a new wave of actions were set into motion.

Cappa watched Luucar like a hawk and was ready to force his way back into the arena when Luucar's bodyguard re-entered the melting pot and headed straight for the third in line. Luucar's face was instantly ashen as he received what was clearly terrible news.

*

The moment Luucar had forwarded Seban's report the panic had risen to a whole new level. Cappa was desperate to learn of the news delivered, to hear what had brought Kirkoban and Dreda to this new summit of anxiety.

Luucar and Seban had since headed out of court with Feldahd snapping at their heels. There was no sign of Binka or the other nobles - Zuda and Menka included.

Kirkoban was distraught as Dreda tried to make sense of events, both men desperate for updates - and then it came.

Luucar came bounding into court clutching half-burned documents, his face etched with dread. The court was emptied, the doors sealed shut by Feldahd and Seban.

*

The remainder of the day proved the most frustrating experience Cappa had endured. Although prisoners to the cause within the core of the palace compound, as Mecdia they were not privy to any new information revealed and discussed.

Cappa's mind was working overtime, his anxiety building despite the obvious air of fate. He'd discussed his options with his colleagues and even considered revealing his true identity, though he'd been persuaded to exercise a little more patience.

"This could be the very sign you were waiting for," Laonardo echoed. "Focus. Remove yourself from the chaos, so you may see when and how to act."

It was difficult, but Cappa did as he was instructed.

However, as the morning quickly became late afternoon, he was growing all the more concerned.

Then, with his breaking point looming, it happened - Sultan Kirkoban summoned the Mecdia Captain back into court.

CHAPTER 24

Cappa was summoned alone. Before him were Kirkoban, Feldahd and Dreda, with Luucar and Seban flanking them.

He bowed before dropping to one knee.

"Rise, Mecdia Captain," Kirkoban instructed. "I've brought you here to discuss a most delicate matter. As you well know my daughter Ruomaani-Skye is missing. So far, we've managed to keep this news contained. Only my personal guard know of her disappearance. As you can well imagine, this is a most precarious time for her - for all of us. Her future husband arrives tomorrow night, as do many more of my Sultan brethren. The trouble that would follow if news of her disappearance were to leave this compound would be extremely grave. The situation has been made all the more hazardous by Ward Sultan Binka's presence. Fortunately, he's been out with my son since dawn and has no knowledge of this. I must act quickly if there is any chance of saving my daughter from disgrace."

He swallowed, "In many ways, the fact you are not blood makes you the ideal candidate. That and the obvious truth, you know how to see a job through." Kirkoban's eyes shifted to Dreda who offered encouragement. "You are clearly as noble as you are effective. As such I will ask for your solemn vow. What we discuss in this room stays between us."

"Upon my honour, I'm at your service in this difficult time."

Kirkoban smiled weakly. He cleared his throat to prepare for the difficult sentence to come, "My daughter has eloped with Menka, we believe we know where they are headed, and we want you to go and get her."

'Eloped?' Cappa's suspicion was immediate.

"I cannot risk my own men on this. Besides the three of you, only my highest ranked know she's missing. Only we in this room now know precisely why. I need to keep it that way."

Cappa stared into the eyes of the men before him. He witnessed the sadness haunting Feldahd, the sheer concern gripping Dreda, the panic engulfing Kirkoban, and there, as clear to Cappa's well-honed instincts as a sign above his head, was the deception lurking within Luucar.

Cappa buried his realisation and played along.

"Should she be returned to us before Bunsaar arrives, we might just be able to save her." Kirkoban looked to Cappa imploringly, "Can you bring me back my daughter?"

"What about Menka?"

"We do not want him harmed if at all possible. But Ruomaani-Skye is all that matters if such a choice were to be made."

Cappa's eyes were like stone, "I would need absolute knowledge of all you have learned."

"Of course."

"To see all evidence of this elopement to aid me in my quest."

Luucar seemed annoyed, "You will have the information we give you."

Cappa almost barked at him, "All the evidence!"

"You shall have it," Dreda declared forcing Luucar to back down.

"I'll need Laonardo and Bayer to assist me."

"We presumed you would call upon their service," Kirkoban looked nervous, "There's more. Not content with the ruination of my daughter and our clan, Menka has also stolen the dowry securing Ruomaani-Skye's marriage to Bunsaar. Menka is no strategist, no great thinker. He's lived a sheltered life. Should Bunsaar learn of this betrayal, it won't be long before he finds them. When he does, I cannot bare to think what he may do. My daughter is far more precious to me than any treasure, but this dowry was paid to save our tribe from ruin."

Kirkoban looked sombre, "I'm placing a great deal of trust in you. We believe such faith is not misplaced. If you return all to me safely, you will have saved my daughter and my clan, and you'll be rewarded handsomely."

Cappa spoke with assurance, "Your money is of no concern to me Sultan, of that you can rest assured. Without your daughter's courage I would have been struck down by that landslide and may well have been torn apart by that second mataba. She was as responsible for saving my life, as I ever was hers. If helping you helps Ruomaani-Skye, then you have my vow I shall do my utmost to see the quest through."

Feldahd allowed a slight smile to appear. It was strange how he and the Sultans knew Cappa's words to be true, trusting the Mecdia Captain as their only hope.

Dreda acknowledged him, "You do yourself and your people great credit, Thiazarran."

Cappa noted once again there was no such warmth in Luucar's expression. "I'll need guarantees the three of us will be granted safe passage to Zarrapathia once the job is done. As outsider's privy to such sensitive secrets, I'd rather be far from here once we've played our part. This is the least we can expect if we deliver all you ask."

"We had hoped you'd stay on in our service, but naturally I understand your concerns," Kirkoban replied. "And you will be rewarded if successful, whether you want it or not."

"Rest assured, young Thiazarran," Dreda said, "No harm will come to any of you after such a service. I guarantee it."

Cappa looked to Dreda, the Thiazarran's command and prowess seeming to grow before their very eyes. "After my men are sworn to the cause, once I've had time to examine the evidence, I must request a private audience with you, Sultan Dreda, so we may discuss these guarantees."

Kirkoban, Luucar and Feldahd looked confused at the request. Dreda, however, was happy to go along with anything the Thiazarran demanded in order to save his beloved hanouri, and the incompetent family that surrounded her.

"Whatever it takes."

*

With his men sworn in, Cappa demanded he be allowed to investigate Ruomaani-Skye's disappearance with as free a reign as circumstance could allow.

Luucar was aghast as Cappa was given time to satisfy his own brand of deduction. "Isn't time supposed to be of the essence here?" Luucar's protests had been ignored.

The Thiazarran proved particularly interested in the half-burned documents; supposed letters between Ruomaani and Menka, the final entry of which offered hints of elopement and clues toward their intended route of escape.

Once satisfied, Cappa insisted on a private discussion with his men before being granted his audience with Dreda.

Luucar was clearly agitated.

When at last Cappa and his men left and returned to the blacksmith's stables to prepare, Luucar found he'd had quite enough. He barged into the enclosed chamber at the side of the court to discuss developments with Dreda himself.

The Sultan was in no mood, "It's better he study the evidence now rather than make mistakes when anticipating their next move. It's imperative she be returned to us."

Luucar's mood seemed to ease, "So he agrees with our assumption. That they're headed toward Durant?"

"It appears so."

"Then why the private audience?"

"He wanted written documentation by my own hand, parchment enclosed by my personal seal and for this action to be mirrored by Kirkoban. A dual passport of sorts, a guarantee of free passage so the three may head safely for Zarrapathia without hindrance once the job is done."

"Is that not what we were offering in the first place?"

"He's being cautious."

Luucar was suspicious, "Did he ask for an escort?"

Dreda raised an eyebrow, "I don't think he seeks our help in such matters, do you? Isn't that one of the reasons we decided to send him on this unfortunate errand?"

Luucar scowled, "Surely granting him such a passport here and now will only increase the likelihood they will flee with the dowry if successful."

"I know a thing or two about Thiazarrans, particularly wealthy ones. Believe me, the last thing you need concern yourself with is the safety of the money."

Luucar raised an eyebrow, "Those two dustbowlers, wealthy?"

He eyed Luucar, "Only the rich and righteous refuse reward."

"Then why are they out here?"

"Adventure, Luucar, they are here for adventure."

Luucar visibly eased a little more, "I'm sorry for my impertinence, Sultan Dreda, all this drama must be getting to me."

Dreda smiled weakly as Kirkoban and Feldahd entered.

"Well?" Kirkoban demanded.

"He just wanted written guarantees. He asked you to do the same." Dreda pointed at his own handiwork, "Copy mine."

Kirkoban read over the document, a little surprised this simple request had been the sole result of such a meeting. "Our Thiazarran is cautious," Kirkoban said after a moment.

"He wanted every possible reassurance," Dreda clarified. "You can't really blame him, what with all the treachery going on here."

Kirkoban agreed as he wetted the quill, "I suppose not." He began writing, "It will be a shame to lose them. They are good men."

Dreda sighed, "Probably for the best all things considered. If any of this were to get out, we'd be thrown into a tribal war."

*

Dreda insisted Luucar deliver the seals in person. "Take the documents over to the smith's stable. The Mecdia are preparing over there as we speak."

Luucar looked to Kirkoban who nodded, so he took the papers and set off to fulfil the task.

He marched to seek out his bodyguard.

Seban was waiting patiently as Luucar instructed, "Follow me!" The pair headed for the blacksmiths quarters.

As they approached, they could see the Mecdia horses already saddled at the fore of the shop. Luucar entered the smith's stable and saw Cappa in the far corner near his pack ponies. "Mecdia, here are the documents you demanded of Dreda." Luucar was displeased with the notion of playing messenger boy, waving them at Cappa as he approached.

"I'm glad you are here, Luucar, for I believe I may have uncovered further clues with regards Ruomaani-Skye."

Luucar did not appreciate Cappa addressing him by his first name, but he was in a hurry.

"Information?" he sneered. "Well spit it out I don't have…" Luucar didn't finish his sentence - instead, he was interrupted by a sudden commotion to his rear. He turned to see his bodyguard collapsing in a heap, felled at the hands of Laonardo and Bayer.

In his confused panic, Luucar was set to yell out, however Cappa's blow soon put halt to that.

The two were quickly abducted into the forge basement.

Once in the underground chamber, they transferred Seban to a tool room where he was tied to a joist, his forehead strapped to the upright before being gagged and blindfolded. Luucar was taken to the cutting room at the far end of the forge store.

Here he was dragged to the centre of the chamber, placed in a kneeling position with his ankles bound together. He was also blindfolded and gagged after having his hands tied behind his back. Both prisoners were still out cold.

Cappa turned to his accomplices, "You know what to do."

*

Cold water smashed Luucar from his sanctuary. As he woke, Luucar tried to groan but was met by the stiff resistance of the gag. He tried to adjust his tongue, but it was strapped firmly to the base of his mouth. He breathed heavily through his nose and tried to recollect what had happened, when suddenly, he remembered the Mecdia Captain, *'Cappa!'*

As if his thoughts were transparent, the voice entering his senses confirmed the memory, "How's the head?"

He snorted angrily through the gag.

'What treachery was this?' He lifted his blinded vision toward the direction of Cappa's voice.

"Luucar, soon I'm going to ask a few questions." The voice moved to his side now, "As you can probably guess these queries will relate to Ruomaani-Skye."

Luucar snorted again as an element of panic joined his anger. He heard soft footsteps before the voice returned, this time to his rear. *'He's circling me.'*

"Now, you and I both know all is not as it seems here. Only, you don't know the half of it." A long pause followed, "I also know you are in league with Bunsaar, that the two of you are responsible for Ruomaani-Skye and Menka's disappearance."

Luucar tried to slow his breathing. He had to stay calm, play it out until help arrived.

"Now, in a moment I'm going to remove your blindfold. But I want you to think on something first." Cappa leaned in close, suddenly breathing in Luucar's ear as he said darkly, "Firstly, how severe a punishment would you receive if you were to betray Bunsaar? What would he do to you and your people?"

Luucar was startled by his situation - the accusation - the blindfold and gag - the damp darkness amplifying his fear.

Cappa's very being seemed to surround him as he whispered closer still, "What danger does this dustbowl Sultan of yours represent?" Cappa allowed him to snort and wriggle some more before adding, "Think on it a moment."

There was a cold edge to the Mecdia Captain's voice that was distinctly unnerving. Again, Luucar sensed calculated movement. In this temporary blindness, he was startled by just what his senses could define. His interrogator's voice was supremely calm. A dark confidence that was terrifying. It did not belong to a man scared of being discovered. Luucar wanted to swallow his trepidation, but the gag did not allow it.

"Now, I'm going to lift your blindfold and I want you to look straight ahead of you." Cappa's voice was directly at Luucar's ear once more as a powerful hand suddenly pulled at his hair, quickly followed by an arm cradling Luucar's head like a vice.

He snorted and struggled as slowly the thick blindfold was pulled clear. Luucar's eyes were sore and bleary and at first he couldn't make them obey his command.

Instead of focussing, they turned to grease. He blinked and battered his eyelids. He knew he was in a dark room but the vice-like grip did not allow him to explore it significantly. The smell taken in by his flared nostrils suggested he was still beneath the blacksmith's store. As his focus returned, his gaze was being aimed toward a silver object directly in front of him. It was large and well-polished, its features flickering with the dance of several large candles that burned all around him like a vast magic circle. The nearby lights made the blackness of the room beyond almost impossible to see which only added to the eerie spectacle.

He stared at the object, took in its detail.

It was a shield, finely crafted, sizeable and round.

"Look at the symbol. I presume even a dustbowl noble will recognise the graphic?"

The voice had moved again clarifying Luucar's suspicion that it was another man holding him. Luucar was confused.

Of course, he recognised the symbol. The entire educated world would recognise the symbol. It was the Pathan Eagle, the plumage worn by the powerful military elite of the Zarapathineon across the sea.

He choked on the gag, tried to make sense of what was now happening.

"Do you recognise the symbol?" The voice was harder this time.

Luucar thought on the fact Cappa and Laonardo were both Thiazarran traders. He started to sweat profusely as he nodded against the arm holding him.

"Good. And are you aware of the power which accompanies such a symbol?"

Again, Luucar nodded, his thoughts racing, '*What angle was this trickster playing? Had he come across such an artefact before journeying here from Thiazarra?*'

"The most powerful, formidable soldiering elite known to the civilised world. Faithful, devout, obedient to their kingdom and he who rules it, the Zarapathineon." Cappa paused, "You have heard this term?"

Once again, he nodded anxiously, the powerful forearm allowing just enough movement.

Cappa's tone softened, only serving to make Luucar more nervous. "Do you see the open talons there? The way they swoop down, strong and capable? They represent the power of the Pathan ideal."

Another pause allowed Luucar to guzzle in a breath.

His hair was damp and sweaty in his warder's grip.

Cappa's voice became more condescending, "Do you know what graces the talons of our Zarapathineon's armour?" His use of the term *our,* was very deliberate.

Luucar shook his head, clearly growing more agitated with each passing question.

"They decorate the armour with an effigy of the sun gripped within one talon, and the moon in the other."

Cappa elaborated, "The sun is to signify the new day - to welcome and embrace the freedoms granted by the ruler and his Pathan Order. As for the moon, well, this is to signify the successful climax of each day. To symbolise how another chapter of our liberty has remained safe under the protection of the Zarapathineon."

Luucar snorted on the gag once more, *'Where are the guards, why does nobody come?'*

Cappa's voice came close to his rear again. "Do you know what decorates the armour of the King's first in line, the Prince to his realm?" he went on, "A smaller effigy of the same sun - to symbolise the new dawn - the future of our great race safeguarded by the Zarapathineon heir, the next great King yet to come."

Luucar sensed movement - his eyes sought Cappa out, but the brief shadow of his being disappeared into the veil of darkness, beyond the candlelight.

"Do you know the name of the Prince who is currently first in line to Zarrapathia?"

Luucar was startled. The voice was now circling the outer shadows of the room, the deliberate drama almost too much for him to bear as he struggled to breath.

"His name is Capatheous." The voice came to a stop directly in front of him. Luucar squinted, desperate to see, not certain if his eyes had made out the shape of his tormentor just out of his vision's reach in the shadows.

"Do you know what the name Capatheous is often shortened to in Zarrapathia?"

Luucar snorted and his eyes opened wide as he made the somewhat obvious guess.

"Cappa!" The Prince declared as he stepped out into the candlelight in front of Laonardo's shield.

Luucar's shock was taking over. His panic growing as he looked upon the lowly soldier with fresh eyes.

Cappa's stare blazed with fury, his teeth snarled like a wolf beneath the fearsome cover of the helmet. He appeared bigger than as a hired mercenary, the midnight blue of his cape shrouding him in menace, the fine silks celebrated by the awesome engraving on his chest armour - and there, just as Luucar feared - was the effigy of a sun gripped within one talon. He almost choked as Cappa towered above him, unable to remove himself from the warder's grip.

"So, tell me, Luucar. How much do you fear your dustbowl master now, with his ragtag rabble of armed men? With his insignificant purse thrown at you as price for your betrayal?" Cappa took a knee and leaned in close, the steel of his helmet butting Luucar. His eyes were demonic, "How does it compare to the nightmare before you now? To the man who has sent word to have ten thousand Pathan mobilised to my cause? Warriors set to land on this continent within days, men loyal to their Prince, men who will stop at nothing to rescue their future Queen."

Luucar's fearful expression transformed into surprise.

"That's right. Out in the desert I had her agree to marry me. I told her who and what I am, that I could bring an army here that would make Bunsaar quake. Offer compensation that would see your Sultan clans weep. I've sent for a force so powerful I could see your water wells and clay palaces buried beneath the baked dust over which you squabble." Cappa was terrifying as he breathed on his captive. "For make no mistake, if any harm befalls that girl, I will burn your world to the ground, beginning with all those closest to you." He stood up and spun away, the cloak whipping Luucar's face.

Cappa turned slowly, his voice suddenly more reasonable, "Or, I could pardon your ills against me, see you and your kin rewarded, granted wealth beyond their wildest dreams." Cappa signalled Laonardo to pull away the gag.

Luucar swallowed several times before looking at Cappa with a bitter heart, "How have I acted against you?" he croaked, "You have no right here. Who are you to ask for her hand in marriage when she has given oath to another? Who is she to break such a vow, to spit on our customs and traditions?"

Cappa's venom exploded, "Who are you to sell her into the life of a whore? For that will be her punishment will it not? The most beautiful noblewoman your dustbowl can produce, sold into a life of slavery and shame?"

Luucar was mindful. He'd considered this to be an elaborate hoax, but as he stared on Cappa, he somehow understood he was who he claimed to be, the devastating danger he posed. He thought of Sooramena, of the life he'd hoped they'd lead, when suddenly Cappa drew his sword and pointed it straight at him, his very being emanating menace and purpose, his warning repeated as if hearing Luucar's thoughts.

"Now, you will answer my questions truthfully. Or I will make good on my promise and destroy everything you've ever known!"

CHAPTER 25

Luucar would not risk the destruction of all he held dear.

He had no way out.

Only his cooperation could see him saved.

He'd asked Capatheous for his word no harm would come to him or those he loved. Cappa had agreed, warning Luucar to be transparent, explaining how if any harm should befall any of them during their quest to save Ruomaani-Skye, that nothing could stop the inbound Pathan troops from scorching all of Ferenta.

Once he began, Luucar found he couldn't stop, his words blurted out as much for his own redemption as for the benefit of the Zarrapathan elite.

The sheer depth of the deception proved a surprise.

Much of Cappa's assumption had been educated guesswork, a bluff. Cappa knew Luucar was guilty the moment he claimed Ruomaani and Menka had eloped. He'd seen her pain in the desert, felt her longing, witnessed how she turned away from the escape Cappa offered her, determined to face her duty to save her clan. To suggest she would betray her people and leave them bankrupt was absurd. Cappa had begged her to be with him, offering to pay a huge sum in compensation, all to no avail. It exposed the lie.

For Luucar to move against Kirkoban and Dreda was one thing, but in kidnapping Ruomaani-Skye he would suffer the wrath of Bunsaar. This made no sense at all unless it was Bunsaar pulling the strings all along.

In his meeting with Dreda, Cappa had revealed his true identity promising the Sultan evidence and perhaps more importantly, wealth, trade and protection, whatever the outcome. It was enough to see Cappa given his opportunity.

Dreda held no affection for Bunsaar, believing the tyrant too powerful for his own good. The implication Bunsaar may hold the likes of Luucar in his pocket while prepared to destroy another clan from within, only served to strengthen such fears.

Dreda had also believed Cappa when he'd spoken of the already mobilised Pathan troops.

"Bunsaar wants the wells at Fraeda and Ninkal," Luucar explained. "They will expand his territory onto Kirkoban's doorstep and make him the predominant water supplier to all. However, he knew Kirkoban would never sell, that the tribal clans, with their codes of conduct, would back such a decision. Bunsaar is powerful, but not yet powerful enough to take on the might of our clans combined." Luucar elaborated, "In addition, Bunsaar is also set to buy a huge area of outland to the north where he's discovered a source to many more underground springs. He intends to build a vast fort there and take control of the entire northern region."

"So where does Ruomaani-Skye come into all of this?"

"I'd have thought that obvious. For the same reason you are probing me now. He wants her - he is intoxicated by her. But the dowry for such a beauty is huge. With such a massive purse granted to Kirkoban for his daughter's hand, Bunsaar knew he would be even further from any chance to secure Fraeda and Ninkal, as the old fool would have his wealth restored. By faking the elopement, Bunsaar is within his rights to take back the dowry and demand compensation. Ruomaani-Skye would be enslaved to him for breaking her sacred vow."

Luucar continued, "As you saw in one of the burned letters, Menka gives instruction as to how Ruomaani-Skye can meet up with him. This falsified information is how we were to catch the two of them at dawn tomorrow. Menka would not be in the camp as we raided it - an investigation would deduce he was foraging nearby and that upon realising my men had captured Ruomaani-Skye, Menka fled, making his escape into the outlands."

"Let me guess, with the dowry conveniently strapped to his horse?" Laonardo stated.

"A sedative will ensure Ruomaani-Skye remains asleep, her hands untied so to those finding her, she would appear to be there of her own free will. Nobody will believe her claims of abduction, any plea of innocence seen as the desperate lies of a girl caught in a disgraceful act."

"So Menka was not in on any of this?"

"Menka and the girl were abducted last night. Drugged and taken separately, neither knew of the other's fate. I ensured enough of the right people were on duty so their kidnappers could escape Malbood without detection."

"What was to be your reward in all of this?" Cappa asked.

"When Bunsaar arrives in Malbood he'll see Kirkoban arrested pending investigation. Further evidence will be uncovered implicating Zuda knew of his sister's plan. This final act will ensure Kirkoban's direct bloodline will be tainted beyond redemption. Unable to cope with the shame, Kirkoban would then hang himself."

Both Cappa and Laonardo looked to one another, taken aback by the coldness of the statement.

"With Kirkoban, Zuda and Menka out of the frame, Malbood and her territories fall to me. I'll be forced to pay back the dowry only I no longer have it, as it's been stolen by the fleeing Menka. Therefore, I'd be forced to agree to Bunsaar's demands."

"Handing over control of Fraeda and Ninkal?"

"For my swift action resulting in the capture of Ruomaani-Skye, as well as the deal for the two wells, I will be rewarded twenty thousand pieces of silver, almost half the dowry, which of course was never stolen in the first place. For my loyalty, I will also receive a small percentage of all Bunsaar's future profits. Bunsaar will take the shamed Ruomaani-Skye to Numbala as his concubine - punishment for her disgracing the solemn vow made to him, as is his right. This way he gets the girl, keeps more than half the dowry to pay off the territories to the north, and realises his ambition in gaining control of Fraeda and Ninkal. I'd have double the amount needed to secure my own marriage to Sooramena, a girl I've loved all my life, but have been unable to marry because Kirkoban squandered our fortune. With the money left over, combined with future income from Bunsaar, I could begin building a better future. Make this clan respectable again."

"And the bandit attack?"

"One of several staged to show just how weak Kirkoban is." Unaware of Cappa's limited knowledge, Luucar once again divulged more than his captives had bargained for, "I was with Kirkoban during the first leg of the journey which saw Ruomaani-Skye delivered to make her vows in Numbala. Bunsaar and I arranged for an attack to take place not far out of Fraeda. I was to be injured during my attempts to protect my Sultan. Once the attack was repelled, I encouraged Kirkoban to deceive Bunsaar, concocting instead the story of a desert storm. This way Kirkoban could even exaggerate the numbers lost, allowing him to manipulate Bunsaar into providing half the purse for a larger Mecdia army taken from a superior talent pool in Numbala. It was not difficult to convince him this was the best route to take."

Luucar went on, "During the inquest that would later follow, the truth of Kirkoban's deception would be uncovered. Any finger pointed my way would be deemed the actions of those desperate to shift blame from Kirkoban. More lies and treachery sealed within the shameful knowledge of how bandits were responsible for Kirkoban's losses all along.

Thieves bold enough to raid a Sultan's caravan on his own territory. A Sultan prepared to deceive his own brethren and abuse the scared rules of the Sultan brotherhood. The scandal would make the transition of our plan even easier." Luucar stated, "The clans do not want a more powerful Bunsaar, but they'd rather this than witness bandits bold enough to attack them on their doorsteps, to see one of their own spit on their sacred traditions. After such an inept fool in charge, I'd be received with open arms."

"And the attack when we were sent to escort Binka?"

"I acted on impulse, using the same secret army Bunsaar placed under my charge. Removing you seemed the logical thing to do. When you presented her that claw, I realised she'd gained a champion. Sending you away would never work. I acted because I understood what you were really saying when you handed her the souvenir from the mataba attack."

"Enlighten me," Cappa urged coldly.

"That you would die protecting her."

Cappa's icy stare remained fixed.

"Naturally your return was a shock. The three tribals I sent with you were as inept a group as any at my disposal. I could never have imagined you would fend off the attack. But when you blurted out the news of this ambush, Kirkoban was weakened further right before Binka. Since it appeared you suspected nothing, I actually thought this had turned out quite well all things considered." Luucar felt shame at how readily he had crumbled, embarrassed by his weakness, by his easily prompted tongue.

With the conspiracy in its entirety exposed, Cappa insisted, "I need details of everything that awaits Ruomaani-Skye."

"I was to lead the force sent to intercept her rendezvous with Menka." Luucar divulged, "On finding her, half my men were to chase the phoney trail of her escaping lover and dowry, while I returned Ruomaani-Skye to Malbood. Unfortunately, I was to be intercepted en route by Vhlarm and his men."

"Vhlarm?"

"Bunsaar is to catch everyone off guard by arriving early tomorrow. This very night he'll make camp at the midway stage through the Salt Canyons. In our original plan, he was to be met by one of his spies who would inform him of Ruomaani-Skye's elopement. Angry, he was to send his Captain with orders to drag her back to Numbala, away from any hope of protection."

Luucar swallowed, "Naturally, when you were called upon to retrieve her instead of me, I had to act. I couldn't predict what you'd do. So, I sent word to both the kidnappers and Bunsaar, warning them it will be you - not I - sent to the rendezvous."

Cappa glared, "When were these warnings sent?"

"While you spoke privately with Dreda."

Cappa realised the head start such informants would have gained. He was angry this could not have been his first line of enquiry. "So, where is she? How do I find her?"

"Once my message is delivered, the kidnappers will now move Ruomaani-Skye to a more direct rendezvous with Vhlarm - north into the Vespa Corridor, through the Clamenta Cliffs to the basin on the other side. It's here she'll be handed over to Vhlarm."

Cappa turned and spoke to an area of darkness which Luucar had presumed unoccupied, "Is that enough for you?"

Luucar was startled as a person he knew only too well stepped out of the shadows. It was Dreda, the man he'd hoped all his life would become his father-in-law.

Luucar closed his eyes, realising now why the plot itself had superseded Cappa's own desire for details of any impending danger to Ruomaani-Skye.

"I can grant you a small number of my own tribal guard but leave Kirkoban's castle garrison behind. We don't know who you can trust, and we'll need numbers if we're to arrest Bunsaar on his arrival." Dreda looked on Luucar with disgust.

"As for you, you've brought shame on our tradition. Shame on the very people you claim to love." He drew his curved sword.

"I thought…" Luucar was desperate. "I thought I was to be absolved if I told all!"

Dreda stared coldly, "They made such a promise, not I. You of all people know the punishment for your actions, and it will be carried out swiftly before Bunsaar can have opportunity to save you."

*

Dreda set plans into motion quickly. He sent messengers to inform the Sultans he trusted, rulers making passage to the agmanta, to be prepared to hold Bunsaar under arrest in Malbood. Those he couldn't trust would be delayed with warnings of a pitfly outbreak, a virus nasty enough to see them sent to the nearest of Kirkoban's wells until the disease was cleansed from the township. The incompetent Kirkoban would be kept in the dark for the sake of realism. When he greeted Bunsaar on his arrival it was essential Kirkoban's fear be genuine, so the conniving Bunsaar could be lured more easily into the trap.

Bunsaar had many men but would travel with an honour guard of only forty to Malbood - as was tradition.

How many would head with Vhlarm to rendezvous with the kidnappers was anyone's guess.

Dreda also had forty men at his disposal, plus those he could trust under the command of Feldahd. He hoped surprise and assistance from the other visiting Sultans would prove enough to neutralise Bunsaar, whose closer reinforcements could arrive in advance of Dreda's own.

Cappa and Laonardo therefore requested the use of only eight men to go up against the twelve kidnappers, a near even match as long as they could intercept them before they rendezvoused with Vhlarm. Bayer believed this to be more than achievable as an update would not reach Bunsaar until the early hours, by which time the Pathan would be well on their way to Ruomaani-Skye.

As they awaited Dreda's men, Laonardo took the Sultan to one side allowing Cappa the privacy required to make last minute preparations with Bayer. "Remember Sultan," Laonardo spoke with purpose, "if we are successful, no one is to ever know the Prince of Zarrapathia was here. Legend will spin he sent envoys to your lands, to assess the worthiness of Ruomaani-Skye, this great beauty spoken of by two Thiazarran traders who gained employment as Mecdia to her father. After Bunsaar's disgrace, she will be brought in great ceremony to Kiniphul, to create an alliance between the Sultans and the vast wealth of Zarrapathia"

"You can trust me," Dreda reassured. "Rules exist between the Sultan clans about conduct, morality and hospitality because we are an honourable people. I appreciate you've seen little of that here, but I beg you to appreciate this is as abhorrent to me as it is to you. Do not judge us by the actions of these despicable few." He added, "I pray the gods be with you and that you bring my beloved hanouri back safely."

Cappa finalised his plans with Bayer. It was of the utmost importance Dreda and all who stood with him believed there was indeed a force of thousands already on their way in Pathan ships. As a result, their plotting was made in whispers.

"If all goes well, this is where we shall intercept the kidnappers." Cappa moved his finger across Laonardo's secret map. "Vhlarm will meet with them somewhere here."

Bayer took charge of the scroll, "When you have her, head for the Clamenta Cliffs along this curve. The corridors through the cliffs link into what's known as the Web, a maze of pathways and ravines that cut through the rock. They'll offer a more even playing field should a fight come your way. The majority of these corridors are narrow and winding, meaning fewer men can attack at once." Bayer pointed, "Trentach is to approach Malbood along this trail. I'll intercept him here, then lead him to you at this location." He pointed to a teardrop shaped plain. "It's known as the Spider's Sack, many of the Web's corridors open onto it. Once you've hit the plain, head toward the rendezvous point via the Gorda Passage. If all goes well, we could be with you by late afternoon tomorrow."

Cappa and Laonardo did not like losing Bayer, but they knew Trentach would listen to nobody else with new instructions in the absence of Cappa and his Patruan.

"We'll be there." Cappa squeezed his wrist, "Thank you, Banteez Bayer, for everything."

CHAPTER 26

Ruomaani-Skye felt trapped between the spirit world and reality. She tried desperately to focus as her mind began to wake but her body would not obey. Her eyes rolled, picking out random shapes on the rare occasion her eyelids managed to open. She tried to concentrate, tried to ascertain what was happening. Was she dreaming? She sensed she was in another place, removed from the comfort of her bedchamber.

It felt like a fat carmol sat on top of her pinning her down, her head as heavy as a barrel of wine, her neck too limp to move it. She felt nauseous as she made attempts to see her body obey and was sucked back into the realm of spirits for another long moment.

She fought the pull of the dream, forcing herself back into the world of the living. *'Focus,'* she willed, *'Focus!'*

She repeated the mantra time and again until finally her senses gave back sporadic control.

She remained limp, but her hearing returned, her eyes flickering, desperate to offer assistance.

She could hear breathing, shallow and erratic. It was a man of that she was certain. *'Concentrate.'* For a moment she thought she could move her head, but it was a false promise.

She demanded her ears hone in on the noises around her.

Again, the heavy breathing returned, accompanied by occasional whispers, lecherous whispers which unnerved her.

Her eyelids flickered, only this time her brain managed to record some of the information around her, '*A tent, a small brazier holding hot coals, the unnatural breathing.*'

How could this be real? It made no sense.

Then it came, the sensation of being caressed.

She fluttered in and out of consciousness still unable to move. Again, she willed her body to obey.

She felt a coarse sensation rub over her breast, fondle down toward the base of her stomach.

The breathing, the lecherous whispers.

It was a hand, a man's hand moving over her body.

She felt sick, utterly helpless, as still she could not move.

Her limbs felt like stone, her head like an immovable mountain. Her eyes began opening for longer periods until eventually her irrational suspicion was confirmed.

She saw a bald head resting below her chin, felt the stubble of a large jaw pass over her exposed flesh, the lecherous whispering now needling the senses.

The large heavy hand took another firm squeeze on her breast before journeying to the inside of her thigh.

'*What before the gods is happening?*'

She tried to silence her panic, desperate to ascertain her predicament. '*I'm in a tent, embers of a small fire are lighting it, there's a chill and a dull light at the chimney above the coals. Looks like the first throes of morning.*' The panic returned, '*I can't move, there is a man caressing me, I feel his touch, hear his repulsive pleasure.*' She swallowed the fear, concentrating her willpower to combat the paralysis.

'*Focus, move.*'

The man's face came close to hers for the first time, his disgusting whispers warning of his tongue's visit to her earlobe.

She cringed, and somehow, she knew he was aware of it.

He bolted upright, startled. His movement ceased. But then it came again and this time it felt worse than before as she realised, he was pleased she was partially aware of his presence.

"Do you like me touching you, Princess?"

The voice was like a demon, his touch like a snake.

"Don't worry, you'll be kept fresh for your Sultan."

The pressure of his hand wondering her body was more intense.

"I just wanted to take a peek, a quick look at the jewel causing all this trouble."

There was a filthy edge to his voice, a fanciful state of mind behind his actions.

"I must say, I see why he's gone to such lengths to have you."

Her senses were sharpening. She could smell the alcohol on him. Her head rolled to the side as his powerful frame lifted her slightly, his tongue visiting her chest. A tear rolled down her cheek, but she would not give in to fear, not succumb to her bewilderment. She focussed on her right wrist. Tied around it was a silk rope but she noted it was otherwise free.

She tried to regain use of her fingers, *'Move!'*

She trained her eye toward him and felt repulsed at the realisation he was touching himself as he was touching her, his breathing erratic, his whispering sickening, *'Move!'*

She returned her attention to the limp hand laying open on the floor. She felt her chin twitch slightly, her right toes clench, her left breast shudder, *'Move...!'*

"Have you ever felt the touch of a man, Princess?"

She ignored the foulness of his words, the smell of stale wine, the rough touch of his palm as it played over her once more. She felt her lips move; her tongue shrink.

She made ready, her eyes darting back to the open palm.

Then it came, as if she was being released from the very gates of the underworld.

She wasn't sure what came first, the scream or the claw of her finely manicured hand.

All she was certain of was the result.

Her attacker stumbled back in the half-light and yelped. He clutched his cheekbone, the deep cut of her talons almost visiting his eye. His gaze was wide and startled.

Ruomaani felt certain he would pounce when sudden movement and enquiry erupted from somewhere outside.

"What was that?"

She didn't know the voice but was relieved to see the effect it had on the large man now standing above her. He scrambled out of the tent as Ruomaani managed to sit up onto the same elbow which powered her attack.

She heard movement, panic and demands. She heard men clutching for weapons. "What are you doing out here?"

"I caught her trying to escape!"

The tent sheet was thrown open revealing a pale sky with dimming stars. A smaller man entered, his face concerned, his eyes betraying his recent sleep. He looked on Ruomaani-Skye as she struggled to get up.

Her big attacker entered once more just as the smaller man leaned over to quickly cover her exposed flesh.

"She was trying to escape!" The ape bellowed once again.

The smaller man snarled, "Was that before or after she removed half her clothes?"

Her attacker was immediately defensive, "They were torn in the struggle," he gestured to his recent wound. "She almost took my eye out!"

"Struggle? She can barely move!"

The bigger man moved close to his accuser, "I'm not sure I like your tone. You'd do well to remember I am not one of your lapdogs to be ordered about."

"You would do well to remember she is for nobody but Bunsaar!"

Their argument was set to escalate when another man arrived outside, "Be quiet… someone approaches."

The big man made a hasty exit as the smaller ensured Ruomaani-Skye's nightclothes were fastened. He looked upon her but said nothing. Her body was still weak, and she could offer little resistance as he re-tied her wrists with the silk rope.

In doing so, she realised through her confusion, this man was to offer no permanent rescue from the nightmare into which she had awoken.

*

Ruomaani was beyond desperate as she tried to stay conscious. Her faceless captors remained restless until they were informed the rider approaching was one of their own.

She tried to listen in on the conversation, make sense of the insane nightmare in which she'd found herself.

She heard the rider dismount close to her tent.

He began relaying instruction but was quickly hushed by the voice of the smaller man who had entered her tent, "Lower your tone… she's awake."

She wanted to give in to her panic, scream, yell or cry, but she needed to focus her bewildered senses, figure out how she'd gone from her bed to a tent in the desert.

More hushed conversation followed, urgent words, spoken with intensity.

Her head rolled back, *'What before the gods is happening?'*

The tent's entrance was thrown open and the smaller man approached. He looked determined, "We're going to move you. Do not test me with any foolishness."

She implored him, "Please, just tell me what is happening."

He looked at her scornfully, "You know damn well."

Even through her confusion she somehow sensed his lack of conviction, the lie behind his drama, "I promise you I do not. The last thing I remember is retiring to my bed. Now I'm out here in the desert, with you people…"

"Spare me your pathetic lies."

"Lies?"

"Your lover has fled, left you to face the consequences alone. Don't disgrace yourself with further deceit."

"Lover? Deceit? What are you talking about?"

"You know full well." He pulled her forcefully before tying a blindfold to her head.

"Please, I don't know what is happening. There's no need for any of this. Just tell me what I have done."

"Menka has gone, taken the dowry with him."

She squinted against the blindfold, "Menka? Why would Menka take the dowry? Why would Menka be with me out here in…?"

"I told you no more lies." He checked the security of her bonds and pulled her upright, "We know all about your elopement, of you and your cousin's scheme. Luckily, we caught you in time." He called for the men outside before adding; "We are to detain you, before handing you over to the Sultan Bunsaar."

"What are you talking about?" Her panic was growing, "Who are you people?"

"Who we are is of little concern. What I'm talking about is punishment for your sinful treachery. You're to become Bunsaar's whore, and before the gods you'll be punished for such disgrace."

CHAPTER 27

Dreda had entrusted his First Lieutenant, Zoobram, to lead the hunt. In the early desert light, he scrunched a handful of dust in his palm noting the dull warmth of the ash mixed with the dirt.

Cappa returned having ridden beyond the perimeter to look for further clues. "There are very deliberate tracks headed north," he declared. "One rider - no doubt supposed to be Menka."

Zoobram cast the dirt to the floor, "Ash from a fire basket... still warm." He pointed, "Recently filled holes, the pattern suggests a cone-tent stood here."

Laonardo approached with one of Zoobram's scouts, "Attempts were made to cover the trail of those now headed toward the Clamenta Basin. As with the camp, the job was clearly rushed."

Zoobram turned to the magnificently dressed Pathan warrior, "How many tracks?"

"I'd say ten to twelve men."

"It appears Luucar spoke the truth of their number and intended direction." Zoobram mounted his horse, quickly flanked by the midnight blue of the Pathan capes, their features menacing beneath the helmets, "We must hurry," he turned to his men, "To the Clamenta Cliffs."

*

With the new rendezvous point reached, Ruomaani-Skye's captors erected two tents to offer protection from the merciless mid-morning sun. The larger offered respite for the guards not patrolling the perimeter, the smaller cone-tent reserved for their prisoner. The group would have preferred the cover of the nearby cliffs but had been instructed to remain in the open.

The changes made to the well-rehearsed plan had seen tension grow within the group. A notion not helped by the additional warning Luucar had sent with his messenger, of how the two Thiazarrans tasked with finding Ruomaani-Skye, should not be underestimated.

The smaller man responsible for Ruomaani-Skye's gag and blindfold tried to ease the mood, "Luucar will ensure anyone hunting us will be sent on a wild goose chase. They could never find us before Vhlarm arrives."

The messenger reignited the drama; "Luucar seemed genuinely concerned these men were chosen to replace him in the hunt for Kirkoban's daughter." He added, "I heard rumour these same men were recently ambushed by ten times their number yet walked away unscathed," the messenger looked at the brute that had assaulted Ruomaani-Skye, "Those killed were mercenaries, in Bunsaar's employ."

A further rumble of discontent followed.

If need arose, they hoped this messenger was as able to fight as he was capable of gossip. That he'd prove a useful addition after losing one of their number who had continued into the desert as planned, playing the role of a fleeing Menka.

The brute responded with disdain, "Together, we have four men patrolling the perimeter, one guarding the prisoner and seven hiding in here from the sun. Like our leader said, Vhlarm will arrive long before anyone can pick up our trail." There was scorn to his tone when he aimed the word *leader* at the smaller man who'd berated him over events with Ruomaani-Skye. The thought of her seemed to prick the fresh scars worn across his eye. "So, let's not start shitting our tunics just yet."

Laughter followed the comment, but it was an uneasy brand.

"Speaking of which, taking a shit is my next intention, so if you'll excuse me a moment, I'm going to hide behind a rock and prey these devils don't attack me while my drawers are down." He stood and laughed, "I'd ask for protection, but I fear the sight of my big arse letting out a stink while burning in the sun may prove enough to see all of you flee."

In the ensuing debate that followed the brute's exit, nobody noticed his discreet change in direction as he looped around toward the smaller tent. The guard there was one of his own men and after glancing to see he'd reached the tent unseen, the brute entered, gesturing for the man at the door to remain silent. He closed the canvas and approached the blindfolded girl strapped to a stake in the centre of the cone.

Ruomaani-Skye was awake now, her senses sharp, she remembered the stale-wine smell clearly.

She pulled away from his approach with a start.

The blindfold was pulled down slowly, the brute delighted by the wide-eyed greeting, which followed her squinted adjustment to the light.

"Hello, my pretty," he whispered, pulling a dagger from his belt. He ran the blade across the scores left by her strike, "Remember me?" He smiled sickeningly; the dagger now aimed at her throat. "Now, don't make a sound, or I'll hurt you, understand?" He licked his lips as he pulled away the gag. "You and I have unfinished business."

Ruomaani breathed deeply, this lecherous pig would not cow her, "One scream and you'll be discovered."

"One scream and I'll cut your whore throat." He smiled as his eyes undressed her.

"If I'm to be a whore, then I'm to be Bunsaar's whore. I don't think he'll take too kindly at having his property manhandled before he has had chance to sample it."

Her confidence angered him. If he'd been a more intelligent man, he would have expected it. He was accustomed to his brutish frame and nature injecting fear into the women he tried to own. He grabbed her chin and squeezed it, his other hand pointing the knife into her gullet.

Despite his resolve Ruomaani saw the hesitation.

The drugs hadn't long since left her system, and it had proved difficult to think until being tied to this stake in the loosely strung shelter. When her mind had finally cleared, she'd dwelled endlessly over her predicament, tried to ascertain what was happening, brooding only interrupted by the ape now holding a knife to her throat.

Ruomaani stared at the brute defiantly, seeing him squeeze her chin tighter - she responded by spitting in the very eye she'd almost claimed.

The effect this had was as terrifying as it was satisfying.

The ape stood suddenly, cursing at the top of his lungs. Next, the acidic strike of his hand crossed the socket of her left eye. It was a heavy blow, interrupted by the guard suddenly entering the tent warning, "The others are coming over!"

He snarled, "It is Ferentae custom is it not, to see adulterous whores cleansed by the desert sun!" The brute stormed out and began chopping the tent's guy ropes in a rage.

The smaller leader was quickly on him yelling, "What are you doing? Get away from there."

This time the brute was in no mood, and he pushed the smaller man away yelling, "Step back or we'll kill you all." The ape's men quickly drew their weapons.

It was a near even match, but nobody made the first move, as Luucar's smaller man shouted, "And what the hell do you see happening after this? Vhlarm will kill you!"

"Vhlarm and I have been brothers-in-arms for ten years," he snarled as the final section of tent was cut away. He then tore down the canvas and dragged it over Ruomaani, leaving her exposed to the sun while still tied to the stake.

"I tried to stop this whore escaping and look what she did to my face. I demand satisfaction but since I cannot have it, I will simply adhere to custom." His rage was terrifying as he pointed the dagger her way, "This adulterous whore will be staked out in the sun, so the desert may scorch the sin from her flesh." He ripped the remaining canvas clear, leaving her squinting beneath the glare. "She will sit while the sun does its work, and both Vhlarm and Bunsaar will thank me for it."

The standoff remained poised for a long moment.

This time, however, the smaller man was not prepared to put himself on the line for his prisoner, not with this crazed ape ready to explode. So instead, he placated the brute, "Very well." He gestured for all weapons to be lowered. "If you wish to see the sun cleanse her then so it shall be. But *you* can explain to Vhlarm why his master's desert beauty has been sent to him with a black eye and burned skin!"

"The black eye was sustained during her attempt at escape, delivered after she tried to take out my own." He gestured to the scar, "Isn't that right boys?"

His men seconded the notion.

The smaller man tried to calm the situation. "If that is how you want it, fine, but on your head it will rest. I object to her mistreatment, but I will not resort to infighting. There are other dangers out there." He pointed to the cliffs before gesturing to the prisoner strapped upright to the post, "If you think your friendship with Vhlarm can help you resolve this, then so it shall be." He nodded to his men who then followed his retreat, cursing as he returned to the shade of the tent.

The brute smiled at his victory, his four men sheathing their swords. He looked on his prisoner, helpless within her bondage. "This is all an adulterous whore can expect in the outlands." He laughed before retreating with his men.

*

Kirkoban was at his wits end as Bunsaar arrived at the gates, his procession greeted with great pomp and ceremony.

Dreda stood with him on the citadel steps instructing Kirkoban to remain calm.

"Calm? How can I be expected to stay calm?"

"Greet him with open arms as I instructed," Dreda reminded, "Leave the rest to me."

Kirkoban was not at all reassured, "I appreciate your backing on this. Genuinely I do. But I really don't see a way out of this, for any of us."

With the gates opened, the caravan entered the citadel square. Dreda's heart rate quickened as he caught the first glimpse of Bunsaar and his approaching guard, "Just greet him at the steps. We'll then lead him to the inner yard." There was a gritty determination to Dreda's tone.

Dreda counted Bunsaar's guard as twenty, half the permitted number he could lead into a visiting Sultan's territory, the rest no doubt headed with Vhlarm to claim Ruomaani-Skye.

Dreda needed to discover the conniving Sultan's strategy. Would he play his hand directly, or try to catch Kirkoban off guard? According to Luucar's confession, Bunsaar would already know of Ruomaani's elopement thanks to the fictional report received via Bunsaar's equally fictional spy.

Dreda had made the necessary arrangements to contain the treacherous Sultan. If possible, he hoped he could lure their guest into the palace, away from the majority of his soldiers in the main courtyard. For this, he needed a distressed Kirkoban to welcome him into Malbood, precisely what Bunsaar would be expecting.

The procession came to a halt, Bunsaar quickly approaching, all smiles and happy greetings.

Dreda noted the confident theatre on show as the guest of honour approached. He glimpsed at Kirkoban who thankfully was unable to replicate such a performance.

"Sultan Bunsaar, we are honoured to receive you."

Bunsaar was pleased at the nervous edge to Kirkoban's welcome. Bunsaar reciprocated the greeting before offering the same to Dreda.

"It is good to see you, old friend." Dreda announced.

Bunsaar let nothing slip, though his cunning was working overtime as he mused, *'So, you've decided to fall on Kirkoban's sword also… All the better.'* Despite the news of Luucar not being sent to collect the shamed Ruomaani-Skye in person, it appeared everything else was going to plan.

"Where are Zuda, Menka and Luucar?" Bunsaar's tone was a little edgier.

"Come, I'll take you to them." Kirkoban responded, "Get you some water."

"Where are the rest of your honour guard? Where is Vhlarm?" Dreda asked. Bunsaar never went anywhere without Vhlarm.

"On their way. Something came up in Fraeda, they'll not be too long behind me."

"I hope all is well? We weren't expecting you until sunset." Kirkoban had rehearsed the line several times. "You honour us with your early arrival."

Bunsaar followed them up the steps, "It is not every day a man begins his agmanta. Considering the fine company waiting, I figured, why not make an early start to the festivities." It was a most worthy performance. "We camped in the western caves of the Salt Canyon last night."

The three entered Malbood's humble palace, with ten of Bunsaar's high tribals following as close quarter bodyguards, the unusually high number noted by both welcoming Sultans.

Kirkoban could not know the distress Dreda was now experiencing. The western caves were much closer than the expected camp midway through the canyons. This meant Luucar's messenger would have reached Bunsaar and Vhlarm some hours earlier than hoped and planned for. He wondered if Luucar had deceived them but quickly removed it from his mind. Bunsaar had probably altered this detail in the belief he was outplaying everyone, even his co-conspirators.

They entered the cooling shade of the palace and moved on toward the inner courtyard garden, Dreda glancing at the honour guards - wondering when Bunsaar would make his move.

"How is your daughter?" Bunsaar enjoyed the shudder his words brought to Kirkoban's composure.

"She is… well," Kirkoban stammered despite his best effort.

Bunsaar stopped and eyed him closely, "Great Sultan, is everything alright?" The query stank of accusation rather than concern.

"Of course…" Kirkoban was beginning to perspire.

"It's just, you seem like you want to tell me something."

Kirkoban nearly imploded.

"I am indeed a lucky man to be granted the hand of a beauty such as your Ruomaani-Skye." Bunsaar bowed.

Kirkoban tried to smile, but much to the delight of Bunsaar he appeared more like a hare cornered by a hound.

As they were led into the inner yard, Bunsaar could almost hear the hands of his guards as they slipped toward their weapons. However, while lost within the enjoyment of his game, Bunsaar could never have imagined what was to come.

Before his men made their move, a sudden commotion was unleashed - Bunsaar's guard quickly surrounded by men at arms, on all sides. At more than double their number, Dreda's men had come from nowhere, their weapons drawn, demanding Bunsaar's surrender. At that very moment, the citadel doors were sealed.

"What before the gods?" Bunsaar's ten guards were neutralised before they could draw a sword. In a panic he turned to his rear and yelled toward the now closed doors. "Save your breath, Bunsaar. Your men outside will be suffering the same fate. Perhaps you should have brought more guards, sent fewer of them with Vhlarm," Dreda declared.

Bunsaar was instantly alarmed. "What treachery is this?"

"Treachery? You dare speak of treachery?" Dreda's men confiscated their frozen opponent's weapons without a single action against them as Kirkoban looked on dumbfounded. "Perhaps we should discuss your plans made with Luucar." Dreda acknowledged the wide-eyed response, "That's right. We know all about it, as do the other Sultans." He glared at the tyrant, "Unfortunately, Luucar is no longer on hand to assist you."

Bunsaar snarled, "I will see you roasted on a spit for this!" He then turned to the bewildered Kirkoban and growled, "Do not think I'm unaware of your daughter's elopement."

Dreda almost spat at him, "You have kidnapped and shamed Ruomaani-Skye and murdered Menka to see your ends met. So spare us your threats and accusation. We possess all the evidence and have implemented the necessary countermeasures to ensure you fail!"

Kirkoban looked to Dreda horrified, his shock at the words freezing his senses.

Bunsaar's subsequent snarl almost saw Kirkoban melt, "You dare to cross me?"

"Oh, he dares," Dreda answered for him. "And once all the evidence has been presented, you may find it is you who is to be roasted on a spit!"

CHAPTER 28

Cappa, Laonardo and Zoobram watched the distant camp from their rocky knoll. They registered four guards on the outer perimeter and were able to estimate the size of the large tent that could certainly house several more.

Their journey to the basin had not gone without hazard.

One of Zoobram's men was thrown from his horse after a snake attacked the animal. He'd broken his hip in the fall. Unable to ride alone, Zoobram instructed another of his men to take the guard back to Malbood. Nobody would see the injured man risk death alone in the open, however desperate they were for numbers.

Both Pathans suspected the abductors would offer little resistance to their brand of warfare, as long as they could reach Ruomaani-Skye before Vhlarm and his men arrived.

They hoped they would still be well ahead of any such threat, though appreciated nothing should be taken for granted.

Cappa focused on the distant plain, "What's that close to the main tent?" He didn't wait for a response, the horrible realisation striking him, "My gods, it's Ruomaani," he felt the venom rise, "Why would they stake her out in the open like that?"

Zoobram looked solemn, "When a woman is said to be adulterous, she is staked out in the sun, so it may burn the sins from her flesh." He sensed the Pathan's anger, "As disgusting as it is, it may work to our advantage. At least while she's in the open we can see her, spot any threats which may come her way during our rescue."

Laonardo agreed, "Focus Cappa. Soon she'll be with us."

Cappa swallowed his rage for the fight to come. "I can only see the four perimeter guards and the man watching Ruomaani. The rest must be in the tent."

Zoobram acknowledged this before his gaze was drawn to something in the distance. "Wait!" There was urgency to his tone. He pointed, "Do you see the dust trail?"

The Pathans honed in on the danger, realising their worst nightmare may have been realised. They cursed as they watched the dust cloud approach, the dirt turning into the figures of riders heading toward the small encampment.

The guard at the camp's eastern perimeter signalled a warning to the others who came bundling out of the tent pulling weapons.

Zoobram counted their number, "Eight out of the tent."

They watched as the perimeter guard retreated back to the camp, the other border sentries following suit to bolster those minding the prisoner. However, as the approaching horseman drew closer, those guarding Ruomaani-Skye lowered their arms, realising there was no danger - recognising the new arrivals as more of their own.

Zoobram observed, "Seven of them. Very lightly armed, no water-ponies or carmols."

"No sign of Vhlarm." Laonardo asked, "Advance riders?"

Zoobram nodded, "No doubt sent to bolster the camp numbers until the rest arrive."

Cappa took in the detail, how the perimeter guards had responded to the threat, a plan quickly formulating. "That could mean Vhlarm and his wolves will be closer than we hoped. We must act swiftly. We may not have much time."

*

The relentless sun scorched Ruomaani's flesh, her lips dry and blistering, her focus squinting in and out of vision. Her eye socket throbbed as the bruise began to show.

She swallowed stiffly, desperate to drink, the bonds pulling her upright into the stake.

As the heat sapped her strength, she was unaware of how the same argument had broken out amongst her captors - the newly arrived reinforcements questioning the judgement of having Bunsaar's trophy exposed in such a manner.

She was equally unaware as her cause was championed, that she was to be released from the stake and given some water.

Ruomaani was unable to grasp how this action was then delayed, interrupted by a sudden warning of danger - How men were being mobilised against an incoming force, seeing the majority of her captors move out to meet the threat.

Nor could she fully grasp how her brutal attacker, together with the smaller leader and two others remained near, as the perimeter guard beyond came closer to the encampment.

What Ruomaani *could* comprehend, was the dazzling object on the horizon, fading in and out through the distant heat ripples. Her eyes flickered, and her head ached as another attempt to swallow was for the most part unsuccessful. She was struggling and could make little sense of those around her. Her chin slumped to her collar, and she almost blacked out but something inside her demanded she take another look.

Her eyes opened.

She searched the ripples bouncing off the salt sand and was set to succumb when she caught sight of it again, the mirror-flash now much closer, approaching from the same location which delivered the recently arrived reinforcements.

She shivered despite the heat, the sun keen to strip her resolve. She fought it, her eyes rolling before capturing the image once more. This time a silhouette accompanied the dazzling mirage, and for reasons beyond her, the detail was enough to pull her focus back in line.

She denied the sun as the figure drew closer on the horizon, slowly taking form through the hazy heat.

It was a man on horseback, inviting her gaze, wanting her attention. He was still some way in the distance, but somehow, she understood he was here for her.

Ruomaani could have cried at such a fanciful notion.

She closed one eye to aid her focus.

The horse was now sideways on, the figure within the saddle held a magnificent shield gleaming in the hot sun. From his rear a cape rode the wind, a dark, alluring cape that seduced her with its movement. The vision was majestic as the horse began to prance.

This was a vision demanding to be looked upon, an angel whose soul desire was attention - and attention it soon received.

Ruomaani was pulled back to reality by a chorus of yells, suddenly aware once more of her surrounding captors.

Ahead, between their camp and the shimmering vision, the perimeter guard grew animated. His horse seemed to sense the danger, happy to assist in a slow backward retreat as the sparkling, caped rider made a zigzagged, prancing approach.

Weapons were drawn and orders yelled as Ruomaani somehow found strength enough to observe the unfolding events.

Her shining mirage suddenly advanced at the full, an action, which saw one of the camp guards pull back on his bow, sending an arrow into the air.

In the near distance the approaching rider came to a stop. The figure dismounted and sent his horse dashing away.

The arrow missed its mark and the caped figure now approached steadily on foot.

Another arrow was sent his way, then another and another.

The mirror of the man's shield was taking shape and as a fifth arrow was launched the gleaming defence was this time employed, the figure disappearing beneath it as the arrow struck.

Ruomaani could sense the hope in her captors - felt their disappointment as the figure stood, chopping away the arrow with the short lance now evident in his opposing hand.

What happened next, further invigorated Ruomaani's focus.

The figure changed his posture, moved low then sprung in a powerful forward motion. It was difficult to see precisely what had happened, but the answer was not long in coming.

As her captors squinted from the reflection of the aggressor's shield, a sound came upon them, it was a distinctive sound, which introduced the Pandral spear with devastating effect.

The projectile hit the still-retreating perimeter guard with such power it smashed him from his horse, sending him on a high-speed collision with the dirt. It caused panic, the archer replying with a desperate volley of arrows.

Most missed the mark, the only strike met once again with supreme calm, the warrior simply retreating beneath his shield to take the hit, before emerging unscathed.

The aggressor once again zigzagged toward them.

He was close now, clear and bright, his helmet, the armour, the blue menace of his cape.

More arrows flew as again the shield absorbed the rare hits.

The archer searched desperately for more arrows as his world was overcome with the yells of his panicking colleagues. As he fumbled, the aggressor accelerated, moving past the dying perimeter guard, pulling the spear from his writhing torso as he went. Within moments, the spear was travelling at speed toward the archer who blinked as his eyes caught the dazzling effect of the shield once more.

The others yelled, but it was too late.

The Pandral struck with almighty force, the archer's contribution ended as he was sent crashing to the floor.

The gleaming devil drew his sword and made a faster approach, his muscles powering him forward without fear, without mercy.

He was inside the camp now, the menacing helmet framing the glare of his eyes, the flash of his teeth as he moved in on his next opponent. The magnificent shield sang as it repelled an incoming blow aimed by his ensuing victim's sword.

Another of her captor's dying groans immediately followed, the predator having despatched of his foe with ease.

He then moved toward his next adversary, his poise and control terrifying.

Another blow rang out against the shield, this time followed with a second strike aimed to the predator's shin.

Both were repelled, the action ending as swiftly as the last, the blue cape snapping with the forward lunge that saw the next guard killed on the spot. The predator didn't even pause as his fluid turn directed him toward the small leader who'd tied Ruomaani's gag and blindfold.

The captor raised his shield, but he would not even be granted the dignity of a fight, as the blue-caped attacker stopped to stab his sword into the dirt.

The small leader looked on confused when suddenly a razor-sharp projectile sliced through his knee. The lead-captor stumbled back and yelled, his shield dropping slightly.

The exposed target was met swiftly by another dagger, the weapon slicing his throat leaving a blaze of blood that splashed into the dirt. The lead-captor gurgled and spluttered as the predator retrieved his upright sword before moving toward his final opponent.

Ruomaani suddenly felt her bonds released, her frame heaved up into the air with tremendous force. The grotesque ape had moved quickly to utilise her as his shield, yelling at the approaching marauder to *back away*.

The warrior slowed but did not obey.

Instead, he crouched low, approaching Ruomaani's warder like a mataba, his menace sublime - his approach so dangerously confident it immediately reminded her of the cat that attacked in the canyons.

His shield was raised covering most of his frame, the eagle carved on its mirror resplendent. The plumage of his helmet peered at her over the rim of his defence, the blue spikes cut short and pristine. The matching colour of the cape flowed as he circled the ape now squeezing her.

Onward he came, slow and smooth, hidden by the impressive glare of the armour.

Ruomaani panted against the brute strength of her captor and was quickly aware of his all too familiar dagger aimed at her neck. "Be still or I'll cut her throat."

The sharp reflection of the shield moved the predator in closer.

"I said hold, or I'll kill her right now!"

There was a shrill panic to his voice, not usually heard in one so grotesque and fearsome.

This time the predator ceased.

The shield tilted showing the bridge of one side of his helmet, exposing the eye shrouded within its frame, the cat-like prowess still flexing throughout his entire form.

Ruomaani thought again of the mataba, when suddenly she noted something inexplicable. She focussed on it as her abductor issued another demand for retreat.

She shivered from head to toe - convinced her eyes were deceiving her - that the sun had done its work.

The object was unmistakable, its presence indecipherable.

Her mouth opened as she took in its form.

A mataba claw like her own, worn on a leather lace around the neck, cast onto the rescuer's shoulder during his exertions.

In a surreal sense, her brain remembered the flying daggers that had slain the mataba and suddenly confirmed where she'd seen the design on the shield before.

In an instant she felt like bursting into tears as she recognised the eye behind the armour.

It was the same eye that had captured her soul in the salt canyons, intrigued her during the passage back from Numbala, the eye that had met her own with disastrous consequences when they'd first met in the Torantum arena.

However, on this occasion the eye gave no deviation, this time, the predator had eyes only for his prey.

The brute pulled her across his torso to protect himself, unable to accept the struggle was lost. "If you move once more, I'll kill her right before you. You may strike me down, but I swear I'll take her with me. Your choice."

The lack of response was disturbing, the predator's silent coil terrifying.

"You are good. But not so good to stop this blade before you can reach me." The ape pressed against her jugular squinting against the flash of the shield.

Cappa lowered his defence exposing a small part of his face beneath the fearsome attire. Ruomaani wanted to yell at him but was more than aware she should not.

Cappa's eyes remained fixed on the brute, "There's nowhere to go. Just put the girl down."

The ape snarled at him, "I will put this girl down when…"

His words would never be completed.

Instead, he was propelled forward in a demolished heap.

Laonardo's spear had been fired with unbelievable force, clean through the back of his head. Half the ape's skull was disintegrated, the momentum sending his dead form to the floor taking Ruomaani-Skye with it. She closed her eyes expecting the impact, but as the brute fell, she was pulled clear before the collision was felt.

"Ruomaani!" She heard the familiar voice.

"Ruomaani?" Her eyes snapped open, and she could have cried as she realised it was truly him. Her hands clasped his shoulders as she struggled with her emotion.

"Ruomaani!" Cappa demanded again.

As Laonardo approached, Zoobram and his two remaining guards arrived on horseback.

Zoobram dismounted and brought water to Ruomaani as she clung to Cappa, her hands shaking. She gulped down a drink.

Laonardo gathered his Pandral spear with a sickening pull, the dead brute now nothing more than a carcass.

The Patruan had taken most of the projectiles and made fast work of the rear offensive. Zoobram and his men fought valiantly as the Patruan moved from one victim to the next in devastating fashion. Three had fallen to the enemy's fourteen and as Laonardo made his stealthy approach, Cappa had merely held the hostage taker's attention while his Patruan trained his spear.

"Ruomaani - Can you ride with me?" Cappa stroked her head, his eyes imploring beneath the fierce gaze of the helmet.

She focussed, adrenaline powering her resolve, "I'll damn well ride out of here."

He was relieved as he lifted her gingerly to her feet.

Her hand caressed the side of the helmet; her fingers ran the length of his exposed lips. "I can't believe you're here."

The sun had clearly done its work, but she refused to succumb.

"I'm here," Cappa helped her onto his stallion's back, "Now let's get you to safety."

She took a firm hold before leaning close to the familiar ear, "Hello Coba."

Zoobram instructed her to drink more from the water flask then had his men gather their defeated opponent's horses.

Zoobram chose a fresh-looking mount and tethered it to his rear, instructing the others to do the same. He had them cut the saddles and bits from the remaining animals, slapping their hides and shooing them away. The group then set about watering their paired animals in the trough as Laonardo handed Cappa several of the retrieved projectiles.

Ruomaani enjoyed the surreal peace brought about by watching Coba drink and found it hard to comprehend the arm now holding her belonged to Cappa who had climbed aboard to her rear.

They prepared to make their exit when suddenly Zoobram yelled, "Riders!" He pointed to the approaching dust cloud,

"It's Vhlarm!" Zoobram turned his horse about.

They had no understanding of why Vhlarm had arrived early, but they knew they had to level the playing field by making the maze of ravines known as the Web.

They dug in and headed for the curve of the Clamenta Cliffs.

"Hold on!" Cappa was concerned Ruomaani may slip into unconsciousness.

She reassured him, the much-needed water and exhilaration of her rescue replenishing much of her strength.

*

They rode hard, leaving the camp quickly, the fleeing riders checking over their shoulders as they went.

"How many?" Laonardo yelled to Zoobram.

"My guess would be close to twenty!"

The Patruan drew alongside Cappa. "Stay at the front of the line. Your pace is our pace!"

"They're gaining on us!" one of Zoobram's guards yelled.

Ruomaani turned to Cappa. "You have to put me on my own horse."

He was sceptical, "Ruomaani you…"

"Coba cannot carry two of us at pace in this heat. If you demand it of him, we'll never make it." She gritted her teeth, "Cappa, I can ride!"

He shouted to his Patruan, "Bring your spare horse closer."

He did so, slowing the pace as he saw Ruomaani-Skye was set for a change of saddle.

"Closer!" She yelled.

Laonardo admired the grit of a girl who was half unconscious only moments ago. He slowed the pace further allowing her to make the leap.

Cappa prayed she was up to the task after being so viciously dehydrated, watching with bated breath as she leapt onto the horse trailing Laonardo's rear.

'Yes, Ruomaani!' Laonardo silently praised her courage.

'*Praise the gods*,' Cappa sighed relief.

Then as she kicked in her heels, the chase was on.

CHAPTER 29

Dirt plumes trailed the pursuit across the edge of the basin as each set of riders made haste for the cliffs.

The race proved an even one, Cappa's band maintaining their lead, reaching the ravines ahead of the chasing pack.

With the promise of the Clamenta Cliffs breached, a game of cat and mouse had begun within the maze of the Web.

Zoobram had steered the band deeper into the tight alleyways, and after several wily and winding manoeuvres, it appeared the fleeing group had, for the time being, managed to elude their pursuers.

Zoobram's main concern was Vhlarm utilising his greater number to swarm the passages in an attempt to pen them in. However, he also appreciated his own advantage. In the two Pathans he had warriors the likes of which he'd never seen. Both had disposed of their enemies in breathtaking fashion, and he shared their optimism the narrow ravines would serve to even the odds.

Once deeper within the alleyways, Ruomaani had taken the opporunity to drink more water and looked all the better for it.

The group kept up a steady pace, their senses sharp, speaking only in occasional whispers.

Laonardo followed Zoobram's lead with Cappa minding their rear, Ruomaani-Skye central within the protective layer of the two remaining guards.

As the narrow walkway now opened into a broader corridor, the Patruan took his opportunity to go over their location, pulling his horse alongside Zoobram who quickly updated their position with several gestures to the map.

Once satisfied, Laonardo had Zoobram retake the lead as he then dropped down the line to update Cappa on their situation.

As the Patruan passed Ruomaani in the centre, she caught his eye, her beauty beyond contestation despite the cruel behaviour of her captors.

She smiled, marvelling once more at the Pathan attire, at the prowess employed during her rescue. She had so many questions. "Laonardo."

"My lady," he tilted his head.

"I want to thank you for what you did."

"You don't have to thank me."

"Yes, I do, all of you. You saved me from despair, a sentence of cruelty and shame."

He admired her noble nature, was impressed by the formidable willpower shown when she'd pulled herself from the brink at the moment it was required, a trait worthy of any Pathan. "My lady, you've displayed magnificent fortitude today," he offered a piercing gaze, "I am, and shall always be, at your service."

His tilt returned, the comment affecting Ruomaani intensely. She wasn't certain what was happening, wasn't entirely sure what she was involved in. There had been no time for detailed talks. However, there was a gravitas to this man's words like none she'd heard before and her emotions almost got the better of her as a result. Ruomaani returned his gesture and bowed, watching as he continued down the line.

She pondered over the extracts she'd learned of the fabled Pathans from across the sea and observed as Laonardo approached Cappa, again noting the effigy of a sun beneath the eagle's talon, a symbol not present on Laonardo's crest.

Cappa smiled as he approached. "What was that about?"

"Turns out she wants me and not you," Laonardo shrugged, "Who could have known?"

Cappa laughed quietly despite their situation.

"She wanted to thank us for the rescue. I can only presume she did so to me personally after recognising my superior input. I informed her that such observance might upset you and implored her to keep it to herself."

Cappa's smile remained, "Thank you, Laonardo," there was weight to the comment, substance which only gratitude in the face of danger can bring, "For everything."

The Patruan echoed his earlier sentiment, "A day will never dawn when you've to thank me." He reached into his tunic, "Now, let me update you with this map."

*

As the day wound slowly on, the tension remained high.

Zoobram had adjusted their course on two cautious occasions, the group following their astute guide without question. For the most part they'd managed to stick to winding corridors barely wide enough for single file. However, they were fast approaching a section of the Web where many of the paths and ravines widened considerably.

There was still no sign of Vhlarm, but the group were only too aware their pursuers could be around any bend, ready to pounce at any crossroad. The pathways of the maze would aid their chances. However, until the rendezvous was reached, they also offered Vhlarm opportunity to see them trapped, and hidden away from their reinforcements.

The sun had long since passed midday, and as the chasm broadened, the shade began to dissipate, the narrow corridor trailing away as it opened into a wider gorge.

Cappa took the opportunity to edge up the line and check on Ruomaani's wellbeing.

She heard his approach and turned to him saying softly, "So, you are a Pathan?" She'd recovered considerably.

He smiled at her and nodded.

"Something you neglected to mention?"

"Would it have made any difference?"

She smiled and thought of her refusal in the canyons, of how she would have always put her duty first, "Probably not."

"How are you feeling?" he asked after a moment.

"Better," she replied before adding, "Bewildered."

He acknowledged her need to understand. "As soon as we're safe I'll tell you everything." He gestured to the silent cliffs, "For the moment it's best we stay focused on what's out there."

She agreed. "He'll find us, won't he? Even in a maze such as this."

"Probably. The key is to be ready, to ensure he can only attack in these narrow thoroughfares, even the odds."

She took in his resplendent attire, tried once more to familiarise herself to the transformatory effect it created. If she had any doubts of her growing love for him, they had vanished since her liberation from the camp. "These men we are hoping to rendezvous with, they'll meet us at all costs?"

He looked deeply into her eyes, his gaze all the more powerful beneath the cut of the helmet, "They'll be there."

The conversation halted as Laonardo held up an arm bringing the procession to a stop. Their senses were immediately heightened, their focus sharp.

A long eerie silence followed as Laonardo studied the cliffs on either side.

Swords were drawn; shields pulled closer; spears readied.

Ruomaani held her breath.

The horses grunted and pranced, sensing the change of their master's mood.

The moment passed.

Cappa whispered, "Forgive me, we'll talk soon." He gestured for her to follow him to where the path grew wide enough to cater for the whole group. He then had them gather around before prompting Zoobram and Laonardo to once again clarify the plan.

Laonardo handed the map to Zoobram who whispered, "Just ahead, this path opens into a wider gorge. The eastern corridors running from this gorge lead to the plain known as the Spider's Sack. Our chosen route will bring us out close to the base of this plain, only a short ride from the trail, which will deliver Trentach. But beware. This area is where the Web truly lives up to its name, with multiple corridors crossing one another in close proximity. The route we've chosen contains fewer of these intersections with less risk of running into dead ends. Nevertheless, there'll be ample places from which an ambush could be sprung."

Laonardo pointed at the map, "Ride in single file maintaining a steady pace toward this fourth exit. If we get separated, head for the rendezvous any way you can."

Ruomaani had never negotiated the corridors of the Web, but she knew of the tear shaped plain known as the Spider's Sack, "Into this Gorda Passage?" she asked.

"Yes," Zoobram replied, "Once inside head southwest until you reach the caves."

She took in the details of the map.

They steered back into single file and rode prudently into the widening pass, the hooves chattering with the loose stones despite their best efforts.

The two remaining guards now kept the rear, Cappa remaining close to Ruomaani, as Laonardo and Zoobram led them forward into the gorge at the heart of the Web.

Shadows flirted with sunlight as they crossed the first of the intersecting alleyways.

The horses grunted, the bridles and weaponry playing a gentle chorus with the hooves.

Another intersection was crossed, another potential ambush left behind.

The gorge widened, the band's pace remaining steady as they made a beeline for the fourth corridor.

The sunlight pressed the path ahead seeing the shade reduced to nothing as the fissure opened fully.

They were more cautious, more exposed.

Then, just as they approached their chosen route, the nightmare was realised.

The sound of urgent movement was on them as quickly as the horses that brought it, as suddenly they found themselves at the centre of an ambush.

The broad chasm quickly filled with Vhlarm's men. They rode in from all angles before the bull horned helmet of Vhlarm entered the fray from the far corridor directly ahead.

Zoobram yelled out as he drew his weapon.

Laonardo pulled a projectile from his belt despatching of the first ambusher bold enough to come near.

Zoobram threw himself into the cause, engaging a second with an almighty clash of steel.

At the rear, arrows struck their two guards.

"They have archers!" Cappa pulled Ruomaani's horse close, desperate to offer protection with his shield.

Ahead, Zoobram won his fight but was quickly engaged in another.

Laonardo saw a second victim fall and as Cappa protected Ruomaani from a second volley, his Patruan sensed his need, turning his horse about, galloping toward the flight of the arrows.

As Vhlarm advanced he marvelled at the bravery, observing as the formidable blue caped warrior made a charge toward his surprised bowmen.

Laonardo's shield protected the head of his horse his own skull pressed low exposing only the plume of the helmet.

One arrow whizzed past as another struck the defence.

With the now desperate archers trying to reload Laonardo drew his Pandral spear, hurtling it into the chest of one of the bowmen.

The second archer made ready but as he drew his string another projectile hit with breath-taking accuracy, the small weapon as deadly as the larger spear.

Laonardo turned his horse and moved back to the core of the fight, "Head for the exit!" He yelled to Cappa who pulled Ruomaani's horse, dragging her toward the path now blocked by two men on horseback.

"Take the shield!" Cappa passed her the defence before reaching into his belt.

His first projectile struck the target seeing the rider fall to the floor in agony, the second however, was deflected by the quick use of his enemy's own shield, the flying dagger clanging against the steel as the ambusher ducked behind it.

Cappa surged into a direct assault, his sword at the ready as he now powered into his opponent's horse. Coba grunted as Cappa steered his stallion into a body slam, hacking at the rider as he struggled to maintain his balance.

As the rider cowered for cover, Cappa saw his opportunity, almost removing his opponent's left leg with one swipe.

He wailed in agony as he fell from the saddle.

Cappa spun about and saw Vhlarm approaching Laonardo and Zoobram at the gallop. He was huge, his menacing frame adorned by the bullhead helmet. In an instant Cappa was off Coba's back, withdrawing his Pandral spear and taking a steady aim.

Ahead, Laonardo prepared to welcome Vhlarm and the remainder of his men as Zoobram struggled to fend off another attacker.

With Vhlarm's attention firmly on the man responsible for the death of his archers, Cappa unleashed his throw.

The Pandral soared toward its target and was set to end Vhlarm's advance until the formidable warrior proved his worth, sensing the incoming projectile just in time.

Vhlarm's shield was raised to deflect the killing blow but the impact of the Pandral sent him tumbling out of the saddle, hitting the ground in a painful heap.

Three of his men also fell as they reared, desperate to avoid trampling their master.

In the confusion, Laonardo launched more of his projectiles eliminating two more attackers as Zoobram finally finished off his troublesome foe.

With an opening now secure Laonardo screamed again at Cappa, "Get out of here. Head for the rendezvous!"

Cappa was reluctant, but on seeing Laonardo turn his horse toward them he did as instructed; leaping aboard Coba and leaving the arena.

He and Ruomaani charged into the shelter of the ravine, their horses leaping over the wreckage of Cappa's recent victims.

Laonardo twisted in his saddle his shield deployed to defend his rear as he dug in to make his own escape, Zoobram close behind him.

To their rear, Vhlarm was up on his feet, grabbing his horse furiously as he retook the saddle. He spun about and bolted for another of the exits, determined to intercept the escaping warriors. He yelled for half his men to follow his intercept course as the others gave chase to ensure the rescuers could not double back.

*

Cappa and Ruomaani ducked and weaved through the narrow corridor, their eyes wide as they flashed across each adjoining intersection. "Do you see anyone?"

"No!" Ruomaani replied as she monitored their path.

Laonardo and Zoobram were inside the narrow pass desperate to catch Ruomaani and Cappa, the ruckus of those giving chase to their rear bouncing through the high walls of the passage.

Cappa and Ruomaani bolted past an intersection, desperate to avoid an attack from the adjoining alleyways. They came to a fork and took a left before choosing the next right; Ruomaani stating confidently it was the correct path to take.

Laonardo reached the same fork with Zoobram. He caught glimpse of the tracks left by Cappa and Ruomaani, pleased they'd chosen the correct route.

Cappa and Ruomaani rode at speed along a narrow straight as they once again passed the adjoining alleyways safely. They rode hard before slowing into a turn that led into a steep zigzag. They negotiated it quickly, its final bend leading them onto the broad plain of the Spider's Sack.

The sunlight struck causing them to squint as they pulled their horses to a halt on the white open flats.

Cappa checked his rear. He could hear the approach of horses not far behind. "Laonardo is that you?" The sound was drawing close to their position.

Cappa turned Coba about, sword in hand, "Laonardo!"

The yell echoed into the zigzag as Laonardo and Zoobram entered it, "It's us… we are right behind you!"

On hearing how close Laonardo was Cappa kicked his heels, he and Ruomaani riding out across the southwest corner of the tear shaped plain.

Within moments Laonardo and Zoobram appeared from the fissure following in their white wake, quickly pursued by a chasing pack.

Ahead on their left flank Vhlarm could be seen entering the plain, bearing down in an attempt to head them off.

The white plume kicked up by the leading duo intensified making it difficult to see, but even with his vision hindered Laonardo could determine how Vhlarm was not close enough to cut them off, but he would certainly reach the passageway immediately after them.

The fissures leading to the Gorda Passage approached.

Cappa and Ruomaani entered the first fracture, the returning shade instantly welcome.

They followed the passage over loose rock and thorny shrubs, kicking on toward their destination.

Laonardo dropped to Zoobram's rear to offer protection with the shield as the pair entered, relieved to have the stinging salt abate as the alleyway encompassed them.

The pack chasing their tails entered the corridor, with Vhlarm and his men entering directly behind them.

Cappa and Ruomaani reached a trident junction in the road. The most northerly exit was the direct route to the Gorda Passage - the second a longer route to the same destination, the third a dead end. They took the direct route just as they heard Laonardo and Zoobram closing in behind them.

As the chasing duo reached the triple fork a single thought struck Laonardo, *'I need to buy Cappa some time.'* He visualised the map and remembered how the central thoroughfare of the trident took a more obscure route to the same destination. He wasn't certain if it was the correct action to take, his Patruan training instilling in him the notion of never leaving Cappa's side, but in the heat of the moment his decision was made. He slowed, turning his horse about.

Zoobram sensed the movement and checked behind seeing Laonardo come to a halt, "Laonardo?"

"I'm going to try and draw them down the longer passage."

Zoobram glimpsed over his shoulder, the promise of a faster escape tantalising. He rejected it, "I'll stay with you."

As Vhlarm's men came into view Zoobram set off. Laonardo held for an extra second then, "Yargh!" the Patruan allowing his cape to sail the air for the benefit of the chasing pack. Vhlarm's men powered around the slope taking the bait with gusto, steering their horses into the central thoroughfare desperate to catch the prey for their master.

As the majority turned into the central route ahead, Vhlarm pulled on his reins, several of his men following suit as the bull helmeted leader came to a stop.

Vhlarm had always been good in the hunt.

He gritted his teeth, "This way!"

The mighty warrior followed his gut, ignoring the pull of the pursuing pack, instead choosing the more northerly turn.

He realised he'd made the right decision as fresh horse tracks and snapped foliage gave away the trail of those fleeing, "Come on," he yelled, all the more delighted as he saw a shred of Ruomaani-Skye's silks strewn across a thorn branch.

Five of his remaining thirteen followed their master.

Cappa and Ruomaani had no idea Laonardo had chosen a different path. They concentrated solely on reaching the Gorda Passage, pinning their hopes on the promise of Trentach, of Banteez Bayer and the powerful force of Garpathans to come.

CHAPTER 30

Laonardo urged Zoobram to maintain his pace as they entered into a wider passage. "Keep going!" he yelled, as the sound of the chasing pack came closer. The Patruan halted his horse and withdrew his penultimate projectile.

He breathed, calmed his senses, made ready with his throw. His horse grunted, nervous at the decision, the hooves gingerly retreating despite Laonardo's instruction. The noise of the approaching pursuers should have been terrifying, but to Laonardo it presented an opportunity.

As the pack leader entered the straight he was stunned to see the blue caped warrior waiting calmly like death himself. He tried to yell out, tried to warn those behind of the danger but instead his head was split in two as the projectile smashed beneath his helmet into his skull. He was still dying as he hit the floor, his hand gripping the reins, pulling his mare down with him. What followed was a melee as the chasing pack crashed into the falling leader, the alleyway quickly blocked allowing Laonardo to take aim with his last projectile.

A killing throw stabbed into the throat of the man unfortunate enough to have found himself at the fore, his groans spreading abject panic amongst the ranks.

The Patruan had no idea Vhlarm was not caught at the rear of this pile up and he turned his horse about, pleased at the chaos he'd left behind.

Cappa and Ruomaani made quick work of the winding alleyway and soon struck the open run which would take them to the Gorda Passage. From there they would head southwest, ready to make the turn toward the caves.

Cappa checked over his shoulder, desperate to see Laonardo break onto the path behind. The sweat gathered around the brow of his helmet, the reins clammy within his fist.

He glanced to Ruomaani who naturally shared his concern.

Eventually he heard horses approaching the same exit. However, as he turned expecting to see his Patruan, he was mortified to see the bull horned helmet of Vhlarm.

They kicked on.

Cappa was desperate to understand what had happened to Laonardo but for the moment he had to ensure Ruomaani's wellbeing. Such thoughts were short lived however, when to his horror he heard her horse whinny before seeing Ruomaani sent sprawling to the floor as the mare upended.

Vhlarm was delighted. As his men had passed at the gallop, he'd taken a moment to take a masterful shot at Ruomaani's mount, binding the hind legs with his sling. It was an aim worthy of any warrior alive, and it caused his pulse to quicken as he saw the blue caped warrior leap from his horse to aid the stricken beauty. *'I have you now.'*

Cappa was with her in an instant. She yelled in agony clutching at her abdomen. She could barely breathe as Cappa heaved her up throwing her over Coba's back. He turned to face the advancing pack, pulling two daggers and hurling them into their path. The first struck the rider below his jaw, the second into the unsuspecting soldier's cheek sending both men crashing from their mounts. Once again the fall of the advance riders bought them precious moments as the pack behind had to heave on their reins.

As the chasing pack made the necessary adjustments to avoid their fallen comrades, Cappa was already in the saddle. He dug in, his pursuer's now right behind him.

Vhlarm was at the rear, happy for his men to take the fore. "Wear them down. Don't do anything rash, they only have one horse!"

Hunter and hunted understood the peril - one mount carrying two people could not hope to compete in a chase.

Ruomaani groaned against the excruciating pain building below her abdomen, sustained against a rock in the heavy fall.

"Hold on!" Cappa urged. Their situation was desperate.

He bolted Coba forward turning into the broad ravine that was the Gorda Passage. He rode for the tantalising caves but realised he had little chance of reaching them. He glanced over his shoulder to see the frontrunners of Vhlarm's men closing in. "Come on Coba!" His magnificent animal had put up an almighty fight, but this was too much to expect of him.

Cappa cursed.

"Hold on Ruomaani!" He took a steep turn into an adjacent fissure away from the Passage. He had to get off the broad thoroughfare to give Coba a chance.

Ruomaani yelped as they cut through several winding paths, the pain almost too much to bear, but she would not let go of the saddle.

Laonardo followed Zoobram through the winding alleyway happy at the distance he'd placed between them and their pursuers. He hoped Cappa and Ruomaani would be on the Gorda Passage and prayed Trentach would be close by.

After negotiating several more turns both men were delighted to finally reach the widening approach before hitting the broad ravine. The Gorda Passage was long and sun-drenched and both men studied the horizon for riders.

As Laonardo and Zoobram rode for the caves what they saw was nothing less than a revelation. For there, in the distance at the far end of the gorge, was a dust cloud - a cloud fronted with the midnight blue of the Pathan Warrior.

It was Trentach and the Garpathans.

Laonardo almost yelled out with joy, '*Surely Cappa will be with them having taken the faster path.*' He called to Zoobram and they galloped toward their approaching saviours.

Cappa was doing well to fend off the chasing pack, but Coba was tiring fast. He moved quickly from one narrow passage to another desperate to lose his pursuers - But it was no use.

Ruomaani had somehow managed to hold on despite the crippling pain, but their fortitude and luck was set to run out.

As Cappa steered Coba around a rocky precipice, he looked on in despair at what awaited them. They'd moved directly into a large looming bowl, the cliff walls on every side offering no escape from the dogs hunting their rear.

It was a dead end.

He could have yelled out in despair.

Cappa kicked one last time, urging Coba into a final sprint for the far side of the bowl. His stallion obeyed, grunting and panting as he provided his master a brief moment of respite.

Cappa was out of the saddle quickly, lowering Ruomaani to the floor. She whimpered in pain.

He noted the blood close to her groin, observed her pale, perspiring skin. "There now," he said tenderly as she winced when placed on the stones, "Easy." He stroked the hair from her face and whispered to her gently.

She was badly hurt.

He continued to comfort her as the pursuing pack now entered the arena with Vhlarm at the rear.

They didn't rush. There was no need.

There was nowhere for their quarry to run.

"Hush now," Cappa whispered gently, his piercing eyes observing the closing dogs as they moved in. He gritted his teeth as he heard her cry, refused to let his heart break as she begged him to leave her, to make his escape.

"Please, Cappa, take Coba and get out of here."

Her voice betrayed the agony, her pain like torture.

The four hunters spread out cautiously, keeping their horses at a sensible distance, looking to their master who smiled, delighting in the tension so evident in the form of the cornered Pathan.

*

Laonardo's joy at reaching Trentach and Bayer was short lived. "Cappa is not with you?" The concern was evident in the Patruan's voice. "But he was in front of us. He took the quicker path?" Foreboding instantly replaced his relief. He looked back down the passage realising his gamble had failed. "Come on!"

As they rode down the Gorda Passage the remaining pursuers slowed by Laonardo's earlier action breeched the path. They could not know it, but this timing would seal all of their fates as the might of the Garpathans bore down on them.

"Keep still," Cappa spoke softly, "Steady your breathing."

"Cappa, don't do this, try to escape." She implored.

Ruomaani tilted her head and saw the hunters as they circled their position. Her eyes welled with tears as she watched the Pathan warrior leave her, crouching low behind his shield.

Vhlarm was delighted at his refusal to surrender. He lived for such moments. For the rare occasions he could claim such a prized kill. He thought back to the youngster in the arena of the Torantum... skilled, bold, but young and naïve.

The dogs surrounding him did not share their master's confidence, they were wary of the warrior as he moved confidently like a powerful cat, shrouded by the blue of his cape, the fierce helmet partially hidden by the magnificent shield.

The soldier closest to Cappa paused, questioning himself about whom he feared most, the boy warrior or the mighty Vhlarm.

His answer came quickly, pushing him to attack.

His heels kicked, his horse's head lifted, and before he truly knew what he was doing, the soldier was committed.

He bore down on Cappa at speed, using his horse to his advantage, keeping his shield high.

Cappa was ruthless, sending a dagger coursing into the chest of the horse. It reared, forcing the rider to jump free. He did so with great skill and landed on the floor evenly and without injury. On seeing the others were not yet moving in, Cappa engaged the soldier - His sword flashed toward the man who was able to defend himself. Several choice clashes of steel rang out before Cappa, skilfully dropped his shoulder, feigning a move to the left before turning at speed to the right. The soldier was duped, Cappa spinning around his opponent's shield. He struck with venom, ending the contest with a swift and fatal blow.

One down.

Vhlarm smiled coldly. Perhaps this young buck was indeed a full-blooded Pathan after all. He gestured to his remaining horsemen, "Dismount!" he yelled. "He will only take out your horses with projectiles."

Vhlarm would be more than happy to see the Pathan fight it out with his men before he himself would step in. Have chance to weigh up his prize prey, see the youngster use up the last of his flying daggers.

The remaining three soldiers did as Vhlarm asked, jumping from their saddles, pulling their shields close. They moved slowly around the Pathan not yet daring to attack.

Ruomaani struggled against the pain and watched as Cappa repositioned himself between her and the closing pack. The burning in her abdomen was almost unbearable but she managed to push herself onto her elbow. She was desperate to help him but could barely move her body.

The soldiers continued to circle Cappa, moving in closer, one small step at a time.

The Pathan prowled behind his shield.

He had two projectiles remaining.

He crouched lower behind the defence, its mirrored surface dazzling his opponents as he disappeared from view. He stuck his sword into the earth and with a flick of his wrist the cape dropped to the floor behind him. Before the dogs knew what was happening, he reappeared from the shield launching the daggers at two of his tormentors at breath-taking speed.

The first dug into the shield of the attacker closest to him who cowered for safety, but the second had more success, slicing into its victim's thigh.

With the sword stood upright in the dirt the third aggressor moved quickly for the kill but was astonished at the countermeasure.

Cappa launched his body behind the shield, propelling himself forward like a battering ram, plucking the weapon from the earth as he passed.

As the clash of shields rang out the man stumbled backward.

Cappa made him pay, spinning around the unsteady defence, unleashing the killing shot before his aggressor could regain his balance.

This time there would be no respite.

As the two remaining soldiers froze momentarily, he was on them, his blade flashing in a swathe of attacking blows.

The man with the dagger in his thigh could barely stand and was desperate for assistance. He received it in the nick of time, his comrade flanking Cappa with a forceful shot of his own.

Cappa countered the blow before using his shield to bounce the attacker out of the immediate arena. He wasted no time with another attempt on the wounded man, Cappa's power, strength and speed despatching the injured foe before his comrade could get back into the fight.

Again, Cappa offered no respite, but as he moved in for the final showdown, he was aware of Ruomaani screaming at him to watch out.

His instincts took over, his awesome shield taking care of the rest as this time he was struck with real force.

As Cappa allowed his defence to deflect the blow, he saw the flash of bullhorns pass as Vhlarm's attack sped by.

The last of the soldiers was clearly invigorated at Vhlarm's assistance and moved in with accuracy before Cappa could avoid a collision. The soldier's sword thrust for his rib cage.

Cappa smashed the lower edge of his shield onto the blade as it sliced against his Pathan armour, the flesh wound a small price to pay for seeing the attacking blade hit the ground. The soldier continued forward under his own momentum and Cappa brought up his forearm, smashing his opponent under the chin, propelling him into the air in a wail of arms and legs.

Vhlarm returned, unleashing the powerful blows of his customised spear-come-battering pole. He used the two parallel rungs, which protected the holding hands to spin the weapon with speed and skill just as he had against Bayer.

The power of Vhlarm's blows were something to behold, but Cappa was able to utilise this power as a counter force, dropping low, twisting his hips and turning the shield to see Vhlarm spinning away from the close-quarter arena.

Cappa used his precious seconds with deadly force, moving in quickly on the remaining soldier. He forced the soldier into a retreat, cutting away at the calf muscles as he scrambled from the Pathan. As his screams took him to the floor, Cappa spun around at speed, killing the man while simultaneously preparing his position for Vhlarm's incoming attack.

This time the blade of the powerful spear was thrust forward, Vhlarm throwing it at Cappa like a missile.

Once again, the shield was utilised, the battered eagle with its effigy of the sun doing its utmost to protect the heir. Vhlarm moved quickly for a man of his size and Cappa struggled to see off the next incoming blow.

More crashes of steel followed as the two warriors engaged in a fierce exchange.

Ruomaani watched desperately as Cappa fought the mighty bull, desperate to move against her pain. She yelped as she managed to claw herself almost fully upright.

Vhlarm realised his opponent's use of the shield was beyond any he'd encountered.

So successful was his defence, it completely negated the superior striking distance and power provided by Vhlarm's custom made spear and blade.

Vhlarm had to see it removed from the fight.

Further exchanges rang out, the skill and prowess of both fighters a spectacular sight to behold. Cappa had fought several men now and was beginning to tire against the huge, fresher giant, battering at his defence.

Another attack came, then another and another, Cappa successfully reeling from the brute force of the skilful hulk.

He knew Ruomaani was close by, but there could be no distraction.

Again, Vhlarm attacked, the bull helmet glancing left as the spear and blade twisted right.

It was a clever move which wrong footed Cappa.

Vhlarm's immediate follow-through was precise. He jumped forward smashing his armoured shoulder into the shield.

As his Pathan opponent tried to adjust, Vhlarm shocked Cappa, dropping his powerful lance downward against his exposed pelvis. Cappa managed to pull his sword back to his defence in the nick of time, deflecting the blade at the end of the powerful lance before it could do serious damage. Unfortunately, this saw the lance deflected behind the grip of the shield seeing Vhlarm lunge quickly into position, twisting the blade into Cappa's forearm, shattering the outer bone.

Cappa yelled out, but summoned all his strength and skill, powering his sword into an outward swing that forced Vhlarm to leap for cover.

The ogre rolled clear astonished by the youngster's grit.

However, any disappointment was brief - for as Vhlarm retreated from the arena what he saw filled his brutal heart with renewed purpose. The Pathan's shield arm was wrecked, the weight of his once mighty defence now only serving to pull the young warrior low to the ground.

Cappa was also struggling against the damage to his pelvis and as his shield arm began to fail, the Pathan knew he was in trouble. Cappa released the shield and could see the confidence pumping through Vhlarm as he began to stalk Cappa once more.

"It won't be long now, Ruomaani-Skye," Vhlarm goaded in a deep, sickening tone.

She'd forced herself up onto her knees but was clearly struggling to move.

Cappa watched as Vhlarm circled in closer for the kill, and replayed the attacks inflicted with his mighty custom weapon.

Cappa swallowed hard as all of his training illustrated the awful truth to his mind's eye. Cappa could not take such a skilled opponent with a sword alone in this damaged state.

Summoning all his tenacity and teaching, he once again replayed Vhlarm's attacks, searching for an answer.

Cappa struggled as he listened to the continuing goading now aimed Ruomaani's way. Filthy tones designed to torture the pair's fading resolve.

Vhlarm stepped in closer. He would enjoy this kill, would take his prize with pleasure.

He circled the stricken Pathan then moved in at speed.

The thrust was deflected by Cappa's sword, the young warrior fighting the pain as he spun about for the next encounter.

The same pattern followed twice more before it was clear Cappa could go on no further.

As the two circled each other for the final time, Vhlarm made ready to inflict the killing blow. He pounced forward, the blade of his lance piercing the Pathan armour with a sickening sound. Vhlarm wasn't certain whether it was this or the sound of Ruomaani-Skye's scream that satisfied him most.

Cappa had watched the blow come in, utilised all his learning to ensure it hit exactly the right spot, guiding the blow with his sword as best he could - But as the blade pierced his flesh and ran him through, nothing could prepare for the agony, the sheer brutality of the pain.

He cried out, Ruomaani's screams sounding as distant as the building breeze. He groaned as he felt the weapon thrust deeper into his body, piercing the rear skin of his armour, leaving him suspended on the pole.

Vhlarm almost yelled with delight but instead focussed his pleasure into a taunting growl as he repeated over and over through gritted teeth, "Pathan, Pathan!"

The brute looked to Ruomaani, satisfied as she yelled out again distraught, before returning his glare to the young warrior whose arms and torso dropped back limply…

Cappa's hand defiantly clutching the sword…

The sword… '*His hand still clutching the sword!*'

Vhlarm's delirium had got the better of him.

He remembered his own disgust when he'd witnessed how this young fighter had allowed himself to be distracted by Ruomaani-Skye, back in the arena at the Torantum.

He'd barely processed the thought when suddenly he felt his lance twisted and pulled upon, the weapon travelling onward through the stricken body of his opponent.

In that first instant Vhlarm was slow to react, but as the realisation struck, he let go of the lance, only to see his wrists now trapped within the guards designed to protect his hands.

His eyes widened as the pole was pulled upon once more, the heave powered by the Pathan's near to shattered limb pulling him off balance, the twisted angle trapping his wrists from release. In that same flash of realisation, he saw the wounded warrior spark back into being, the majestic sword powering upright and overhead at lightning speed.

The bull helmet had been dragged into range at the expense of the Pathan's own body and in that same sickening instant, Vhlarm realised what was to happen - He was to be killed by the mightiest of opponents, Vhlarm's head removed with a spectacular final throw.

*

As Vhlarm's head hit the dirt, Cappa slouched forward.

The spear had sliced clean through his side. Cappa fell to his knees and struggled to focus as death's embrace threatened.

He slumped over the corpse of his opponent, Vhlarm's hands still trapped within the guards of the lance.

Ruomaani agonizingly clawed her way across the baked salt toward him. She moved in close, her tears engulfing her as she cried out. She ignored the pain of her injuries and managed to embrace him, all the while begging the gods for mercy,

"Please don't let him die."

Cappa was drawn to the darkness but managed to look upon her, "You're safe now."

She snorted against the pain, "I love you," she whispered, "Please, stay with me."

The light faded from Cappa's eyes.

Lost to the brutality of the moment, Ruomaani didn't notice the arrival of the small army of Garpathans. She did not see Laonardo until he came sprawling next to her in abject panic.

Nor was Ruomaani aware of the shock and anguish worn on the faces of the surrounding warriors, of the tears welling in the eyes of Trentach and Banteez Bayer.

She was numb as Laonardo gingerly moved her away from the bloodied pole skewering his fallen friend, as two Garpathans moved in quickly to assist him.

All Ruomaani-Skye was truly aware of was the cruel pain…

As she swore before the gods, she would never love again.

Printed in Great Britain
by Amazon